Valvèdre

George Sand

Translated and with an Introduction by
Françoise Massardier-Kenney

State University of New York Press

Published by
State University of New York Press, Albany

© 2007 State University of New York

All rights reserved

Printed in the United States of America

No part of this book may be used or reproduced in any manner whatsoever without written permission. No part of this book may be stored in a retrieval system or transmitted in any form or by any means including electronic, electrostatic, magnetic tape, mechanical, photocopying, recording, or otherwise without the prior permission in writing of the publisher.

For information, address State University of New York Press,
194 Washington Avenue, Suite 305, Albany, NY 12210-2384

Production by Judith Block
Marketing by Fran Keneston

Library of Congress Cataloging-in-Publication Data

Sand, George, 1804–1876.
 [Valvèdre. English]
 Valvèdre / George Sand ; translated with an introduction by Françoise Massardier-Kenney.
   p. cm. — (SUNY series, women writers in translation)
 Includes bibliographical references and index.
 ISBN-13: 978-0-7914-7059-6 (hardcover : alk. paper)
 ISBN-13: 978-0-7914-7060-2 (pbk. : alk. paper)
 I. Massardier-Kenney, Françoise. II. Title.

PQ2411.V413 2007
843'.8—dc22   2006025534

10 9 8 7 6 5 4 3 2 1

Valvèdre

SUNY series, Women Writers in Translation
Marilyn Gaddis Rose, editor

To My Son

This story originated from an idea that we savored together, that we drank, so to speak, at the same spring: the study of nature. You expressed it first in a scientific study that is soon to appear in print. I express it in turn and in my own way in a novel. This idea, which seems to be as old as the world, is, however, a fairly new conquest of the times in which we are living. During long centuries, man took himself for the center and the goal of the universe. Today we are taught a more accurate and broader notion. Several people profess it brilliantly. As fervent followers, we shall also bring our grain of sand because this notion needs to go through many minds in order to gradually do everyone the good that it contains. It can be summarized in a few words that your book explains and that mine will attempt to demonstrate: "getting out of oneself." It is lovely to do this together as we have so often done.

Contents

Acknowledgments	ix
Introduction	xi
I	1
II	29
III	47
IV	67
V	91
VI	107
VII	129
VIII	151
Last Part	171

Acknowledgments

I wish to thank my colleagues at the Institute of Applied Linguistics at Kent State University who provided an environment in which translation is taken very seriously, and the Sand specialists who encouraged me in my endeavor to bring into English this major but forgotten novel by George Sand. Thanks also to David Powell and Thelma Jurgrau for their generous and invaluable suggestions; to the editorial staff at SUNY Press, Judith Block, production editor, and Laura Glenn, professional freelance editor, who copyedited the novel so carefully. Last, as always, I am grateful to Bill Kenney, who read my manuscript carefully and who provided unstinting intellectual and moral support throughout this project.

Introduction

George Sand's works have influenced a number of English and American writers (George Eliot, Kate Chopin, Margaret Fuller, the transcendentalists, and Henry James, to name a few), and she was widely translated in the nineteenth century. Although George Burnham Ives translated eighteen of her novels during the second part of the nineteenth century (along with novels by Maupassant, Mérimée, Gauthier, Balzac, and Dumas), Sand's other novels, when they were available in English at all, were translated one at a time by different translators. These translations do not include *Valvèdre*, a late novel that Sand wrote when she was fifty-two and that is crucial for constructing her canon. Even today the novel is still inaccessible: there is no reedition or critical edition available even though the novel enjoyed both popular and critical success. It saw three editions in 1861, one in 1862, 1863, 1875, two in 1884, and finally one in 1900, before Sand's works were sanitized by French pedagogical institutions into innocuous examples of exquisite prose, pastoral settings, and children's tales.

Valvèdre is significant among George Sand's novels because it marks the culmination of her lifelong questioning of narrative voice and of her examination of patriarchal institutions. It offers a scathing critique of Romantic conceptions of love, explores the price paid by women for internalizing male Romantic models, and challenges traditional notions of male narrative authority. Among the best of her late novels, it certainly deserves to be rediscovered.

The novel starts with a dedication and a preface that undermine the voice of the first-person narrator whom Sand uses throughout the novel to present the characters and interpret their stories. However, Sand is careful to make the novel enticing by both holding the reader's interest and expressing the attraction that Romanticism has exerted and continues to exert. The narrator is an aspiring young poet who is doing his *grand tour* and who goes to visit a friend, Henri Obernay, a Swiss botanist who is working in the Alps with his mentor, a scientist named Valvèdre. At the mountain inn where the scientists have established their base, the narrator meets a rich, Jewish businessman named Moserwald who gossips about Valvèdre and his wife. When Alida Valvèdre, a beautiful woman who feels neglected by her husband, arrives unexpectedly, the narrator is prepared to fall in love with her; and she obviously shares and embodies his Romantic beliefs about love and femininity.

The novel recounts the narrator's complicated involvement with Madame Valvèdre, who reciprocates his attachment but insists on keeping the relationship platonic, mostly because of her Catholic faith. With the help of Moserwald, himself hopelessly in love with Madame Valvèdre, the narrator and Alida elope and live together, still platonically, while waiting for her husband to give her a divorce, which is permitted under Swiss Protestant law. Before this can happen, the penniless narrator borrows money from Moserwald and takes Alida to North Africa as her health is declining. Even though the two lovers care for each other, the relationship does not bring them happiness. Alida is depressed at having abandoned her two young sons, and the narrator fights against his awareness that Alida's husband is a superior human being and that he has made a terrible mistake in taking his wife away. Alida dies after being forgiven by her husband; the narrator is thus freed from his burden and spends the next seven years working in a metallurgic factory; his friend Obernay then calls him back to tutor one of Valvèdre's sons. The narrator ends up marrying one of Obernay's sisters and repairing the harm he has done Valvèdre by bringing him together with Obernay's other sister, Adélaïde, a beautiful, superior woman.

In the narrative of this ill-fated affair, Sand questions Romantic representations of women and exposes the disastrous consequences such notions of femininity have for both the male narrator and the female character. She suggests that when women internalize traditional patriarchal discourses and expectations about femininity, they are doomed, while the female characters who, for one reason or another, do not fit nineteenth-century conventions of womanhood, live happier, contented lives. Sand's Alida, however, is no Emma Bovary. Although she is trapped by Romantic notions of femininity, she is intelligent, articulate, and chaste, an aspect of her character for which Sand is willing to sacrifice vraisemblance. Unlike male authors of the period, Sand creates a female character who is strong and who dies, not because of her weaknesses as a woman but because she has embraced all too readily the patriarchal constructions of femininity and because she has adopted a narrow conception of what men and women should be.[1]

To counteract the Romantic demonization of woman developed by her contemporaries, Sand creates male characters who are shown to be responsible for their actions. While the narrator attempts to make Alida responsible for his infatuation through the repeated use of words suggesting that she possesses supernatural powers, her husband, Valvèdre, depicted as a superior human being, recognizes his own responsibility in falling in love with someone who is totally ill-suited for him. He admits that he read into her his own aspirations without knowing her. And indeed, his wife's account of her marriage is sobering: "He took a fancy to me, he found me beautiful, he wished to be my husband in order to be my lover," which can clearly be read as part of Sand's support for the reinstatement of divorce (abrogated by Napoleon in 1804 and only reinstated in 1884).

Sand links the conception of essential femininity adopted by Alida to her religious belief and her sense of sin. This connection between Alida's belief in Romantic notions of love and femininity as well as her allegiance to the dictates of the Catholic church are not contradictory since both are expressions of patriarchal structures that limit women's autonomy and are based on a denial of their ability to be rational. Sand's critique of the church's role in the subjection of women and her mistrust in the alliance of women with the church is not original: it inscribes itself in the French post-Revolutionary tradition that long denied women political and civil rights because they were associated with the conservative power of the Catholic church. What is original, however, is that by depicting women's subjection under the church and under Romantic rhetoric, Sand shows the links between religious and Romantic ideology.

Sand's theme of the inadequacy of binary oppositions, be they gender or race opposition, is related to her demonstration that the cultural construction of woman as an essential creature is embedded in a structure that is religious and social as well as aesthetic. Thus *Valvèdre* is a crucial text for understanding a number of anxieties characterizing the second half of nineteenth-century France with regard to the link between Catholicism and women, anticlericalism, motherhood, women's sexuality, the relations between science and art, and anti-Semitism.

Through the character of Moserwald, a rich businessman who is involved with the fate of the main characters, Sand demonstrates the irrationality of her narrator's anti-Semitism (and perhaps her own) and foreshadows the cultural anxieties that were to culminate in the Dreyfus affair a few decades later. Although the narrator and Alida express their distaste for the Jewish character, who is presented as vulgar and materialistic,[2] Sand's resolution of the main plotlines in which Moserwald turns out to be the most faithful of friends and provides the material means to reintegrate the narrator in the Valvèdre household is revealing; in narrative terms, his role is that of an adjuvant, which contradicts the prejudices proffered by the characters and signals Sand's distance from their anti-Semitism.[3]

Valvèdre expresses Sand's lifelong belief in the capacity of literature to educate sensibilities and to be an integral part of life. Her injunction to go beyond the self, her representation of science as a creative activity on par with literature, and her belief in the power of work to create oneself all mark her opposition to the development of literature as an autonomous aesthetic object removed from the preoccupations of her time.

Valvèdre was first published as a series in the *Revue des Deux Mondes* in six parts from March 15 to May 15, 1861, then in book form in September of the same year with the publisher Michel Lévy Frères. This novel was composed during a very creative period: in five years from 1857 to 1862, Sand published thirteen novels and a series of articles. It was also a difficult time in her life during which Sand lost her granddaughter Jeanne Clésinger and her longtime friend, Jules Néraud. As Wladimir Karénine, Sand's first biographer, reminds us, it was a time when Sand found a renewed interest in botany and geology, and would offer solace to her friends by advising them to alleviate their sorrows by contemplating nature and avoiding focusing on their own egos. In the dedication to her son Maurice, Sand suggests that the theme of the novel is the study of nature, which she offers as a corrective to the narcissism of men who took themselves for the center of the universe. She summarizes her project in three words: *sortir de soi* (getting out of oneself). These words are a resounding response to Baudelaire's famous affirmation that "an artist never *gets outside of himself*" and offers a vision that is anti-Romantic and against art for art's sake. They are also found in English in the writer Henry James, who knew Sand's works well, wrote critical articles on her novels, and in his own works reused the expression both in *Roderick Hudson* (1875) and *The Princess Casamassima* (1886), showing us the influence that *Valvèdre* had on Sand's famous contemporaries.

Henry James noted Sand's stylistic fluidity, her eloquence, and her capacity to describe passionate feelings but reproached her for her lack of precision, a remarkable weakness when one wants to study nature. The translation process is helpful in providing an answer to this contradiction. One of the stylistic and semantic regularities that must be preserved when translating *Valvèdre* is the presence of organic comparisons and metaphors used to describe the characters' mental states or to show their emotions. The references to botany, mineralogy, entomology, and geology are found at the content level (as the main characters are involved in geology and botany and the description of their various activities requires knowledge of a certain number of flowers, insects, or geological formation), but they are also an integral part of Sand's network of metaphors. For instance, Sand qualifies feelings with a term coming from chemistry; she uses a series of mineral or physical metaphors (coral banks, flowers, shell fish) to describe a woman character in order to question the development of femininity. This signifying network has to be reconstructed in English because it is part of Sand's injunction to "get out of oneself." The presence of specific terms that indirectly or directly anchor the novel in the "real world" also includes a set of financial and legal metaphors, which expand at the stylistic level the theme of the legitimacy of divorce. Sand may make little use of realistic details per se but she employs with great precision a number of legal terms throughout the novel.

The presence of specialized terms in the novel is not surprising considering the care with which Sand continued to read about botany as well as divorce law and visited metallurgic factories while rewriting the novel. However, she distills this knowledge and keeps concrete details to a minimum. As she explains to her publisher, Buloz, in a letter dated July 30, 1860, "The more I see, the more I think we must face the so-called doctrine of realism by showing that one can be very precise and very conscientious without trampling poetry and art" (*Correspondence* 33), to which she adds "dissecting is not understanding; analyzing is not seeing" (*Correspondence* 54). Another striking characteristic of the novel is the presence of many exclamation points and demonstratives, which suggests the importance of feelings and the author's desire to bring the reader closer to the characters. While the number of exclamation points may be characteristic of the times, the overabundance of demonstratives is a stylistic trait particular to Sand that the translation must account for. Normally English allows for few demonstratives that refer to a clear antecedent, and translators usually erase such demonstratives. However, in this case, their presence is like a symptom in the text of the author's desire to force the readers into the world of the novel, to make them get out of themselves. Thus I have kept these demonstrative markers.

Similarly, the abundance of expressions such as "it seemed to me" and "it appeared to me," which express the novel's insistence of the problematization of perception, requires that they be kept in English, even though this repetition may seem awkward. In the same vein, I have retained the narrator's overuse of impersonal expressions, which may not seem natural in English but which is crucial in order to reveal his status as passive subject.

The whole text is endowed with the fluidity that James admired without specifying its elements but that the translator must re-create in English. Surprisingly, when we consider the reputation of orality and simplicity usually attributed to Sand, we find very long sentences, which can take a whole paragraph and which make ample use of semicolons. However, unlike the complex compound sentences of James, these sentences achieve their simplicity through series of parallelisms of whole clauses or of phrases, a parallelism that is at the heart of Sand's style and that I have endeavored to maintain.

The many corrections on the complete manuscript of *Valvèdre* and a first version of about sixty pages indicate that Sand carefully revised her manuscript. She made a number of additions meant to clarify dialogues, to provide greater transitions, and to add "realist details" to her text. Most of the additions reveal the care with which Sand worked on crafting the parallel structures that are characteristic of her style and create an impression of rhythmic harmony in descriptions as well as in dialogues. Also remarkable is the number of adjectives placed before a noun, a characteristic noticeable in French since adjectives tend to come after the noun they modify. Obviously in the English version, this trait loses its distinctiveness.

Valvèdre's introductory injunction to "get out of oneself" summarizes Sand's persistent questioning of the prejudices of the century in which she lived, be they religious, cultural, or aesthetic, and still today invites the readers to reflect on their own attitudes toward their world.

NOTES

1. For a study of gender in *Valvèdre*, see chapter 3 of *Gender in the Fiction of George Sand*.

2. These characters' anti-Semitism run the gamut of what historian Pierre Birnbaum terms "reactionary Catholic anti-Judaism, classic anti-Semitism, or economic anti-Semitism."

3. This is not to say that Sand escaped the common prejudices of her times. As the work of Thelma Jurgrau has shown, Sand's correspondence contains a number of common anti-Semitic expressions. What is interesting is that at the narrative level, rather than endorsing it, Sand deconstructs the anti-Semitism of her characters.

WORKS CITED

Birnbaum, Pierre, "Un Antisémitisme à la française," in *L'Antisémitisme éclairé, Inclusion et exclusion depuis l'époque des lumières jusqu'à l'Affaire Dreyfus*, ed. Ilana Y. Zinguer and Sam W. Bloom (Leiden; Boston: Brill, 2003), 3–18.

Jurgrau, Thelma, "Anti-Semitism in George Sand's Letters," in *Le Siècle de George Sand*, ed. David Powell (Amsterdam: Rodopi, 1998), 345–56.

Massardier-Kenney, Françoise, *Gender in the Fiction of George Sand* (Amsterdam: Rodopi, 2000).

Sand, George, *Correspondence*, vol. XVI, ed. Georges Lubin (Paris: Garnier, 1964).

———. *Valvèdre* (Paris: Michel Lévy Frères, 1861).

I

For reasons easily understood, I have to disguise all the proper names that will appear in this story, and the reader will be kind enough not to require of me any geographical details. There are several ways to tell a story: the one which consists in making you travel through a country carefully explored and faithfully described is, in one respect, the best one; it is one of the aspects through which the novel, this thing long reputed to be frivolous, can become useful reading, and, in my opinion, when one names a place that really exists, it cannot be described faithfully enough. But the other way which, without being purely fanciful, refrains from giving a specific itinerary and from naming the real location of the main scenes, is sometimes preferable in order to communicate some received impressions. The first approach is useful enough for the gradual development of feelings that can be analyzed; the second one leaves to the impetuousness and disorder of strong passions a broader path.

In any case, I would not be free to choose between these two methods because I propose to recount here the story of a passion that was experienced more than explained. This passion created in me so much tumult that I can still only perceive it through some sort of veil. It was twenty years ago. I took it to several places which seemed splendid or miserable according to the state of my soul. There were even days, weeks perhaps, when I lived without really knowing where I was. I shall thus refrain from reconstructing, by means of cold research or laborious attempts to remember, the details of a past where everything is inner confusion and frenzy in and around me; and it might not be a bad thing to leave in my story some of the disorder and incomplete notions that were my life during these terrible days.

I was twenty-three years old when my father, a professor of literature and philosophy in Brussels, gave me permission to spend a year traveling; in doing so, he yielded to my desire as well as to a serious consideration. I was planning to have a career in literature, and I had the rare happiness of having a family who believed in my vocation. I felt the need to see and to understand life in general. My father recognized that our peaceful and patriarchal life offered a rather narrow horizon. He had faith in me. He put the bridle on the neck of the impatient horse. My mother cried, but she hid her tears, and I left: alas! To meet such perils to moral life!

I had been brought up partly in Brussels, partly in Paris, under the care of one of my father's brothers, Antonin Valigny, a distinguished chemist who had died prematurely as I was finishing my studies at the Saint-Louis school. I felt no curiosity for the modern centers of civilization. I yearned for the poetic and the picturesque. I wanted to see, in Switzerland first, the great monuments of nature, and then in Italy, the great monuments of art.

The first and almost the only time I had gone to Geneva was to visit a friend of my father whose son had been in Paris, my classmate and my closest friend; but adolescents don't write much. Henri Obernay was the first one to neglect our correspondence. I followed his bad example. When I looked for him in his fatherland, it had been years since we had last written each other. It is thus likely that I would not have looked for him with much determination, had my father not insisted very strongly, when saying good-bye, that I renew my acquaintance with him. Monsieur Obernay senior, a professor of science in Geneva, was a man of true merit. His son had given indications that he took after him. His family was dear to mine. Finally my mother wanted to know if little Adélaïde was still charming and pretty. I guessed some plan or at least some hope for a match, and, although I was not in the least ready to begin the novel of my youth with its end, curiosity somewhat reinforcing duty, I visited the professor of science.

I did not find Henri there, but his parents welcomed me almost as if I had been his brother. They kept me for dinner and insisted that I stay with them. It was in the part of Geneva called the old town, which, at that time, still had so much character. Separated by the Rhone river from the Catholic part of town, from the new world, and from the palaces of the tourists, the town of Calvin lined the hillsides with terraces of austere houses and narrow gardens, shaded by high walls and trimmed hedges.

There, no noise, no sightseers, no idlers, and thus none of the commotion that characterizes modern industrial life. A studious silence, quiet piety or activities requiring patience and precision, a hospitable *home* but which did not seem to suffer any overindulgence, a meditative and proud sense of well-being, such were generally the characteristics of these prosperous houses.

The Obernay's house was a gentler and somewhat modernized version of this respectable and serious life. The heads of the household, as well as their children and their close friends, protested against the excess of exterior rigidities. Too much of a scholar to be a fanatic, the professor followed the cult and the customs of his forebears; but his intelligence and his culture had made a large breach into the world of taste and progress. His wife, more housewife than scholar, had nonetheless the same respect for science as for religion. It was enough for M. Obernay to engage in some studies for her to consider this activity as the most important and the most useful one that could fill the life of a gentleman; and when this revered husband asked for some relaxation and diversion around him to rest from his research, she naïvely strained her ingenuity in order to please him, convinced that she was working for the greater glory of God when she was working for him.

In spite of the momentary absence of their children, this old couple seemed to me to be extremely likable. They had none of the narrow-mindedness that is often found in the provinces. They were interested in everything, and nothing was foreign to them. They even took a kind of pride in this, and you could have compared their frame of mind to their house, spacious, clean, austere, but brightened up by the most beautiful flowers, and opening unto the majestic vista of the lake and the mountains.

The two daughters, Adélaïde and Rosa, had gone visiting their aunt in Morges. I was shown the portrait of little Rosa, sketched by her sister. The drawing was charming, the young face lovely; but there was no portrait of Adélaïde.

They asked me if I remembered her. I boldly answered that I did even though this memory was very vague. "She was five at the time," Madame Obernay told me, "you can imagine that she is quite changed! Still she is considered a beautiful girl. She looks like her father, who is not bad for a fifty-five-year-old man. Rosa is not as attractive; she looks like me," the excellent woman added with a laugh, "still youthful and beautiful, but she is at an age when you can change!"

Henri Obernay had left on a naturalist expedition with a friend of the family. At that moment he was exploring the Mont-Rose region. They showed me one of his letters, a very recent one, in which he described with such enthusiasm the places where he was staying that I decided to join him. Already familiar with the mountains and speaking all the dialects of the border, he would make an excellent guide, and his mother assured me that he would be happy to have to direct my first excursions. He had not forgotten me; he had always spoken about me with the greatest affection. Madame Obernay knew me as if she had never lost touch with me. She knew my inclinations, my character, and remembered my childhood whims, which she would recount to me, with a charming good-heartedness. Seeing that Henri had made them like me, I thought with good reason that he really cared for me, and my former affection for him was reawakened. After a twenty-four hour stay in Geneva, I found out where I had a good chance of finding him, and I left for Mont-Rose.

Here, reader, you cannot follow me with a guidebook in hand. I shall give the places that I remember the first names that come to mind. I did not promise a travel narrative but a love story.

The base of the mountains, on the Swiss side, gives shelter to a little village, les Chalets-de-Saint-Pierre, which I shall call for short "Saint Pierre." That is where I found Henri Obernay. He had settled there for a week, as his travel companion wanted to explore the glaciers. The wooden house that they had taken over was large, picturesque, and cheerfully clean. They found room for me, for it was a sort of inn for tourists. I can still see the majestic vistas unfolding from every side of the exterior gallery placed on the coping of this beautiful chalet. An imposing ridge of rocks protected the hamlet from the Eastern wind and from avalanches. This natural rampart made a sort of pedestal to the denuded mountain, but green like an emerald and covered with herds. From the bottom of the house, started a meadow in bloom which quickly sloped down toward the bed of a stream full of noise and anger, and in which rushed swift and swirling cascades falling from the rocks facing us. These rocks, just below the glaciers, first confined in narrow grooves and gradually arranged in vast, dazzling arenas, were the first tiers of the frightening mass of the Mont-Rose. Its perpetual snows were still visible in shades of orange-tinted carmine in the sky when the valley was bathed in the blue of the evening.

It was a sublime sight that I was able to enjoy during a free and quiet day, before entering the storm that almost took my reason and my life away.

The first hours, Obernay and I devoted, and so to speak, laboriously employed, to getting reacquainted. You know how quick the development that comes after adolescence is, and we had really changed. However, I had remained rather short compared to Henri, who had grown like a young oak; but, half-Spanish through my mother, I had acquired a fresh beard which was a deep black and which, according to my friend, made me look like a knight-errant. As for him, though at twenty-five years of age his chin was still smooth, the development of his whole body, of his hair, previously pale blond, now golden with glints of red, his speech, formerly hesitant and timid, now concise and confident, his frank and open manners, his imposing presence, finally his herculean strength acquired through exercise rather than from a strong constitution, all this made of him a being who was quite new to me, but equally attractive as my former classmate, and visibly looking like my senior physically and morally. In sum, he was a rather handsome man, a real Swiss mountain boy, sweet and strong, full of a quiet and constant energy. The only thing that had not changed and that was quite distinctive was his skin white as snow and a glowing complexion that women could have envied.

Henri Obernay had become quite a scholar in several respects but botany was his dominant passion of the moment. His travel companion, a chemist, physicist, geologist, astronomer, and I don't know what else, was on a climb when I arrived and was not supposed to come back before evening. The name of this eminent person was not unknown to me; I had often heard it spoken by my parents: his name was M. de Valvèdre.

The first thing one asks after a long separation is whether the person is happy with his life. Obernay seemed delighted with his. He was devoted to the pursuit of science, and with this passion, when it is sincere and disinterested, there are few disappointments. The ideal, always beautiful, has the advantage of always being mysterious, and of never satisfying the saintly desires that it fosters.

I was less calm. The study of literature, which is nothing but the study of man, is painful when it is not terrifying. I had already read a great deal, and, although I had no experience of life, I was somewhat stricken with what has been called the "*mal du siècle*," the malady of the century, boredom, doubt, and arrogance. It is already quite far behind us, this illness of Romanticism. It has been mocked; fathers at that time complained about it a great deal, but the fathers of today should perhaps regret its passing. Perhaps it was preferable to the reaction that followed, the yearning for money, for pleasures without ideals, for boundless ambition, things that do not seem to me to be such fine characteristics of the *health of the century*.

However, I did not share with Obernay my secret suffering. I only intimated that I was somewhat hurt to be living at a time when there was nothing great to do. We were then during the first years of the reign of Louis-Philippe. We still had vivid memories of the epic adventure of the empire; we had been brought up in generous indignation, in the hatred of the retrograde ideas of the last Bourbon; we had dreamed of a sweeping advance in 1830, and we did not feel the realization of this progress under the triumphant influence of the bourgeoisie. We were mistaken surely: progress occurs anyway during almost every period of history and you can only call retrograde those that close more doors to progress than they open; but there are times when a certain balance is established between advances and obstacles. These are phases in suspension during which youth suffers and yet does not wither since it can express the suffering that it feels.

Obernay did not understand much of my criticism of the century (we always call "century" the time during which we happen to live). As for him, he lived in eternity, since he was at grips with natural laws. He was surprised at my complaints and asked me whether the true goal of man was not to learn and to love what is always great, what no social position can diminish, nor make inaccessible; that is the study of the laws of the universe. We argued a little about this point. I wanted to prove that indeed there are social situations in which science itself is bound by superstition, hypocrisy, or, worse, by the indifference of those who govern and those who are governed. He answered with a slight shrug.

"These obstacles," he said, "are temporary accidents in the life of humanity. Eternity does not care, and consequently neither does the science of eternal things."

"But what about us? We who only have one day to live, can we be that resigned? If you had now, in front of your very eyes, proof that your work will be buried or suppressed, or at the very least without any effect on your contemporaries, would you still carry on with such eagerness?"

"Of course, I would!" he cried out. "Science is a mistress beautiful enough to be loved with no other reward than the honor and exhilaration of mastering her."

My pride was somewhat hurt by my friend's enthusiastic fervor. I was tempted, not so much to doubt his sincerity as to believe in some illusion, in some beginner's enthusiasm. I did not want to tell him and start our renewed friendship with an argument. Besides I was quite tired. I did not wait for his companion the scientist to return from his walk, and I put back to the next day the honor of being introduced to him.

But the next day, I learned that M. de Valvèdre, who had been preparing for several days a major exploration of the glaciers and the moraine of Mont-Rose, which had been set the day before for two days later, as he saw everything ready and very favorable weather, had decided to take advantage of one of the rare periods of the year when the peaks are clear and calm. Thus he had left at midnight and Obernay had escorted him up to his first base. My friend was supposed to be back around noon, and, on his behalf, I was told to wait for him and not to venture in the precipices alone, as all the local guides had been taken by M. de Valvèdre. Knowing that I was tired, they had not wanted to wake me up to tell me what was happening and I had slept so soundly that the bustle of the expedition leaving, a veritable caravan with mules and luggage, had failed to rouse me from my sleep.

I bowed to the wishes of Obernay and resolved to wait for him at the chalet, or, to be more precise, at the hotel d'Ambroise; such was the name of our host, an excellent man, quite intelligent and majestically corpulent. When chatting with him, I learned that his house had been embellished through the generosity and the care of M. de Valvèdre who had fallen in love with the region. He came here often enough, as his own house was not very far away, and he had arranged to have at his disposal a comfortable pied-à-terre. He had done things so handsomely that Ambroise considered himself his servant as much as the recipient of his favors; but the scientist, who, it seemed to me, was a rather pleasant eccentric, had demanded that the highlander turn his house into a summer inn for the lovers of nature who would find their way into this little known region; Valvèdre had even asked Ambroise to serve with devotion all those who would attempt to explore the mountain, the only condition being that they had to write down their observations on a register now showed to me, and to which I admitted that I had nothing to add. Ambroise was no less eager to accommodate me. I was Obernay's friend, I could not be but somewhat of a scientist, and Ambroise was convinced that he would become one himself, if he wasn't already one, because he had often given shelter to people of merit.

After spending the first hours of the day writing to my parents, I went down to the dining hall for lunch and I found myself alone with a stranger, a man in his mid-thirties, rather handsome, and whom, at first sight, I identified as an Israelite. This man seemed to me to be halfway between the extreme distinction and the loathsome vulgarity that characterize among Jews two markedly distinct races or types. He belonged to an intermediary or mixed type. He spoke French rather purely, with an unpleasant German accent, and was by turns slow- and quick-witted. At first, I did not like him. Little by little I found him rather amusing. His originality consisted in physical indolence and an extraordinarily active mind. Soft and fat, he had people wait on him as if he were a prince; curious and gossipy, he asked about everything and did not allow a moment of silence in the conversation.

As he showed me, from the very beginning, the honor of being quite sociable, I quickly learned that his name was Moserwald, that he was wealthy enough to take a rest from his business, and that, at the moment, he was traveling for pleasure. He was coming from Venice where he had busied himself with pretty women and fine arts rather than attending to his fortune; he was going to Chamonix. He wanted to see the Mont Blanc, and he was coming through the Mont-Rose, which he had wanted *to get an idea about*. I asked him if he was tempted to do the climb.

"Not at all," he answered. "It is too dangerous, and to see what, I am asking you! Ice blocks piled on top of each other! No one has yet climbed up to the top of this mountain, and it is not certain at all that the caravan that left last night will come back intact. Besides, I don't wish much for its success. I arrived at ten last night and I was barely asleep when I was awakened by all the local hobnailed boots which, for two hours, kept going up and down the wooden stairs of this house, which is full of openings. All the animals of the creation lowed, pattered, neighed, cursed, or clamored under the window, and when I thought it was over, they came back to fetch some instrument they had forgotten, a barometer or a telegraph! If I had a scaffold at my disposal I would have sent it to that M. de Valvèdre, God bless! Do you know him?"

"Not yet, and you?"

"I only know him by reputation; people in Geneva where I live talk quite a bit about him, and they talk even more about his wife. And her, do you know her? You don't? Ah, my dear, what a pretty woman! Eyes as long as this (he was showing me the blade of his knife) and shinier than that!" he added, showing a superb sapphire surrounded by diamonds that he wore on his little finger.

"So her eyes must be sparkling because you have here a beautiful ring."

"Do you want it? I'll give it to you at cost."

"No, thank you. I wouldn't know what to do with it."

"That would make a nice gift for your mistress, though, wouldn't it?"

"My mistress? I don't have one."

"Ah, really? It's a mistake."

"I'll mend my ways."

"I don't doubt it; but this ring can bring closer the happy moment. Let's see, do you want it? It is a 12,000-franc trifle."

"But, once again, I have no fortune."

"Ah! It's a greater mistake still; but this can be corrected too. Do you want to go into business? I can set you up."

"Are you a jeweler?"

"No, I am rich."

"It is a nice situation, but I have another one."

"There is no good situation if you are poor."

"Excuse me, but I am free!"

"So you must be comfortable because with real poverty there is only slavery. I have been there, as I speak to you, and I lacked education; but I remade myself some as I was overcoming bad luck. So you don't know the Valvèdres? They are a strange couple, from what I hear. A gorgeous woman, a real society lady, sacrificed to an eccentric who lives in the glaciers! You think..."

Here the Jew made a few jokes in rather bad taste, but which did not offend me, as the persons about whom he was speaking were no direct acquaintances of mine. He added that in any case, with a husband like hers, Madame de Valvèdre was in her right, if she had had the affairs that Geneva gossip attributed to her. I learned from him that this lady appeared from time to time in Geneva, but less and less often, because her husband had bought for her a villa, near Lake Major, which he demanded that she not leave without his permission. "You must understand," he added, "that she manages a few escapades when he is not there... and he is never there; but he has given her a warden, an old sister of his who, under the pretext of taking care of the children, there are four or five of them, conscientiously plays her role of jailer."

"I can see that you feel very sorry for this interesting prisoner. Perhaps you know her better than you were willing to admit at lunch?"

"I don't, my word of honor! I only know her by sight; I have never spoken to her, though I can't pretend I haven't felt like it. But patience!

The opportunity will arise one time or another, unless the young man who is traveling with the husband—I saw him from afar last night—M. Obernay, I think, the son of a professor..."

"He is my friend."

"Maybe, but I say that he is handsome and it is only those who are close to us who betray us. An apprentice, he can always bring solace to the boss's wife; it's normal."

"You are a free spirit, quite the skeptic."

"Not free at all, but damn suspicious; otherwise life would be unbearable. People would take virtue seriously, and it would be sad, when one is not virtuous one self. Do you have the pretension to...?"

"I have none."

"Well, keep it that way, trust me. Go at it openly, satisfy your passions and don't do it in excess. You see, I am giving you sound advice."

"You are too kind."

"Oh, yes, you are making fun of me, but I don't mind. Your smiles won't remove a cent from my pocket nor a hair from my scalp whereas your deference could not bring back in my life a single of the hours that I have lost or wasted."

"You are quite the philosopher!"

"Excessively so, but a little late. I have lived a great deal since I have been able to indulge my fancy for things, and I am punished through a lesser desire for things. Yes, true, I have already become blasé. There are days when I don't know what to do to amuse myself. Do you want to go outside and smoke a cigar? We shall look at this famous Mont-Rose; people say it is so pretty! I looked at it yesterday throughout the trip; I found it to be like all the fairly high mountains of the Alps; but maybe you will make me find it different. Let's see, what has it got that is different and that is beautiful in your opinion? I am all too eager to admire. I haven't been brought up as a poet or as an artist, but I like beauty and I have eyes like everybody else."

There was so much naïveté in the chattering of Moserwald that, when smoking outdoors with him, I gave way to the silly conceit of explaining to him the beauty of the Mont-Rose. He listened to me with his handsome Jewish eyes, clear and eager, riveted on me. He looked like he understood and appreciated my enthusiasm, after which he suddenly resumed his air of mocking good-nature and said to me, "My dear Fellow, you may do all you can, you will not succeed in proving to me that there is the least pleasure in looking at this white mass. There is nothing as stupid as the color white, and it's almost as dull as black. People say that the sun sows diamonds on this ice; as for me, I admit that I can't see a single one, and I am sure that I have more on my little finger than this huge block of sixty or seventy square miles shows on its whole surface. But I am glad I made sure of it: you have proven to me one more time that the imagination of well-educated people can work miracles because you said the prettiest things about a thing that is not pretty at all. I wish I could remember parts of it so that I could recite it on occasion; but I am too stupid, too slow, too practical, and I could never find a word that would not make people laugh at me. Here is why I refrain from being enthusiastic; it is a jewel that you must know how to wear and which doesn't fit well people of my kin. I like what is real; that is my job. I like fine diamonds and can't stand imitations, metaphors included."

"Which means that I only seek fake adornments and that you are a jeweler, don't deny it. Every word you said implies it."

"I am not a jeweler: I don't have the dexterity, nor the patience and the poverty necessary for it."

"But before, before wealth?"

"Before, I never did any manual labor. No, it's quite simple; my only survival tool was my reasoning. Wealth is not in the hands of those who pass their time producing, making, or creating but in the hands of those who don't touch a thing. There are three races of men, my dear: those who sell, those who buy, and those who act as intermediaries between these two. Trust me, sellers and buyers are the lowest on the human scale."

"Which is to say that the one who gouges them is the king of his century."

"By golly, yes! He must be smarter alone than the two together! So you are determined to be witty and to sell words? Well, you will always be wretchedly poor. Buy in order to sell or sell to buy back, that's the only thing that counts; but you don't understand me and you despise me. You say: here is a secondhand goods dealer, a money lender, a shark! Not at all, my dear, I am an excellent fellow, known for my honesty. I have the trust of many people of great distinction; people of talent, philanthropists, even scientists consult me and receive my services. I have a heart, I do more good in one day than you'll ever be able to do in twenty years. My hand is big, flabby, and soft. Well, open your hand if you need a friend, and you'll see what a good Jew, who may be dense, but not foolish, is like."

It did not occur to me to get angry at this strangely patronizing tone which was both insolent and friendly. The man was really everything he said he was, dense to the point of being offensive without realizing it, kind enough to make sacrifices with pleasure, subtle enough to be generous in order to be forgiven his conceit. I resolved to take his strangeness lightly and, as he saw that I had no need of him but that I thanked him without disdain nor pride, he gave me a little more regard and respect than he had at first. We parted on excellent terms. He wished he could have had me as a companion for his walks; he feared being bored on his own. But it was close to the time Obernay had promised to return, and I doubted that he would like this new face. After taking leave of the Jew and finding out which path Obernay was supposed to take on his way back, I left to go meet him.

We met at the foot of the glacier, in a most picturesque pine grove. Obernay was coming back with several guides and mules that had carried part of his friend's luggage. This group continued on its way toward the valley and Obernay collapsed on the grass next to me. He was extremely tired; he had walked ten hours out of twelve on a path that wasn't cleared, and he had done so out of friendship for me. Split between two affections, he had wanted to gage the difficulties and dangers of M. de Valvèdre's venture and to come back on time to avoid leaving me alone an entire day.

He pulled some food and wine out of his bag, and gradually regaining his strength, he explained to me the exploration techniques of his friend. Contrary to what M. Moserwald had told me, it was not a question of reaching the highest peak of Mont-Rose, which might not have been possible, but, through a detailed analysis, to do a geological survey of the massif. The importance of this research was linked to a series of other explorations, past and future, of the Pennine Alps range, and was supposed to prove or disprove a specific scientific system that today I would be quite incapable of explaining to the reader; in any case, this excursion in the glaciers could last several days. M. de Valvèdre was quite cautious because of his guides and servants, whom he treated quite humanely. He was equipped with several lightweight and ingeniously designed tents, which could hold his instruments and accommodate all of his people. With a boiling water machine of extremely small dimensions, a marvel of portable industry which he had invented, he could generate heat almost instantly anywhere he was and combat all the accidents resulting from the cold. Last, he had all kinds of supplies for a given time: a small pharmacy, a change of clothes for everyone, and so on. He had just established a veritable colony of fifteen people above the glaciers, on a vast ice field, beyond the reach of avalanches. He was supposed to spend two days there, then look for a passage to move his camp farther up with part of his material and of his people; the rest would join him in two or three trips, while he attempted to go farther still. Condemned perhaps to make only two or three leagues of daily discoveries because of the difficulty of transportation, he had kept a few mules, sacrificed in advance to the dangers and sufferings of the venture. M. de Valvèdre was very wealthy, and could do more than so many other scientists, who are always held back because of their honorable poverty and the parsimony of governments; he felt it was a duty to spare no expense for the sake of the advancement of science. I told Henri that I was sorry that I hadn't been informed of their departure during the night. I would have asked M. de Valvèdre permission to go with him.

"He would have refused," he answered, "as he refused when I asked for myself. He would have told you, as he told me, that you are your parents' son and that he did not have the right to put your life in danger. Besides, you would have understood, as I did, that when one is not truly necessary in these sorts of expeditions, one is quite a burden: one more mouth to feed, shelter, protect, take care of, especially under such conditions."

"Of course, of course, I understand it in my case, but how is it that you are not extremely valuable, you, a scientist, to your scientist friend?"

"I am more valuable to him by staying in Saint Pierre, from where I can follow almost all of his movements on the mountain, and from where, at a given signal, I can send supplies, if he is running short, or come to his rescue, if need be. Besides, I must do a series of comparative analyses simultaneously to his own, and I gave him my word of honor that I would not fail to do so."

"I can see," I said to Obernay, "that you are extremely devoted to this Valvèdre, and that you consider him a man of the greatest merit. It is my father's opinion as well; he sometimes spoke about meeting him at your father's in Paris, and I know that his name carries some weight in scientific circles.

"What I can tell you about him," Obernay answered, "is that, second to my father, he is the man I respect the most, and that, after my father and you, he is the man I like the best."

"After me, thanks Henri! Here is an excellent statement that I was afraid I no longer deserved."

"And for what reason? I haven't forgotten that of the two of us, I am the one who was the laziest in regards to writing; but, as you understood this weakness of mine, I trusted that you forgave me. You knew me well enough to figure out that I may not be demonstrative but at least I am as faithful a friend as you can ever find."

I was quite moved and felt that I loved this young man with all my soul. I forgave him the kind of superiority of views and personality that he seemed to assume over me and I began fearing that he really had the right to do so. He rested for a few moments and, while he was sleeping, head in the shade and legs in the sun, I studied him again with interest, as you would someone you feel will influence your life. I don't know why, but I put him alongside in my literary and descriptive thoughts of the Israelite Moserwald. It came to me as a natural antithesis: one fat and indolent like a well-fed gourmand, the other active and lean like an insatiable researcher; the first one, yellow and shiny like the gold which had been the goal of his life; the other, fresh and full of color like the flowers on the mountain in which he delighted and which, like him, owed to the sun's harsh caresses the richness of their hue and the purity of their fine tissue.

This was for my imagination, young and cheerful at that time, the sign that my friend had a strong vocation. I have always noticed that the strong urges of the mind have exterior manifestations in some physical characteristic of the individual. Some ornithologists have birds' eyes; some hunters have the appearance of the game they are pursuing. Musicians who are simply virtuosi have an ear shaped a certain way, whereas composers have in the shape of their forehead the sign of their summarizing ability and seem to hear through the brain. Farmers who raise cattle are slower and heavier than those who raise horses, and they are born thus from generation to generation. Last, without getting lost in many examples, I can say that Obernay was living proof of my system's validity. I fully recognized later that his face, without real beauty, but eminently pleasant, had the bloom of a rose; his soul—without creative genius, had the deep charm of harmony, and, one could say, a subtle and splendid scent of honesty.

After sleeping one hour with the placidity of a soldier on active service who is used to making good use of his time, he felt quite refreshed and we resumed our conversation. I told him about Moserwald, my new acquaintance, and I repeated the jokes this great skeptic had made about his position as necessary bearer of solace to Madame de Valvèdre. He almost jumped with indignation, but I held him back. "After what you told me about your affection and your respect for the character of the husband, it is quite unnecessary to defend yourself against a shameful betrayal that would even be insulting to me."

"Yes, yes," he answered sharply, "I don't doubt you; but if this Jew comes my way, he'd better not joke about this subject!"

"I don't think he would push his overflowing wit that far, although, after all, I don't know of what he may be capable with his insolent candor. Do you know him, this Moserwald? Isn't he from Geneva?"

"No, he is German; but he often comes to our place, I mean in our town, and, without ever speaking to him, I know quite well that he is a conceited wretch!"

"So he is, but with such naïveté!"

"This cynical naïveté may be a trick. What does one ever know about a Jew?"

"What? You have racial prejudices, you, the man of science?"

"Not the least prejudice nor the least hostile opinion. I am only stating a fact: that is, the most insignificant Israelite always has in him something deeply mysterious. Summit or abyss, the representative of ancient times obeys a logic that is not like ours. He has kept something of the esoteric doctrine of the hypogaea, into which Moses was initiated. Moreover, persecution has given him the science of practical life and a very strong feeling for reality. He is thus such a powerful being that I fear for the future of society, as I fear for this forest in which we are the fall of granite blocks that the ice above holds back. I don't hate the rock; it has its raison d'être; it is part of the structure of the earth. I respect its origin, and I even study it with a certain religious anxiety, but I can see the law which drives its course and which, while disintegrating it, brings together in a common fate its ruin and that of more modern creatures that have grown on its sides."

"Here is, my friend, a metaphor that is overly scientific."

"No, no, it is accurate. Our wisdom, our religious and social sciences have taken root on the ashes of the Hebraic world and, ungrateful disciples, we have attempted to destroy this world instead of coaxing it into following us. It is taking its revenge. It is exactly like those trees with wild, grasping roots that lift rocks and dig their way to the avalanches that will engulf them."

"So, in your opinion, Jews will be the future masters of the world?"

"For a while they will, I have no doubt; afterward other cataclysms will quickly sweep them away, if they remain Jewish. Everything must be renewed or else it dies; it is the law of the universe. But, to get back to Moserwald, whoever he may be, beware of striking up a friendship with him before getting to know him well."

"I don't intend ever to become his friend, although I think better of him than you do."

"I am not judging him; I know nothing about him that allows me to suspect him as an individual. On the contrary, I know that he has the reputation for keeping his word and for being more generous in business than any member of his race; but you are telling me that he speaks lightly of M. de Valvèdre, and I don't like it. And then he offers you his services, and it worries me. One can always need money, and Shylock's fable is an eternally true symbol. The Jew instinctively needs to eat a piece of our heart; he has so many reasons to hate us and hasn't acquired with baptism the sublime notion of forgiveness. I beg you, if you were led to have an unforeseen expense, well beyond your means, ask me for the money and never ask this Moserwald. Promise me, I urge you to."

I was surprised by the intensity of Obernay and I hastened to reassure him by telling him about the respectably comfortable circumstances of my family and the simplicity of my tastes.

"No matter," he continued, "promise me to consider me your best friend. I don't know what your life will be like . . . From what you let me guess yesterday of your angst toward the future and of your discontent with the present, I am afraid that passions will play too great a part in your destiny. It doesn't seem to me that you have made efforts to create for yourself the necessary restraint."

"What restraint? Botany or geology?"

"Oh, if you are going to laugh at me, let's speak about something else."

"I am not laughing when it is a question of loving you and of being moved by your generous affection; but you must admit that you think too much like a scientist and that you would readily say 'there is no salvation outside science.'"

"Well, yes, I would say it readily. I have the honesty and the courage to admit it. I have seen a number of examples of these false theories that have troubled your soul."

"What theories do you reproach me with? Do explain."

"First, the personality theory, the pretension that you can forge a life with personal glory and resolve to be angry or full of despair if you fail."

"Well, you are mistaken; I have two strings to my ambition. I accept glory without happiness and happiness without glory."

In turn, Obernay laughed at my so-called modesty, and, while talking thus, I can't remember how we came to speak about M. de Valvèdre and his wife. I was rather curious to know if there was any truth in

Moserwald's gossip and it so happened that Obernay was inclined to observe the utmost discretion. He gave the highest praise to his friend, and he avoided having an opinion about Madame de Valvèdre; but in spite of himself he became upset and almost irritable when saying her name. He showed a nervous reticence; he would blush when I asked him why. I misunderstood. I imagined that in spite of his virtue, his reason, and his will, he was in love with this woman, and, in a moment when he denied it the most, I let slip out quite ingenuously, "She must be very attractive!"

"Ah," he exclaimed, hitting with his fist on the metal box which held his plants and which he had used as a pillow. "I can see that the Jew's bad thoughts have had an influence on you. Well, since you are pushing me, I will tell you the truth. I don't respect the woman about whom you are speaking. Now, do you still think that I can love her?"

"Huh, sometimes it is one more reason to do so; love is so unpredictable."

"The wrong kind of love, the love found in novels and modern melodrama; but unhealthy love only arises in unhealthy souls, and, thank God, mine is pure. Is yours already corrupted that you admit this shameful fatality?"

"I don't know if my soul is as pure as yours is, my dear Henri, but it is a virgin one; that's all I can tell you."

"Well, don't let it be tainted in advance by these wrong headed ideas. Don't allow yourself to be convinced that artists and poets are meant to become prey to passions and that they are allowed, more than other men, to live a so-called grand life without moral fetters; don't ever admit to yourself, even if it is the case, that you can fall under the spell of a feeling that is beneath you!"

"But, really, you are going to make me afraid of myself if you go on like this! You put before me dangers that I was not thinking about, and, for all that, you'd think that I was the one in love, without knowing her, with the famous Madame de Valvèdre!"

"Famous! Did I say she was famous?" continued Obernay with a slightly disdainful laugh. "No; fame has nothing to do with her in either a good or bad sense. Know that the affairs attributed to her in Geneva, according to M. Moserwald (and I think she is not attributed any) only exist in the imagination of this triumphant Israelite. Madame de Valvèdre lives in isolation in the countryside with her two sisters-in-law and her two children."

"I can see, indeed, that Moserwald is misinformed; he had mentioned four children and one sister-in-law. But do you realize that you are contradicting yourself a great deal when speaking about this woman? She is beyond reproach but you don't respect her!"

"I don't know that there is anything to blame about her behavior; it is her personality, her intellect, if you will, that I don't respect."

"Does she have intellectual qualities?"

"No, I don't think so, but others do."

"Is she very young?"

"No, she married when she was twenty, let's see, already some ten years ago. She must be around thirty."

"Well, you are right; it's not so young. And her husband?"

"He is forty years old but he is younger than she is: he is active and strong like a primitive man whereas she is indolent and tired like a Creole."

"Is she?"

"No, her mother was Spanish and her father a Swede; he was consul in Alicante where he got married."

"Some peculiar racial mix! It must have produced a strange type!"

"Quite successful in terms of physical beauty."

"And morally?"

"Morally? Less, I think . . . a soul without energy, a brain without breadth, an uneven temper, irritable and indolent; no serious capacity for anything, a silly scorn for the things that she doesn't understand."

"Even for botany?"

"Oh, for botany more than for anything else."

"In this case, I am quite reassured about you. You do not love and you will never love this woman."

"I can guarantee it," my friend said happily as he was clasping his bag and putting over his shoulder the vasculum,* which he then crossed over his chest. "Flowers are allowed not to like women, but women who don't like flowers are monsters."

It would be impossible for me to say why and how this conversation, interrupted and resumed several times during the course of the day, and always without planning on our part, fostered in me a kind of agitation and something like a predisposition to experience the unhappiness from which Obernay wanted to protect me. It was as if, endowed with a sudden foresight, he could read in the book of my destiny. And yet, I was

---

*The wrought iron box in which botanists collect their plant specimen to keep them fresh.

neither passive by nature nor incapable of reacting; but I believed strongly in fate. It was fashionable in those times, and to believe in fate is to create it within ourselves.

So, who will take possession of me? I thought as I was struggling to find sleep around midnight, while Obernay, in bed at six o'clock, was getting up again to make the scientific observations, the program of which his friend had put him in charge. Why did Henri seem so concerned about me. Has his eye, trained to read the clouds, seen beyond the horizon the storms that are gathering over my head? Whom shall I love? I don't know any woman who has struck my imagination, apart from two or three great opera singers and theater actresses to whom I have never spoken and to whom I shall probably never speak. I have led a life that has been, if not the quietest one, at least the one of the purest. I have felt in myself the forces of love, and I have been able to keep them intact for an ideal object whom I haven't met yet.

In my sleep, I dreamed of a woman whom I had never seen, whom, apparently, I was never destined to see, that is, Madame de Valvèdre. I loved her passionately during I don't know how many years, the vision of which lasted perhaps less than an hour, but I woke up surprised and exhausted by this long drama, of which I could not remember any details. I chased away this ghost and went back to sleep on my left side. I was unnerved, upset. Moserwald the Jew appeared and offended me so cruelly that I boxed his ear. Awakened again, I found myself mumbling words which made no sense. In my third sleep, I saw again the same character, friendly and mocking, in the shape of a fantastic bird that was quite fat, that heavily rose off the ground, and that I still pursued without being able to catch him. He would land on the highest rocks, crushing them under his weight, and laughing, he would surround me with an avalanche of stones and ice. All the metaphors with which Obernay had entertained me were taking on a tangible appearance, and I could not rest until I had exhausted these strange phantoms.

When I got up, Obernay, who had stayed up until dawn, had gone back to bed for an hour or two. He had the wonderful quality of being able to interrupt and then resume sleep as with any other occupation subjected to his will. I inquired about Moserwald; he had left early in the morning.

I waited for Henri to wake up, and after a frugal breakfast, we left together on a beautiful walk which lasted the greater part of the day, and during which we made no more mention of the Valvèdres, the Jew, or myself. We were totally absorbed by the splendid nature which surrounded us. I was enjoying it as a dazzled artist who is not yet attempting to understand the effect produced on his soul by the novelty of great sights and who, overcome by sensation, does not have the leisure to appreciate and to summarize. Familiar with the sublime mountains and engaged in detecting the mysteries of living plants, Obernay seemed less excited and happier than I was. He was without fever and without cries, whereas I was all dizziness and rapture.

Around three o'clock in the afternoon, as he was speaking of climbing one more bank of awesome rocks to gather a small rarissimas saxifrage specimen that was supposed to be found over there, I admitted that I felt very tired, that I was starving and dying of thirst and heat.

"Right. This is not surprising," he answered. "I am selfish; I am not thinking that everything requires training, and that you won't be a good hiker before eight to ten days of increasing difficulty. Allow me first to get my saxifrage; it is a little late in the season and I am quite afraid of finding it completely gone to seed if I wait until tomorrow. This afternoon I might still find some opened corollas. I'll join you in Saint Pierre at dinnertime. You are going to take the path where we are now; it will take you without danger or fatigue, in ten minutes at most, to a chalet hidden behind the large rock facing us. There you will find as much milk as you please. You will then go down toward the valley, always turning left, and you'll find our shelter by walking along the stream. The path is safe and shady."

We parted company and, after drinking and resting fifteen minutes at the chalet he had mentioned, I went down toward the valley. The path was quite good, in comparison to those Obernay had led me through, but it was so narrow that, when I met with flocks marching one after another, I was forced to step aside and to climb on slopes of varying accessibility in order to avoid being thrown into a deep precipitous ledge that ran along the opposite side of the path. I had managed to protect myself, when, as I was in one of the narrowest passages, I heard behind me the sound of bells ringing in cadence. It was a herd of loaded mules to which I immediately prepared to give way. To this end, I caught sight of a rock which put me on a level with the heads of these unflappable animals, and I sat there while waiting. The view was splendid, but the small approaching caravan soon drew all my attention.

At the head, a mule rather picturesquely harnessed Italian style, led by a guide on foot, carried a woman draped in a thin white Arab cloak. Behind that group, another group, almost the same—a guide, a mule, and on this mule another woman taller and thinner than the first one, wearing a large straw hat and a gray riding suit. A third guide, leading a third mule and a third woman who looked like a maid, was followed by two other mules carrying the luggage and by a fourth guide who brought up the rear with a servant on foot.

I had ample opportunity to observe these characters slowly coming down toward me. I could easily distinguish their features, except for the lady with the cloak; her hood was turned up and only left exposed a strange and rather frightening black eye.

This eye stared at me as the traveler was near me, and she abruptly stopped her mount by pulling on the bridle to the point of tripping the guide, at the risk of causing him to fall into the abyss. She did not seem to care, and, speaking to me in a rather harsh voice, she asked if I was a local. When I answered negatively, she was going to move on when, out of curiosity, I added that I had been here for two days and that if she needed some information, I could perhaps help her.

"Then," she continued, "I shall ask you if you have heard whether the Count of Valvèdre is in the vicinity."

"I know that a M. de Valvèdre is now on an expedition on the Mont-Rose."

"On Mont-Rose? At the top?"

"In the glaciers; that's all I know"

"Ah, I shouldn't be surprised," said the lady with a tone of resentment.

"Oh, God," added the second rider who had come closer to hear my answer. "That's what I feared."

"Do not worry, ladies, the weather is superb. The summit is very clear, and no one worries about the expedition. Everything leads the local people to think that it won't be dangerous."

"I thank you for your good omen," answered the person with the friendly face and the soft voice; "Madame de Valvèdre and myself, her sister-in-law, are grateful."

Mademoiselle de Valvèdre gave me these kinds words of thanks while passing in front of me to follow her sister-in-law, who had already resumed her walk. My eyes followed as long as I could this surprising apparition. Madame de Valvèdre turned around and, as she did so, I saw her whole face. So there was this woman who had so piqued my curiosity, thanks to Obernay's disdainful reticence. I did not find her attractive. She seemed ruddy and very thin, two things that don't go well together. Her gaze seemed harsh and so was her voice; her manners abrupt and nervous. This was not a type I would even have imagined, but in contrast, Mademoiselle de Valvèdre seemed so gentle, so graceful and likable. How come Obernay had not told me Valvèdre had a sister? Did he not know it? Or was he in love with her and so protective of his secret that he did not even want to give any hints of his loved one's existence?

I quickened my step and arrived at the hamlet a few minutes after the travelers. Madame de Valvèdre had already disappeared, but her sister-in-law was still hesitating on the stairs, asking about all the things relative to her brother's excursion. As soon as she saw me, she questioned me trustingly, asking if I knew Henri Obernay.

"Yes, absolutely," I answered, "He is my best friend."

"Oh, really," she replied without shyness, "you must be Francis Valigny from Brussels and you probably already know me? He must have told you that I am his fiancée?"

"He hasn't told me yet," I answered, somewhat troubled by such a sudden revelation.

"Apparently he must have waited for my permission to do so. Well, you'll tell him that I allow him to speak about me, as long as he tells you as much good about me as he did me about you; but you, M. Valigny, tell me about my brother and him! Is it really true that they are not in any danger?"

I informed her that Obernay had followed M. de Valvèdre only for one night and that he was going to come back. "But," I added, "should you be so worried about your brother? Aren't you used to seeing him undertake such expeditions?"

"I should get used to it," she answered with simplicity. Just then, Madame de Valvèdre had her called by a very pretty maid with an Italian accent. Mademoiselle de Valvèdre left me with this request: "Go see if Henri is coming back from his walk and tell him that Paule has just arrived."

Well, I thought, not a word when you are with her, my poor foolish heart! You must be a brother and only a brother to this charming girl. Besides, you would be quite ridiculous to pretend you can compete against a rival who is loved and certainly worthier than you are to be loved. Aren't you already somewhat guilty of a slight trembling when brushing against this virginal dress?

Obernay was coming. I rushed toward him in order to tell him the news. His pink face turned bright vermilion, then all of his blood withdrew toward his heart, and he turned pale down to his lips. Seeing this obvious emotion, I shook his hand with a smile. "My dear friend," I said, "I know everything and I envy you because you are in love, and no more needs to be said."

"Yes, I love with all my soul," he exclaimed, "and you must understand my silence. Now, let's speak reasonably. This unforeseen arrival, which fills me with joy, is also a cause of worry. With the whims of . . . some people . . . or of fate."

"Say, Madame de Valvèdre's whims. You fear that she will throw some obstacles to your happiness?"

"Not obstacles, but influence. The beautiful Alida does not like me much."

"Her name is Alida? The name is affected, but pretty, prettier than she is! I have not been impressed at all with the way she looks."

"Well, no matter. But tell me, since you have seen her, do you know why she has come here?"

"How on earth do you want me to know? I think that a deep conjugal concern . . ."

"Madame de Valvèdre concerned about her husband! . . . Usually she is not; she is so used to . . ."

"But what about Mademoiselle Paule?"

"Oh, she adores her brother; but it's not her influence that has had anything to do with her sister-in-law's decision. Besides, both know that Valvèdre does not like to be followed, to be pestered and disturbed in his research. There must be something going on, and I am rushing there to learn more if that is possible."

As for me, I rushed to get dressed, hoping that the travelers would dine in the common room; but they did not appear. They were served in their suite where they kept Obernay. I only saw him again at night. "I came looking for you," he told me, "to introduce you to the ladies. I have been asked to invite you for tea. It is some kind of ceremonious occasion because, from the terrace we shall see at 9:00 P.M., one or several flares launched from the mountain, which will be a telegraphic message from Valvèdre, of which I have the key."

"But what is the reason for the ladies' arrival? I am not especially curious but I would like to know that it is not a cause of unhappiness or fear for you."

"No, thank God. The cause remains mysterious. Paule thinks her sister-in-law was really worried about Valvèdre. I am not so naïve, but Alida treats me charmingly so I am reassured. Come."

Madame de Valvèdre had taken over her husband's apartment, which was rather large, in comparison with the size of the chalet. It consisted of three rooms and Paule was preparing tea in one of them while waiting for us. She had so little concern about her appearance that she had kept her traveling dress, which was all rumpled and her hair was still loose and disheveled under her straw hat. It was perhaps a sacrifice she had made for Obernay to stay like this so as not to lose a single moment of those they could spend together. However, I felt that she accepted all too easily the neglect of her physical appearance, and the thought immediately came on me that she wasn't enough of a woman to become anything other than the wife of a scientist. I congratulated Obernay in my heart but any feeling of envy or personal regret gave way to a clear liking for his future wife's kindness and reasonableness.

Madame de Valvèdre was not there. She stayed in her room until the time when Paule knocked at her door and shouted that it would soon be time for the signal. She then came out of her sanctuary and I saw that she had changed into an adorable negligee. It was perhaps not quite in keeping with the mental agitation that she was showing, but if by chance she had dressed for my benefit, how could I not be grateful?

She seemed to me so different from what she had seemed on the mountain path that, had I seen her again in a place other than her room, I would have barely recognized her. When she was perched on her mule and draped in her Arab cloak, I had imagined her to be tall and strong, but in reality she was small and delicate. Her color heightened by the heat, under the reflection of her parasol had seemed to me red and as if veined with purplish tints. She was pale and with the finest and smoothest skin. Her features were charming and her whole person had, like her attire, an exquisite distinction.

I barely had time to look at her and to greet her. The moment was approaching and people were rushing to the balcony. She was the last to settle on a seat I handed to her and speaking to me softly, she said, "It seems to me that the first base camps of people who undertake such expeditions have nothing alarming?"

"Indeed," Obernay replied, "this base camp is a hole in the rock with a few stones around it. It is not very comfortable but it is safe. But watch. Five minutes have gone by."

"Where are we supposed to look?" Mademoiselle de Valvèdre keenly asked.

"Where I told you. And yet...no! Here is the white flare. It is coming from much farther up. He must have ignored the stop marked by the guides. He is on the high plateaus, if I am not mistaken."

"But, aren't the high plateaus snow-covered plains?"

"Excuse me!... Second white flare... The snow is hard and he has set up his tent without any difficulty... Third white flare! His instruments have held up during the trip; nothing is broken or damaged. Bravo!"

"If this is the case, he'll spend a better night than we will," Madame de Valvèdre said, "because his instruments are what he holds dearest."

"Why, Madame, wouldn't you sleep in peace," I ventured in turn. "Monsieur de Valvèdre is so well prepared against the cold; he has such experience with these sorts of adventures..."

Madame de Valvèdre gave an imperceptible smile, either to thank me for my solace, or to dismiss it, or even because she found me quite naïve to think that a husband like hers could be the cause of her insomnia. She left the balcony where Obernay, who was not expecting any other signal, had remained to speak of Valvèdre with Paule; and, as I was following Alida toward the tea table, I was once more quite undecided about how charming her features were. It seemed that she guessed my uncertainty because she languidly lay on a sort of chaise that was rather low, and at last I was able to see her, all of her, lighted as she was by the lamp placed on the table.

I had been gazing at her for a moment, in silence and somewhat perturbed when she slowly raised her eyes to meet mine, as if to say, "Well, are you finally ready to see that I am the most perfect creature that you have ever met?" This woman's gaze was so expressive that I felt it go right through me, from top to bottom, like a burning shiver, and I cried out, "Yes, Madame, yes!"

She saw how young I was and did not take offense because she asked me with only the slightest surprise what it was that I was answering.

"Pardon me, Madame, I thought you had spoken to me!"

"But not at all, I wasn't saying anything to you!"

And a second look, longer and more penetrating than the first one, further upset me for it was inquiring into the deepest recesses of my soul.

To those who haven't seen this woman's gaze, I could never explain the nature of her mysterious power. Her eyes, extraordinarily long and clear, with dark eyelashes which contrasted with the plane of her cheek through a changing shadow, were neither blue, black, greenish, nor orange-colored. They were all of that in turn, depending on the light or on the inner emotion that made them lighten or shine. Their usual expression was one of extreme languor and no eye was more impenetrable when, to avoid scrutiny, it withdrew its flame; but when it let out the merest spark, all the anguish of desire or all the spells of pleasure went over to the soul it wanted to take over, however well guarded or suspicious that soul was.

Mine was quite inexperienced and did not even think for a minute to defend itself. She, the woman who had just subjugated me, could see it quite plainly. We had only the three exchanges I have just recounted and Obernay was coming near us with his fiancée, but everything was already settled in my thoughts and my conscience. I had broken with my duties, my family, my destiny, myself. I belonged blindly, exclusively to this woman, this stranger, this sorceress.

I don't have any idea of what was said around the small table where Paule de Valvèdre was rattling tea cups while chatting quietly with Obernay. I have no idea if I drank any tea. I know that I handed a cup to Madame de Valvèdre and that I stayed by her, my eyes riveted on her thin white arm, as I no longer dared look at her face, convinced that I would lose my sense and fall at her feet if she looked at me another time. When she handed her empty cup back to me, I received it mechanically and didn't think of moving away. I was immersed in the scent of her dress and her hair. I examined more stupidly than artfully the lace on her ruffles, the fine fabric of her silk stocking, the embroidery of her cashmere jacket, the pearls of her bracelet, as if I had never seen an elegant woman before, and as if I wanted to understand the rules of good taste. A shyness that was almost fear prevented me from thinking about anything but this piece of clothing which gave off a burning fluid that prevented me from thinking and from speaking. Obernay and Paule were speaking for four people. What things did they have to tell each other! I think they were sharing excellent ideas in a language that was still better, but I heard nothing. I observed later that Mademoiselle de Valvèdre was well-educated, had a fine intelligence, a sound, high-minded judgment, and even a charming mind; but at that time when, within myself, I could only think of restraining the throbs of my heart, I was quite surprised by the moral freedom of this happy couple who expressed their thoughts so easily and so abundantly! They had already a communicative, conjugal love: for me, I felt that desire is shy and passion is silent.

Did Alida have an innate intelligence? I have never been certain, although I heard her say striking things, and sometimes I heard her speak with the eloquence brought about by deep emotions; but usually she was silent, and that night either because she was not willing to reveal anything of her soul, or because she was exhausted or overly preoccupied, she only managed to say a few insignificant words. I was and I remained much too close to her; I could have and I should have kept a more respectful distance. I could feel that and felt paralyzed. She must have laughed inwardly, but she did not seem to mind and the two fiancés were too taken up with each other to notice. I felt both so poorly and so well that I would have stayed there all night without moving and without a clear thought. I saw Obernay shake Paule's hand in a brotherly fashion and tell her that she probably needed to sleep. I found myself in my room not knowing how I had managed to say good-bye and to leave my seat; I threw myself on my bed half dressed, like a drunken man.

I only regained my senses at the first chill of daybreak. I hadn't closed an eye. I had been prey to an unknown mix of joy and despair. I could see myself overcome with love, that, until this time of my life, I had only known in my dreams and that the somewhat skeptical arrogance of a sophisticated education had led me both to fear and to scorn. This sudden revelation had an indescribable charm and I felt I was a new man, more energetic, more enterprising, but the ardor of the desire that I was still so unsure of being able to satisfy caused me intense suffering and, when my excitement quieted, it was followed by terror. I did not wonder if, overcome to this point, I might be ruined; this was of little importance. I only took my own counsel about the course to follow in order to avoid being ridiculous, bothersome, and soon rejected. In the midst of my madness, my reasoning was rigorous; I mapped out a line of conduct. I understood that I shouldn't let Obernay suspect anything because his friendship with Valvèdre would certainly turn him into an opponent. I resolved to gain his trust by appearing to share his negative opinion of Alida and to learn from him everything I could fear or hope from her. Nothing is further from my nature than this treachery but, surprisingly, it did not bother me at all. I had never tried my hand at duplicity, and I became quite adept at it from that first time on. After two hours of early morning walk with my friend, I held everything he had begrudged me until then. I knew everything he knew.

II

Without fortune or ancestors, Alida had been chosen by Valvèdre. Had he loved her? Did he still love her? No one knew; but no one had reason to believe that love had not guided his choice since Alida had no other capital than her beauty. During the first years, the couple had been inseparable. It is true that gradually, for the last five or six years, Valvèdre had resumed his life of explorations and travels but without appearing to neglect his companion and without ceasing to surround her with care, luxury, attentions, and condescension. It was not true, according to Obernay, that he kept her prisoner in his villa, or that Mademoiselle Juste de Valvèdre, the oldest of her sisters-in-law, was a chaperone charged with oppressing her. On the contrary, Mademoiselle Juste was a very distinguished person in charge of the children's early education and of the running of the household, tasks for which Alida herself declared she was unfit. Paule had been brought up by her older sister. The three women thus lived as they wished: Paule under her sister Juste's influence out of inclination and duty, Alida completely independent of both.

As for the matter of the affairs attributed to her, Obernay did not believe it at all; that is to say, no exclusive relationship had taken a visible place in her life since he had known her. "I think she is a flirt," he would say, "but she is so out of affectation or idleness. I don't consider her active or energetic enough to be passionate or even to have strong desires. She likes attention; she is bored when there is a dearth of compliments, and perhaps they are rare in the countryside. She may miss them in Geneva also where she has honored us by accepting our hospitality on occasion. Our circle is a little too serious for her, and it is a great misfortune, isn't it, that a thirty-year-old woman should be forced by social conventions to live reasonably? I know that before, in an effort to please her, her husband often took her out in fashionable circles; but there is a time for everything. A scientist owes his time to science; a mother owes hers to her children. To tell you the truth, I have a poor opinion of a woman's brain when she finds her duties boring."

"It seems, though, that she obeys them, since, free to throw herself into the whirl, she lives in seclusion?"

"She would have to face the whirl on her own and it is not easy, unless you have a certain audacious vitality, which she doesn't have. In my opinion, it would be better for her to have the courage to do it since she has the inclination, and it would be better for Valvèdre to have a wife completely dissolute and promiscuous, who would leave him perfectly free and at peace, than an elegy in skirts who cannot make any decisions and whose weakened deportment seems to be a protest against common sense, a reproach to rational life."

All this is easy to say, I thought to myself. Perhaps this woman is yearning after something other than frivolous pleasures; perhaps she has a great need to love, especially if her husband introduced her to love before leaving her for physics and chemistry. Such a woman really starts life at thirty and the company of two brats and of two infinitely virtuous sisters-in-law does not appear to be an ideal to which I would devote myself. Why do we demand of beauty, which is exclusively made for love, what we, the ugly sex, would be incapable of accepting? At the age of forty, M. de Valvèdre is completely devoted to his passion for science. He has thought it quite fair to drop sisters, brats, and wife in the bargain . . . It is true that he lets her have her freedom . . . Well, let her take advantage of it; it is her right, and it is the task of a young and ardent soul like mine to make her overcome the scruples that hold her back!

Of course, I refrained from sharing these thoughts with Obernay. On the contrary, I pretended to agree with all of his pronouncements and I left him without contradicting him in the least. I was supposed to see Alida again, as I had the night before, at the time of Valvèdre's signal. Tired by the daylong mule ride that she had taken in order to travel from Varallo to Saint Pierre, she kept to her bed. Paule was busy sorting the plants that she had asked the guides to pick along the way and that she was going to examine during the evening with her fiancé, who was teaching her botany. Aware of these details and seeing Obernay leave quietly for a walk while waiting for the moment to be admitted for his courting,

I did not feel the need to go with him. I wandered aimlessly around the house and in the house itself, observing the movements of the servant and of Alida's maid; I tried to overhear what they were saying, I was spying in a word, for I had something like sudden revelations of experience, and I thought quite rightly that, in order to assess the question of a woman's behavior, you had first of all to observe how those who served her reacted to her. They appeared to be eager to respond to her needs, for, called by the bell several times, they went through the gallery, and climbed up and down the stairs about twenty times without showing any ill-temper.

I had left my bedroom door open; we were the only travelers, and Ambroise's beautifully rustic inn was so quiet that I could hear everything that was happening. All of a sudden I heard a loud swish of skirts at the end of the hallway. I made a dash, thinking that someone had finally decided to come out; but I saw only a beautiful silk dress in the hands of the chamber maid. She had probably just unpacked it because a new mule loaded with cases and boxes had arrived a few minutes earlier in front of the inn. This circumstance led me to hope for a stay of several days in Saint Pierre; but how long that day seemed, the day whose end I so awaited! Would it be totally lost to my love? What could I invent to fill the hours or to obtain the revocation of the social code that kept me away?

I concocted thousands of schemes, all equally absurd. I wanted to dress as a trader in herborized agates to gain admission into the sanctuary, the door of which opened every minute, or I wanted to run after some bear-leader and make his animal growl so as to draw the women to their windows. I also had the idea of firing my pistol to create some commotion in the house; they might believe it was an accident; they might send for news of my health, and even if I was slightly wounded...

This extravagance was so appealing that I almost put it into effect. At last my choice fell on a less extreme solution, which was to play the oboe. I played very well, according to my father, who himself was a good musician, and it was an opinion which the artists who gathered at our Belgian home seemed to share. My room was far enough from Madame de Valvèdre's own room that my music would not disturb her if she was asleep, and if she was not sleeping, which was more likely, considering the numerous comings and goings of the maid, she might ask who the pleasant virtuoso was. But what a disappointment it was when right in the middle of my most beautiful melody, a manservant, after discreetly knocking at my door, told me the following with as much embarrassment as respect. "I am very sorry, Sir, but if your grace is not absolutely determined to practice in an inn, there is her ladyship who is feeling quite poorly and who begs your Lordship . . ."

I gestured that he had been eloquent enough and I put my instrument back in its case with no little irritation. She was determined to sleep! My vexation became a kind of fury and I hoped that she would have nightmares; but fifteen minutes had hardly gone by when the servant showed up again. Madame de Valvèdre was thanking me very much and, unable to sleep in spite of my silence, she gave me permission to resume my music. At the same time she was asking if I didn't have some book to loan her *so long as it was literature and not science*. The man delivered the message so well that this time I thought he had learned it by heart. My travel library consisted only of one or two recent novels in small format, pirated editions bought in Geneva, and a very thin, anonymous volume which, for a moment, I hesitated to add to the package and which I slid, or rather, I suddenly tossed in, feeling like a man who is burning his bridges.

This thin volume was a book of poems, which I had published anonymously when I was twenty years old, prompted by the encouragements of an uncle of mine, a publisher who spoiled me; and I had been warned by my father that I would be wise not to compromise his name and mine for the pleasure of producing this trifle. "I don't think your poems are too bad," my good father had told me. "I even like some of them, but, since you want to have a literary career, be content to do this as a trial run and don't boast about having written it if you want to know what people really think. If you are discreet, this first experience will be useful. If you are not and your book is ridiculed, you will be vexed and then you will have created a bad precedent that people will not easily forget."

I had religiously followed his good advice. My little poems had not created a big stir, but they had not displeased and a few passages had even been noticed. They had, in my opinion, only one merit: their sincerity. They expressed the state of a young soul hungry for emotions, which does not claim to have more experience than it does and which did not boast too much about being as good as its ideals.

It was indeed quite rash on my part to have sent my poems to Madame de Valvèdre. If she guessed who the author was and found the verses ridiculous, I was lost. Pride did not blind me. My book was the work of a child. Would a thirty-year-old woman be interested in such naïve outbursts, in feelings so candidly expressed? . . . But why would she guess my secret? Hadn't I been able to protect it from my closest friends?

And even if I was more upset at the thought of her sarcasms than I could be about those of anyone else, didn't I have a chance of being cured through the chagrin that her harshness would cause me?

I did not want to be cured, however; I could feel it all too well and the hours dragged on, painfully slow, more cruel still since I had impulsively sent my twenty-year-old heart to a languid and high-strung woman who would probably not even look at it. As no new communication come forth, I went out in order to avoid feeling faint. I stopped the first passersby I met and spoke loudly under the travelers's window. Nobody showed. I felt like going back, but I went away, not knowing where I was going.

I was wandering on the road to Varallo when I saw a person coming toward me whom I thought I recognized. As he drew near, my heart gave a singular start. It was Monsieur Moserwald; I was not mistaken. He was walking up a steep slope; his small traveling cart carrying his belongings followed him. Why did the return of this man seem to me an event worthy of notice? He seemed surprised at my questions. He had not said he was leaving the valley for good. He had gone on an excursion in the vicinity, and, intending to go on other excursions, he was coming back to Saint Pierre as it was the only possible stopping point within a ten-mile radius. As far as he was concerned, he was not a great hiker, he said. He was not keen on breaking his neck in order to look from above: he found the mountains more beautiful when looked at from halfway up. He quite admired adventure seekers, but he did wish them good luck and he traveled as comfortably as he could. He could not understand that one could go through the Alps on foot and frugally at that. There, more than anywhere else you had to spend a lot of money to have a little fun. After many platitudes of the like, he said good-bye and climbed back into his vehicle; then, stopping his driver at the first turn of the wheel, he called me back: "I was thinking! It will soon be dinnertime there, and you may be late. Do you want a ride?"

It seemed to me that after displaying much obtuseness, purposely perhaps, he was giving me a look of sudden insight. I do not know what distrust or curiosity this man called forth in me. There was a little of both. My dream had left me with a superstition. I took the seat at his side.

"Do you have some new traveler here?" he asked as he gestured toward the hamlet with its little openwork belfry outlined in brilliant white against the dark green background of the trees.

"*Travelers*? No," I answered, taking refuge in a most awkward casuistry. I felt much less self-assurance in hiding my agitation from Moserwald, whose sincerity I doubted, than I felt in shamelessly deceiving Obernay, the most just, the most sincere of men. It was like a punishment for my duplicity, this struggle with a Jew who was much better at it than I was, and I was humiliated to be engaged in this onslaught of dissimulation. He continued with a smile of simple-minded shrewdness, "So you did not see a certain caravan of women, guides, and mules go by? . . . I saw them last night, ten miles from here, in the village of Varallo, and I was quite sure they would stop in Saint Pierre; but since you are telling me that no one has arrived . . ."

I could feel that I was blushing and I hastened to answer with a forced smile that I had said no about the arrival of male travelers, not that of unexpected women travelers.

"Ah, well! You were playing with words! . . . With you, I can see, one needs to specify the grammatical gender. In any case, you saw these beautiful adventure seekers; when I say these beautiful . . . you might reproach me with not using the appropriate number any better than the grammatical gender . . . because there is only one who is beautiful! The other woman . . . is, I think, the geologist's younger sister . . . , fair at most. Do you know that M . . . .what is his name? . . . your friend? Anyway, you know who I mean: he is marrying her!"

"I know nothing at all, but if you think so, if you heard it, how could you have had the bad taste the other day to joke about his relations with . . ."

"And with whom? What did I say? Really! I don't remember! People say so many things when they talk! *Verba nolant*! Don't think that I know Latin! What did I say? Come on! Tell me!"

I did not answer. I was quite vexed. I was getting increasingly tangled up; I felt like picking a quarrel with this Moserwald and yet I had to take everything lightly or allow him to read my agitated mind. However hard I attempted to cut off the conversation by pointing out to him the beautiful herds passing near us, he came back to the topic relentlessly and I was forced to mention Madame de Valvèdre's name. He was blind or generous; he did not comment on the strange look I must have had when saying this terrifying name.

"Well," he exclaimed with his natural or affected frivolity. "I said, did I say it? that M. Obernay, his name is coming to me now, had designs on his friend's wife! It is possible . . . One always has an eye on one's friend's wife! I did not know then that he was to marry the sister-in-law, I promise! I only heard about it yesterday morning when I got the ladies' manservant to talk. I could easily tell you that this doesn't seem to be an unacceptable reason. . . . I am a skeptic; I am, I told you, but I don't want to shock you, and I am ready to believe. God, you are really not paying attention to me! What are you thinking about?"

"Nothing, and it is your fault. You are not saying anything worth listening to. You don't have any common sense, dear fellow, with your ideas of deep wickedness. What poor taste you have! It is not fitting, especially when one is rich and well-fed."

If I had known how impossible it was to upset Moserwald, I would have done without these unnecessary harsh words, which he found very amusing. He liked people to pay attention to him even if they treated him harshly or mocked him. "Of course, yes, you are right!" he continued as if he were full of gratitude. "You are telling me what all my friends say, and I appreciate it. I am ridiculous, and that's the saddest part of it all! I am melancoly, dear fellow, and the disbelief of others on my account adds to my own about everyone and myself. Yes, I should be happy because I am rich and in good health, because I am well fed! And yet I am bored, my liver bothers me, I don't trust men, women even less! Ah, my word, how do you manage to believe in women? You will tell me that you are young! It is not a good reason. When one is highly educated and very intelligent, one is never young. Yet, here you are in love . . ."

"Me! Where did you get that idea?"

"You are in love, I can see it, and as naïvely as if you were certain to succeed in having your love reciprocated; but, my dear child, it's an impossible thing. One is only loved out of interest. I have been loved because I have a capital of several millions; you may be loved because you have a capital of twenty-three, twenty-four years, black hair, burning eyes, a capital that promises a sum of pleasures of another kind and no less positive that those my money represents—much more positive, I should say, because money brings high pleasures, luxury, arts, travels . . . Whereas when a woman prefers to all this a poor, handsome boy, you can be sure that she sets great store in reality. But this is not love as we understand it, you and me. We would like to be loved for ourselves, for our minds, our social qualities, our personal merit, in a word. Well, that is what you will probably buy at the price of your freedom, what I would willingly pay with all my fortune, and what we shall never encounter. Women have no heart. They use the word *virtue* to hide their infirmity, and with that they still fool some men! Fools I envy, I must admit."

"Ah," I cried out interrupting this flow of nauseating philosophy, "what have you been saying for the last sixty minutes? You are telling me that you have been loved, that I shall be . . ."

"Ah, dear God! You think that I was speaking about Madame de Valvèdre? I was not thinking of her, dear fellow, I was speaking in general. First, I don't know her; you have my word that I have never spoken to her. As for you, you cannot know her yet; you may have spoken to her, however? By the way, do you find her pretty?"

"Who? Madame de Valvèdre? Not at all, dear fellow, I found her ugly."

I answered with such self-confidence, a desperate self-confidence (I wanted at all cost to avoid Moserwald's inquiries), that he was fooled and he let me see how pleased he was. When we got out of the carriage, I had finally managed to take away from him the light he thought he had seen, that he had seen for an instant, and he had fallen back into darkness, while leaving his secret in my hands. He had quite evidently come back to Saint Pierre because he had met Madame de Valvèdre in Varallo, because he had questioned her manservant, because he was in love with her, because he hoped that she would like him, and he had sounded me out to see whether I would not get in his way.

Having found out from Antoine that the Valvèdre ladies would not dine downstairs, I wanted to avoid the unpleasant experience of another tête-à-tête with Moserwald by being served discreetly in a corner of my host's small garden when he told me that I would be alone in his low-ceiling dining hall with Obernay; the Israelite had said that he might dine later in the evening. "And what is he doing? Where is he now?" I asked.

"He is in Madame de Valvèdre's room," Antoine answered with a comical expression of surprise on his face when he saw my astonishment.

"Oh," I exclaimed, "does he know her?"

"I don't know, Sir; how could I know that?"

"True, it is of no matter to you, and, as for me . . . But do you know him, this M. Moserwald?"

"No, Sir, I don't; I saw him for the first time the day before yesterday."

"Had he told you when he left that he was to come back soon?"

"No, Sir, he said nothing at all."

A kind of irrepressible anger swept over me when I heard that this Jew had had the audacity or the cleverness, when he had just arrived, to gain admittance with Alida whom he pretended not to know. Obernay was very late; it was night when he came back. I had waited to have dinner with him; I deserved no credit for that, as I was not in the least hungry. I did not speak to him about Moserwald, as I feared to reveal my jealousy.

"Sit down to dinner," he said to me. "I must have fifteen minutes to sort a few extremely fragile water moss specimens that I am bringing back."

He left me and Antoine served me my meal, saying that he knew of Obernay's fifteen minutes of unpacking his botanical spoils and that it was no reason to serve me an overcooked roast. I had hardly sat down when Moserwald appeared, exclaiming that he was delighted not to dine alone, and ordered our host to serve him across from me, and this without asking my permission at all. This familiarity, which I might have found amusing had I been in an another frame of mind, struck me as intolerable, and I was going to let him know when, my curiosity overtaking all of my other anxieties, I resolved to hold back my feelings and to make him talk. It was a painful and angry curiosity; but I was quite the stoic and quite casually I asked him if he had managed to see Madame de Valvèdre.

"No, I did not," he answered while rubbing his hands together, "but I shall see her soon with you, in an hour."

"Ah, really."

"Are you surprised? Yet, it is quite simple. My face and my voice were already familiar to the sister-in-law, who had noticed me at Varallo. Oh, I say this without self-complacency. I have no claims on that side. I observe that she had noticed me the day before yesterday when going through the village where we crossed paths. Well, we met again a while ago in the gallery. She is quite open, quite trusting, this young lady; she came to me to know whether I had picked up some news about her brother on my way."

"About whom you knew nothing."

"Excuse me; with money you always know what you want to know. Seeing that the ladies were worried, I had, as early as last night, sent the most daring mountaineer from Varallo to M. de Valvèdre's presumed base camp. Why! It cost me dearly; during the night and through impossible paths, he claimed it was worth..."

"Spare me the francs that you spent. Have you had news of the expedition?"

"Yes, I did, very good news. His sister almost kissed me. She wanted to introduce me right away to Madame de Valvèdre; but this lady, who had spent the day in bed, was just getting up and put me off till later. Here it is, dear fellow! It is as simple as that!"

Moserwald no longer hid his plans; he needed to boast about his cleverness and his liberality too much to be cautious. My jealousy quieted a bit. What could I fear from such a vain and vulgar rival? Wasn't it insulting to a woman as exquisite as Alida to fear on her behalf the appeal of a Moserwald?

I was going to question him further when Obernay, looking preoccupied, came to eat hastily some leftover poultry; then he looked at his watch and told us it was time to go up to the ladies in order to see the flares go off. "I have heard," he said to Moserwald, "that you have been invited to have tea upstairs in order to thank you for the good news you gave, for which I too am grateful; but allow me to ask a question."

"A thousand questions, if you like, *dearest fellow*," Moserwald answered with ease.

"You sent a mountaineer near the Ermitage peak; he went there through numerous dangers and you waited for him in Varallo until morning. Did he see M. de Valvèdre? Did he speak to him?"

"He saw him from too far away to speak to him but he saw him."

"Very well but if the fancy struck you again to send express messengers and if they reached him, please refrain from asking them to tell him that his wife and his sister are looking for him."

"I am not so stupid," Moserwald exclaimed with a laugh that either was unusually impertinent or naïve.

"What do you mean, 'not so stupid'?" answered Obernay with surprise, looking at him straight in the eyes. Moserwald was embarrassed for a moment but his quick-witted mind suggested to him a fairly clever answer.

"I am quite aware," he continued, "that your scientist would be quite upset by the arrival and the worry of the ladies. When you risk your life in such a campaign and when you have in mind the great problems of science about which I admit I understand nothing, but about which I recognize the passion, seeing that I understand all passions, as I am speaking to you . . ." Obernay interrupted him impatiently by throwing his napkin.

"Well," he said, "you guessed the truth. M. de Valvèdre needs all the freedom of mind possible right now. Let us go up; we do not have time left to chat."

Alida's attire was simpler than the day before. I was extremely grateful to her for not having dressed up for Moserwald. She was all the more beautiful. I do not know if her sister-in-law was more groomed than the previous day; I think that I did not see her at all that evening. I was so full of my inner drama that I almost believed I was alone with Madame de Valvèdre.

She first greeted me with coldness and suspicion. She seemed impatient to see the flare launched. I did not follow her on the balcony. I don't know if the signals augured well; I don't remember that I asked about it.

I only know that fifteen minutes later Paule de Valvèdre and her fiancé were sitting at a large table and that they were examining plant specimens, giving barbaric or pompous names to borage and couch grass, while Madame de Valvèdre, half reclined on her chaise with a pedestal table between her and me, was embroidering nonchalantly on thick canvas, as if she wanted to avoid meeting our eyes. I could see from her careless hands that she only worked to withdraw into herself. Her expressive features had at that time a mysterious placidity. There was most certainly no reciprocal affinity between her and Moserwald. I even noticed with pleasure behind the expressions of politeness and thanks that she showed him quite laconically there was a touch of disdain.

I was fully reassured when I also noticed that the Israelite, who had first been full of self-confidence with her, was swiftly losing some of his vitality. As usual he had probably counted on the good-natured and paradoxical bon mot of his natural wit to compensate for his lack of education; but he had quickly become less voluble. He only spoke in platitudes and I cruelly helped him as I could detect an imperceptible smile of irony on Madame de Valvèdre's closed lips.

Poor Moserwald! He was nonetheless better and more honest at this time of his life than he had perhaps ever been. He was in love and quite sincerely moved. Like me, he was drinking the strange poison of irresistible passion that had inebriated me, and when I think of everything that afterward this passion made him do that was contrary to his theories, his ideas, and his instincts, I wonder with amazement if there is a school for feelings and if feelings themselves are not what ultimately reveal who we are.

As he was losing his composure, I was regaining my clearheadedness. Soon I was able to understand and to comment calmly on the situation. He had not dared boast in front of Mademoiselle de Valvèdre about all the zeal with which he had found a pretext to come near Alida. He had even had the good taste not to speak about the money he had spent. He was pretending he had only gone to find information in the surrounding areas and that he had managed to find a hunter who was coming down from the mountain and who had seen from afar the scientist's camp and the scientist himself in a safe place and apparently healthy. He had been thanked for his kindness. Paule spoke innocently of his "good heart." They knew him by name and by reputation but they had never noticed his face, even though he did his utmost to mention various circumstances when he has been at the public promenade in Geneva or at a show in Torino, not far from *the ladies*. He implied as subtly as he could that Madame de Valvèdre had made quite an impression on him; that such and such a day at such and such a meeting he had noticed every detail of her appearance. "They were performing the *Barber of Seville*." "Yes, I remember," she would say.

"You were wearing a light blue silk dress with white trims and your hair was curled instead of being coiled like today."

"I don't remember," Alida answered with a tone that implied "What business is it of yours?"

There was such a *crescendo* of coldness on her part that the poor Jew, quite confounded, left the corner of the fireplace where he had been swaggering for the last fifteen minutes and went to disturb and annoy the botanist couple by asking them crude and mocking questions about their sacrosanct study of nature. I took over the spot that Moserwald had claimed: it was the most favorable from which to see Alida without having in my line of vision the small lamp behind which she hid; it was also the closest one could properly take near her. Until then, not wanting to sit further, I had barely been able to catch a glimpse of her.

At last I was able to speak to her. I had quite a bit of trouble asking her a direct question. Finally my tongue loosened in a desperate effort and, at the risk of being as clumsy and silly as Moserwald, I asked her if I was unfortunate enough for my cursed oboe to have really disturbed her sleep.

"So disturbed," she answered with a smile full of sadness, "that I was unable to go back to sleep; but do not take this reproach for a criticism. It seemed to me that you play quite well; that is precisely why I was compelled to listen to you. Nevertheless I do not want to pay you a compliment either. At your age, it is not good."

"At my age? Yes, I am a child, really, just a child! It is the age when one yearns for happiness. Is it a crime to be happy with a trifle, a word, a glance, be it a distracted or stern glance, be it a word of simple kindness or of generous forgiveness in the guise of praise?"

"I can see," she rejoined, "that you have read the little book that you sent me this morning, for you are full of the pride of the very young and this not very kind for those men or women who are in the next stage."

"Among the books that, at your command, I sent you this morning, was there one that had the misfortune of displeasing you?"

She smiled with an indescribable sweetness and was going to answer. I was hanging on her every word. Moserwald, leaning over the table, was not looking at all through Obernay's magnifying glass, which he had taken without thinking and which he was clouding with his breath, to the botanist's greatest annoyance. He was making faces behind the magnifying glass, but he was staring hard at me, and was squinting in such a funny way that Madame de Valvèdre burst out laughing. It was for me a moment of cruel triumph, but one for which a moment later I cruelly paid. When laughing, Madame de Valvèdre dropped her embroidery and a small metallic object which I took for a thimble and which I rushed to pick up; but I had hardly taken it in my hands that a cry of surprise and sorrow escaped me.

"What is this?" I cried out.

"Well," she answered placidly, "it is my ring. It is much too large for my finger."

"Your ring!" I repeated beside myself and looking with distress at the big sapphire circled with diamonds that I had seen two days before on Moserwald's finger. And I added, overcome by a real despair, "But this thing is not yours, Madame!"

"Excuse me, but whose do you think it is?"

"Ah, you bought it today?"

"Well! What does it matter to you, I wonder! Give it back to me!"

"Since you bought it," I bitterly said when handing it back to her, "keep it; it is yours. But if I were you, I would not wear it. It is in horrible taste."

"Do you think so? It is quite possible. I bought it yesterday for twenty-five francs from an ugly little Jew in Varallo who sets amethysts and other local stones in vermeil; but the big stone is pretty. I shall have it set differently and everyone will think it is an oriental sapphire." I was going to tell Madame de Valvèdre that the little Jew had stolen this ring from Moserwald, when I realized that the low price implied an all too incredible lack of knowledge in a Jewish jeweler about the value of the stones, and I was thrown back into an insoluble enigma. Alida had just spoken with obvious sincerity, and still, whatever effort Moserwald made to hide his left hand from me, I could see that he no longer had his ring. A hideous suspicion weighed on me like a nightmare. I took the Israelite by the arm and led him to the gallery as if to speak about something else. I flattered his vanity in order to wrest the truth out of him. "You are a clever man and a magnificent suitor," I said, "you have your gifts accepted in the most ingenious way!"

He fell into the trap without coaxing. "Well, yes," he said, "that is how I am! Nothing is beyond my capacity to give an enjoyable trifle to a pretty woman, and I do not have the bad taste to put conditions to it! It is up to her to figure it out."

"And certainly you have been figured out? Is it a habit?"

"With this one… it is the first time, and I wonder with a little trepidation if she is really taking this first-quality gem for a hundred centimes amethyst. No, it is not likely. All women know about precious stones; they like them so much!"

"Still, if she does not know anything about it, she is not figuring out who gave it to her and you are at a dead end. Either you must make your declaration or you will run the risk of having the ring go to the chambermaid."

"Make my declaration?" He answered with real terror. "Oh, no, it is too soon! I have received no encouragements until now… unless her mocking tone is a grand lady's way! This is possible. I had never aimed so high, because, you know, she is a countess. Her husband does not use his title but he comes from the high nobility."

"Dear fellow," I continued with an irony that he did not catch, crafty as he may have been, "I can see only one way, which is to have a generous friend enlighten her about the worth of the object that she has so cleverly been led to accept. Do you want me to take care of it?"

"Yes, but not today at least! Wait till I am gone."

"Nonsense! How fearful you are! Don't you know that a woman is always flattered by an expensive gift?"

"No, it depends; she may like the gift and hate the person who gives it. In this case, you need lots of patience and many gifts, always slipped into her hands without her thinking of rejecting them, and never showing any hope. You can see that I have my strategy!"

"It is superb, and very flattering for the women whom you make the honor of pursuing!"

"But… I think it is quite subtle," he continued with conviction, "and if you criticize it, it is because you would be incapable of following it!"

I did not forgive him for this outburst of impertinence and I went back to the small drawing room determined to punish him for it. I felt then an extraordinary composure, and coming near Alida I said, "Do you know, Madame, the topic of my conversation with M. Moserwald under the moonlight?"

"About the moonlight, perhaps?"

"No, we were talking jewelry. The gentleman pretends that all women are experts in precious stones because they love them passionately and I promised to submit to your arbitration."

"There are two questions there," Madame de Valvèdre answered. "I cannot solve the first one because in my case I don't know anything about it, but for the second one, I have to agree with M. Moserwald. I think that all women like jewelry."

"Except me, however," said Paule with gaiety, "I don't care at all for it."

"Oh, you, my dear," Alida went on with the same tone, "you are a superior woman. Here we are only speaking of mere mortals."

"As for me," I said in turn with extreme bitterness, "I thought that as far as women were concerned, only courtesans had a passion for diamonds."

Alida looked at me with great surprise.

"What a strange idea!" she continued. "Among the creatures about whom you are speaking, this passion does not exist at all. Diamonds only mean money for them. Among honest women, it is something more noble: it represents the sacred gifts of the family or the long-lasting tokens of serious affections. It is so true that, once ruined, a great lady will suffer many hardships rather than sell her jewelry case. She will sacrifice it only to save her children or her princes."

"Ah, well said and quite true," said Moserwald with enthusiasm. "Between women and diamonds, there is a supernatural attraction! I have seen thousands of examples of it. According to legend, the snake had a big diamond in his head. Eve saw this fire through its eyes and was mesmerized. She looked at her own reflection as in the mirrors of an enchanted palace."

"Here is some poetry if I am not mistaken," I said, interrupting him. "And you make fun of poets, you of all people!"

"You are surprised, dear fellow?" he continued. "It is because I too am becoming a poet apparently, with people who inspire me!"

With these words, he gave Alida a burning look, which she met and held with an extraordinary impassivity. It was the height of scorn or impudence, as her large quizzical eye was still full of mysteries. I could not stand this dubious situation, horrible for her, if she was not the lowest of women. I asked her if I could again see her twenty-five franc ring, and having looked at it, I told her, "I am quite surprised at the lack of attention you paid to such a beautiful gem after you admitted your taste for these kinds of things. Do you know, Madame, that you have been sold a very valuable stone?"

"What? How is that possible?" She said as she took the ring back and looked at it. "Do you know much about these things?"

"My only knowledge comes from M. Moserwald here, who no earlier than the day before yesterday showed me a ring quite like it, with diamonds like those, and he offered it to me for twelve thousand francs, that is to say for nothing according to him, because it is worth much more."

Faced with this direct interpellation, Moserwald's face crumpled, and Alida's quick glance from him to me finished distressing him. Madame de Valvèdre did not lose her composure. She kept silent for a few minutes, as if she wanted to solve an inner problem; then, presenting the ring to me, she said, "Whether it is valuable or not, I do find it quite ugly. Would you be kind enough to throw it out the window?"

"Really, out the window?" Moserwald cried out, unable to control his emotions.

"You can see," Alida answered, "that it is something that has been lost, then found by your fellow Jew in Varallo, and sold without his knowing its value. Well, we must return this thing to its destiny, which is to be picked up in the mud by people who are not afraid to get their hands dirty."

Moserwald, pushed to the limit, reacted with much calm and presence of mind. He asked me to give him the ring, and as I was giving it back to him, affecting a rightful restitution, he put it back on his finger saying, "Since it must be thrown away, I am picking it up. I don't know where it comes from, but I know that it has been purified forever by being on Madame de Valvèdre's finger for a day. And now, whether it is worth twenty-five centimes or twenty-five thousand francs, it is priceless for me and will never leave my finger." That said, he stood up and added while looking at me, "I think the ladies are tired and it would be time to . . ."

"M. Obernay and M. Valigny are not withdrawing yet," Madame de Valvèdre answered with a heartbreaking intention, "but you are free to go, especially since you are leaving tomorrow morning, I presume! As for the ring, you cannot keep it. It is mine. I bought it and did not give it to you. Give it back to me!"

Moserwald's beady eyes shone like garnets. He thought his triumph was certain in spite of a dismissal given for the sake of appearances and he returned the ring with a smile that clearly meant "I knew that she would keep it!" Madame de Valvèdre took it, and, throwing it out of her room through the open door onto the landing, she added, "It will be picked up by someone. It is no longer mine; but the person who will wear it as my keepsake can claim to own a thing that I thoroughly despise."

Moserwald left in such low spirits that I felt sorry for him. Paule had not understood a thing of this scene, to which in any case, she had paid little attention. As for Obernay, he had tried to understand for a minute, but did not manage to do so and, attributing all of this to some strange whimsy of Madame de Valvèdre, went quietly back to the analysis of *Saxifraga retusa*.

III

I had followed Moserwald without affectation, thinking that if he had any heart, he would ask me for explanations about the way I had served his cause. I saw him hesitate before picking up his ring, shrug his shoulders, and take it back. As soon as he saw me, he drew me to his room and spoke to me with a great deal of bitterness, mocking what he called my prejudices and declaring that my austerity was the most ridiculous thing. I purposefully let him become a little cruder in his criticisms, and when he was there I said, "You know, dear Sir, that if you are displeased, there is a way to settle this, and I am at your service. Do not go any further in words because I should be forced to ask you for the reparation that I am offering."

"What? What is this?" he said very surprised. "You want to fight? Well, here is a ray of light: an admission! You are my rival, and it is out of jealousy that you so brutally or so clumsily betrayed me. Say that it is your motive and I shall understand and forgive you."

I stated that I had nothing to confess and that I did not need his forgiveness; but, as I did not want to waste in his company the precious moments that I could still spend near Madame de Valvèdre that evening, I left him after urging him to think further about the matter and telling him that I would meet him in one hour.

The carved wooden gallery went around the house and I came back through it to Madame de Valvèdre's apartment, but I found her in the gallery coming to meet me.

"I have a question for you," she said to me with a cold and irritated tone. "Sit down here. Our friends are still immersed in botany. As it is at least unnecessary to tell them about a ridiculous incident, we can exchange a few words here. Would you be kind enough, Francis Valigny, to tell me what role you played in this incident, and how you learned what you intimated?"

I told her everything with the utmost sincerity. "Good," she said, "your intention was good, and you really did me a favor by preventing me from falling into this undescribable trap for one more second. You could have been less acerbic in your manner, but you do not know me, and if you take me for a fallen woman, it is no more your fault than mine."

"Me!" I cried out, "I take you for...? I...who...!" I began babbling uncontrollably.

"Enough, enough," she continued. "Do not deny your prejudices. I know what they are. They became cruelly clear when you said that my theory about diamonds, which was quite impersonal, was the expression of a courtesan's taste."

"But, in the name of the Lord, allow me to swear that I did not say this!"

"You thought it, and you said something similar. Listen, I have just been mortally insulted by this Jew and, consequently by you. Do not think that the scorn which saves me from anger protects me from being truly and deeply hurt."

I saw in the moonlight a stream of tears shining like a cascade of pearls on the pale cheeks of this charming woman, and without realizing what I was doing and even less what I was saying, I fell at her feet and swore to her that I respected her, that I commiserated with her, and that I was ready to avenge her. Perhaps at that moment I happened to tell her that I loved her. We were both upset, I because of her grief, she because of my sudden emotion, and for a few moments, we were unable to hear each other and hear ourselves.

She was the first one to overcome this agitation and, in answer to the words that I was repeating to diminish my offense, she said "Yes, I know, you are a child; but just as there is nothing as generous as a child who believes, there is nothing as terrible and cruel as a child who doubts, and you are the friend, the alter ego of another child much more skeptical and brutal than you are... But I do not want to quarrel with either of you. The sweet and lovely Paule Valvèdre must be happy. You are already her friend since you are her fiancé's friend; either I would be wrong in all your eyes, or if Paule sided with me against you two, she would suffer. So let me explain and let me tell you a little about who I am. It will be done in a nutshell. I am *drained, finished*, and consequently harmless. Henri Obernay described me to you, I know it, as a plaintive and boring creature, unhappy with everything and accusing everyone. It is his thesis; he has defended it in front of me, for he may have bad manners but he is sincere, and I know quite well that he is not a deceitful enemy. Tell him that I complain about no one, and, that said, tell him the reason why I came here, you who know and must say nothing of the reason that is going to cause my departure tomorrow."

"Tomorrow! You are leaving tomorrow?"

"Yes, if M. Moserwald stays, and I have no control over him."

"He will leave; I guarantee he will!"

"And I forbid you to take up my cause! What right would you have, if you please, to compromise me by acting as my defender?"

"But why do you want to leave, by God? Do this man's affronts hurt you?"

"Yes, they do. Affronts always hurt a widow whose husband is alive."

"Ah, dear Madame, you are misunderstood and abandoned, I knew it, but . . ."

"But nothing. That is the way things are. M. de Valvèdre is a man worthy of the highest respect; he knows everything, except the art of ensuring that the woman who carries his name be respected. But this woman fortunately knows what she owes her children, and to gain respect on her own, she has only one refuge, which is to withdraw in solitude. Thus, she will go back to it and, since you know why she is going back, you will also learn why she had come out of it for a moment. The solitude that was chosen for her must be at least her own and no one must have the right to disturb it. Well, I am not a complainer, but this time I do protest. I find Mademoiselle de Valvèdre's company unpleasant. My husband assures me that he did not place her near me to keep watch on me but to act as Paule's chaperone so that, he said, I would not have to play a role that is not yet of my age. However, Mademoiselle Juste has become oppressive and offensive. I have borne this for five years, but I am at the end of my rope. The logical and natural moment to end this has come since Paule's marriage to Obernay has been decided and is to be celebrated at the beginning of next year. M. de Valvèdre seems to have forgotten it, and Henri, like all scientists, is very patient in love. I was coming to tell my husband, 'Paule is bored and I am dying of lassitude and disgust. Marry Paule off and free me of Juste, or if Juste must remain sovereign in my household, allow me to take my children and my home near Paule, in Geneva, where she is to live after her wedding. And if this does not suit Obernay, let me find or assign me another retreat, a hermitage in some refuge, as long as I am free of the totally illegitimate authority of a person whom I cannot love.' I was hoping, I thought that I would find M. de Valvèdre here. He took flight toward the clouds and I cannot reach him. I did not and do not want to write: writing magnifies the wrongs of those who are absent. I do not want either to talk directly with Obernay about Mademoiselle Juste: he is very fond of her and would not fail to take her side against me. We would hurt each other's feelings, as we have done before. Since I cannot wait for M. de Valvèdre here, I am at least asking you to explain to Henri the reason, in appearance so disquieting and so mysterious, for my trip. If he loves Paule, he will make some effort to hasten his wedding and my liberation. I have spoken. Forget me and take care."

While finishing this explanation with an animation that held back deep inner tears, she held out her hand to me and stood up to take her leave.

I held her back. "I promise you," I exclaimed, "that you will not leave, that you will wait for M. de Valvèdre here and that you will successfully carry out a plan that is all too legitimate and reasonable. I promise that Moserwald, if he does not leave, will no longer dare look at you because Obernay and I will prevent him from doing so. We have the right to do so since Obernay is to become your brother-in-law and since I am his *alter ego*, as you said. Our duty is thus to defend you and to allow no one even to bother you. Finally, I promise that Henri will not stubbornly side with another person whom you dislike and who cannot be right against you. Henri loves his fiancée dearly; I do not believe in the patience which he is displaying. Please, Madame, believe in us, believe in me. I understand the honor you did me when you spoke to me as if I were a member of your family, and from now on, you can count on my undying loyalty."

The ardor of my zeal did not appear to frighten Madame de Valvèdre. She had cried; she was crushed; she seemed to be led instinctively by the need to confide in a friend. I could not understand, for myself, how such a gorgeous woman, both proud and sweet, could be so isolated in life that she needed the protection of a child whom she was seeing for the first time. I was surprised, indignant against her husband and her family, but extremely happy on my account.

Upon leaving her, I went to Moserwald. "Well," I said, "what is our situation? Are we fighting?"

"Ah, you are coming here boasting," he answered, "because you think that I might back away? You are mistaken, my dear; I know how to fight and I do it when necessary. I have had too many affairs not to know that one has to be brave on occasion; but in this situation, there is not enough of a motive and I am not angry. I am sad; that is all. Comfort me; it will be much kinder and wiser."

"You want me to comfort you?"

"Yes, you can; tell me that you are not her lover and I shall not lose hope."

"Her lover? When I saw her for the first time yesterday! But what kind of a woman do you think she is, corrupted, dirty mind that you are!"

"You are insulting me; you are in love with her! Yes, yes, it is obvious. You took me for a fool; you told me you thought she was ugly; you offered to help my cause . . . and I fell into the trap. Ah, love does make one stupid! You, it gave you wits; it is proof that you love less than I do."

"Do you have the pretension to love when you only know dishonorable ways; and do you believe that love can be bought?"

"Now you exaggerate again, and I am surprised that a young man as intelligent as you has so little understanding of reality. What? It is offensive to a woman to heap presents and riches upon her without asking anything of her?"

"But we know this way of not asking anything, dear fellow! It is used by all the impertinent Nabobs; it shows an inner confidence, a quiet and perfidious expectation which a woman of honor is bound to indignantly reject. It is a way to invest a capital in the certainty of a personal pleasure and in the inevitable cowardice of the person who has been seduced; what selflessness indeed! If I was a woman, I would be quite moved by it!"

Moserwald sustained my indignation with a remarkable gentleness. Sitting at a table, his head in his hands, he seemed to be reflecting. When he held up his head, I was greatly surprised to see that he was crying.

"You have hurt me," he said, "very much, but I don't bear you a grudge. I have deserved all this because of my lack of wit and education. What do you expect? I have never courted a woman so highly placed and what I figure is the most artistic and delicate attention is precisely what offends her the most . . . whereas you . . . with nothing, with a glance, a few words, you who did not know her before yesterday and who certainly do not love her as I have for two years, because I have been smitten for two years. I go mad every time I see her. I am losing my mind, do you understand, dear chap? And I am telling you, you my rival, destined to displace me because you have on your side the music of feelings and because the most sensible women are lulled by this kind of music. It does not always entertain them but it flatters their vanity, sometimes more than jewelry and happiness. Well, I shall repeat it: I don't bear you grudge. It is your right and if you resent what I did, you are foolish. We don't owe each other anything, do we? Then, we have no reason to hate each other. In the end, I like you, I don't know why; some instinct, a whim, maybe a romantic idea, because we love the same woman and we are likely to meet more than once following her footsteps. Who knows? We may both be rejected, and perhaps too you will be the first . . . me later. So I am not giving up, you see! If I promised you to, I would be lying, and I am as honest as can be. I am leaving tomorrow morning. Is that what you want? I want it too! Your Obernay bores me and the sister-in-law bothers me. Good-bye, then, my dearest fellow, and until we meet again . . . Ah, wait! You are poor, and you think it is possible to do without money in matters of love. Quite wrong! You need some or you will soon need some, if only to pay for a post chaise if need be! Here is a signed power. Give it anywhere to any banker. They will give you the amount you deem necessary. I leave it to your tact and your discretion. Will you now say that Jews are no good?"

I took his arm just when he was presenting me with his signature, which he had just quickly scribbled with a few words of financial jargon on a sheet of white paper. I forced him to put this back on the table without having had to touch it with my hands. "Wait a minute!" I said, "before we part, I want to know; I want to understand your strange behavior. I am not speaking idly and I don't think that you are mad. You consider me as a rival, a successful rival moreover, and you want to give me the means that, according to you, are necessary to satisfy my passion. What is your ulterior motive? Answer me, do answer, or I shall be seriously insulted by the offer you are making me. I am losing patience, I must warn you."

I spoke so firmly that Moserwald was disconcerted. He remained in his thoughts for a moment, then he answered me with a nice open smile which showed him in a new light, quite inexplicable. "You do not guess what my ulterior motive is, child? It is because you seek an ulterior motive where there is none! It is such a natural gesture and inspiration . . ."

"Do you want to buy my gratitude?"

"Exactly, so that you will not speak about me with loathing and scorn to the woman I love . . . You refuse my services? It is not important! You will not be able to forget how courteously I offered them and a day will come when you will request them."

"Never!" I exclaimed with indignation.

"Never?" he continued. "God himself does not know this word, but for the moment I take hold of it. It is one more admission that you love her!"

I felt then that whatever my attitude, light or serious, I would not have the last word with this strange man, as stubborn as he was flexible, as naïve as he was crafty. I burned his signed power in front of him; but somehow he artfully turned around the end of our conversation. It is a fact that upon leaving him, I realized that he had forced me to thank him and that, having come with the intention to fight, I was shaking the hand he was holding out to me.

He left at dawn, leaving our host and all the servants filled with enthusiasm by his generosity. It would not have been a good idea to call him a Jew in front of them; I think they would have stoned us.

I cannot say whether I slept better that night than the previous ones. I think that at the time I must have spent whole weeks without sleep and without feeling the need for it, so focused on my imagination was my life. The next day Paule and Obernay came for breakfast in the common room with Alida. They had forced Madame de Valvèdre to give them an explanation which, contrary to her expectations, had not been met by any storm. It is quite true that Henri had come to the defense of Mademoiselle Juste's character and intentions, but Paule had calmed things down by declaring that her eldest sister had overstepped her mandate, that instead of simply relieving Madame de Valvèdre of the family and household cares, she had usurped an authority that was not rightfully hers; in a word, that Alida was right to complain and that she herself had been tormented quite injustly and unfortunately for having attempted to defend the rights of the true mother and head of the household.

Obernay did not like Alida, and he liked even less that his fiancée took her side; but he feared above all being unfair, and faced with this troubled household he judged quite sanely that it was necessary to give in to avoid vexing them. Then, as the question of his wedding was brought up by the incident, he suddenly felt quite grateful to Madame de Valvèdre and completely went over to her camp. He may have been a botanist, but he was a man, and a man in love. With a few words, while breakfast was served, he told me what had happened the night before after I went out, and what had been decided that morning after the news of Moserwald's departure. They were to wait in Saint Pierre for Valvèdre's return in order to submit to him their common hope, that is the immediate wedding of Paule and the amicable expulsion of Mademoiselle Juste. This last measure, if it seemed to come from the head of the family, could not but be irrevocable and kindly expressed.

Alida's stay in Saint Pierre could thus last one week, two weeks, perhaps more. M. de Valvèdre had put in his planning log that he might come down from the mountain by the side that was opposite to us and that there, renewing his supplies and his guides, he would resume the climb on another side if his first efforts had not been successful. How I wished for the failure of the scientific exploration from then on! Alida seemed calmed and almost joyful about this camp in the mountain. She spoke to me gently and freely; she happily suffered my presence at her side. I was seated at the same table. She would plan on taking a walk and would not forbid me to go with her. I was all hope and all happiness at the same time as the sorrow of having offended her stayed in me like remorse.

There is a mysterious language between souls who are looking for each other. This language does not even need to go through the eyes to be convincing; it is quite impossible to discern through the eyes and the ears of those who are indifferent, but it goes through the dark and narrow space of physical perceptions; it sets ablaze some unknown fluids; it goes from one heart to the other without being subjected to exterior manifestations. Alida has since often told me so. From that morning on, when I did not think to express my regrets and my passion with a single word, she felt that I adored her and she loved me. I did not make any *declaration*; she did not make any confession, and still that evening we could read each other's thoughts and we would tremble from head to foot when, despite ourselves, our eyes met.

During the walk, I did not leave her for a moment. She was a mediocre hiker and, unable to bring herself to confine her little feet in bulky walking shoes, she went, graceful and carefree, but quickly bruised and tired, through the rocks of the mountain and the stones of the stream, with her thin boots, her parasol in one hand, a big bouquet of wildflowers in the other, and letting her dress catch on all the obstacles along the path. Obernay walked ahead with Paule, both occupied by their devotion to collecting plants; then they would stop for quite a while to compare, choose, and prepare the samples which they were taking with them. We did not have any guides; thanks to Henri we did not need any. He entrusted me with the care of Madame de Valvèdre, happy that he was not to worry about her and to be able to devote himself entirely to his intrepid and indefatigable pupil. "Follow us or go ahead," he had said to me, "as long as you do not lose sight of us. I won't take you to dangerous areas. However, keep an eye on Madame de Valvèdre; she is quite absent-minded and doesn't see danger."

I had been shamefully hypocritical and told him that I was the victim of the day and that I would much prefer to go collect plants my way, that is to wander and to observe following my own rhythm rather than to accompany this nonchalant, whimsical, and beautiful lady.

"Be patient for today," Obernay had answered. "Tomorrow, we'll manage differently. We'll give her a mule and a guide." How naïve Obernay was!

I arranged things so well that I was alone with Alida during the four hours of the walk without interruption. When our companions stopped, I would make her walk so that, I told her, we would not have to rush to join them when they moved ahead, and when we were slightly ahead, I invited her to rest until we could see them resume their walk. I did not say a word to her. I was at her side or around her like a watchdog, or rather like an intelligent slave busy with removing thorns and pebbles from her path. If she looked at a blade of grass on the side of a boulder, I would rush forward at the risk of getting killed in order to bring it back to her at once. I held her umbrella when she was seated, I removed from her scarf the bits of moss which she picked up when brushing against the pine trees. For her, I found strawberries in places where there were none; I think I could have made camellias blossom on the glaciers. And I showed all the conventional marks of attentions; I was giving her all these tributes, which today are obsolete, and thus rather trite, with an exhilarated happiness that prevented me from being ridiculous. At first she did try to make fun of it; but, seeing that I gave myself over to her scorn and her irony without complaining and getting discouraged, she became serious, and I felt that, with the passing of every minute, she was moved.

In the evening, in her room, after the lighting of the flares that indicated to us that the expedition was in a region less elevated than the day before, but further on the side of the mountain, she resumed her embroidery and the betrothed couple their study. I sat next to her and offered to read to her in a low voice. "All right," she replied softly, pointing to my volume of poetry on her pedestal table. "I have read all the poems but they stand to be reread."

"No, not these. They are mediocre."

"They are young; that is not the same thing. Didn't you extol the merits of youth just yesterday?"

"There is youth and youth; the youth that is waiting for love, and the youth that is feeling it. The first one has many words but says little; the second does not say anything but understands the infinite."

"Still, let us see the dream of the first one."

"As you like! We can laugh at it, can't we?"

"No, we won't! I am taking the child under my protection. I read in the ten lines of the preface that the author is only twenty years old. By the way, do you think he is still twenty?"

"The book is from 1832; but that is all right, if you want the author not to have grown older . . ."

"And you, how old are you?"

"I don't know. I am as old as your highness wants me to be."

I found again the courage to joke because I could see Obernay was halfway listening to me. When he felt convinced that I only had idle chat to share with this woman who was reputed to be frivolous, he stopped listening; but then I could no longer find anything to say, emotion seized me by the throat, and I felt it would be impossible for me to read a single page. Alida became quite aware of this and she said as she took back the book, "I can see that you have nothing but disdain for my little poet; but without precisely admiring him, I did like him. Since you set so little store by *romantic* ingenuity, I shall not give it back, I must warn you. Do you know this young man?"

"He is anonymous."

"It is not an answer."

"True. I can speak about him without compromising him and tell you what became of him. He has remained anonymous and no longer writes poetry."

"Oh, my god. Has he become a scientist?" she asked lowering her voice and as if she were horrified.

"You must definitely hate science?" I resumed also with my voice lowered. "Oh, do not mind me. I don't know anything."

"You are quite right; but I cannot say anything here. We shall talk about this tomorrow during our walk."

"We shall speak! I don't think so!"

"Why? You see," she said while trying to dispel with words the emotion that overwhelmed me and to which she no longer wanted to be subjected in spite of herself, "why didn't we talk today? For me, I am taciturn, but it is out of shyness. An ignorant woman who has spent ten years with oracles has had to get used to being silent, but you? Well, since you are neither reading nor speaking, you should play some music for me... No? Please!"

Madame de Valvèdre, I found out later, was an attractive child who always needed to be occupied and entertained in order to be roused from a deep melancholy. She could feel this need so well that she sought attentions with an idle naïveté which made her appear now flirtatious, now voluptuous. She was neither. Boredom and the need for emotions were the motives of all her behavior, and I would add of her affections... I was unable to deny her request and I only gained permission to make music from a distance. Placed at the end of the gallery, I made my oboe sing like a voice in the night. The sound of the mountain streams, the magic of moonlight contributed to the prestige; Alida became quite moved; the betrothed couple listened to me with interest. When I came back in, the good Obernay showered me with praise; the candid Paule also became party to my success. Madame de Valvèdre said nothing to me; she whispered to the others—but I was able to hear her—that I had the finest talent that she had ever met.

What happened during the next two days? I was not daring enough to declare myself but I was understood; I feared being rejected if I spoke. My ingenuity was great: one read clearly in my heart and one let herself be adored.

The third day, Obernay took me aside after the flares had gone up. "I am worried and I am leaving," he said. "The signal which I just explained to the ladies as announcing nothing unfortunate was almost a distress signal. Valvèdre is in danger. He can neither go up nor down, and the weather is threatening. We must avoid at all cost worrying Paule or alerting Alida; they would want to follow me, which would make things impossible. I have just invented a migraine and I am pretending to withdraw in order to sleep; but I shall be on my way within the hour with the guides who, following my orders, are always ready. I shall walk all night, and tomorrow I hope to be able to join the expedition in the afternoon. You will know, if I can send you a flare in the evening. If you do not see anything, there will be nothing to say, nothing to do; you will arm yourself with courage by telling yourself that it is not proof of a disaster, but that the supply of flares is exhausted or damaged, or even that we are in a declivity that does not allow us to be seen from here. Whatever happens, stay with the two women until I come back, or until Valvèdre comes back, or until some news . . ."

"I see," I said, "that you are not sure you will come back! I want to go with you!"

"Don't even think about it, you would only make me late and would add to my preoccupations. You are needed here. In the name of friendship, I am asking you to replace me, to protect my fiancée, if need be, to build her courage, to help her be patient if, as I hope, it is only a question of a few days of absence, finally to help Madame de Valvèdre to go to her children, if . . ."

"Come! Let's not think the worst! Leave quickly; it is your duty. I am staying since it is mine."

We agreed that the next morning I would explain Obernay's absence by saying that he had received a message from M. de Valvèdre, who was sending him to make some observations on a mountain nearby. And for the rest, I would invent, if need be, other excuses for his absence, drawing inspiration from the circumstances that might arise.

I thus entered into the poem of happy love under the gloomiest of auspices. I must admit that M. de Valvèdre's fate worried me but little. He was following his destiny, which was to prefer science to love or at least to domestic bliss. He was thus risking his conjugal honor and his life. So be it! It was his right, and I did not see why I should have felt sorry for him or spared him; but I was full of dread and sadness about Obernay. It was quite difficult for me to appear calm when I explained his departure. Fortunately, my companions were easily fooled. Alida was inclined to complain about her husband's perilous excursions rather than to worry about the situation. It was easy to see that she was humiliated to have lost the influence that had kept him several years at home. She did not seem to mind it on her own account, but she was ashamed of it in front of other people. As for Paule, she believed so religiously in Obernay's trust and sincerity that she bravely fought a first impulse to worry by saying, "No, no, Henri would not have misled me. If my brother was in danger, he would have told me. He would not have doubted my courage; he would not have left to anyone but me the care of bolstering my sister-in-law's courage."

The weather was foggy and we did not go outside that day. Paule worked in her room; in spite of the wet cold, Alida spent the afternoon sitting in the gallery, saying that she was suffocating in those rooms crushed by a low ceiling. I was at her side, and could not doubt that she accepted our tête-à-tête. The day before I would have been thrilled by such a favor, but I was unbearably sad when thinking of Obernay, and I was making unsuccessful efforts to feel happy. She became aware of my feelings, and without thinking of guessing the truth, she attributed my low spirits to passion restrained by fear. She pressed me with imprudent and cruel questions, and what I would not have dared tell her in a state of rapture and hope, she drew out of me in the fever of distress; but these were bitter admissions and full of the unfair reproaches that express desire more than they do affection. Why did she want to read in my troubled heart if hers, which seemed calm, only had barren pity to offer?

She was not hurt by my reproaches. "Listen," she said, "I provoked this lack of reserve on your part. You will find out why, and if you resent me for it, I shall think that you do not deserve my trust. Since the first day we saw each other, you took a painful, impossible attitude toward me. I have often been accused of being a coquette; people have been quite wrong since the thing I hate most is to cause suffering. I have inspired on several occasions, I don't know why or how, sudden passions, or I should say ardent, even offensive infatuations. I have had to feel pity for some as I could not share them. Yours, . . ."

"Look!" I cried out, "Do not speak about me: unable to understand me, you are maligning me! You may be sweet and good, but you have never loved!"

"Yes, I have," she continued, "I have loved . . . my husband! But let us not speak about love; that is not the question. It is not love that you feel for me! Oh, stay here and let me tell you everything. You experience a very strong emotion when you are with me. I can see it. Your imagination was fired up, and if you told me that you are capable of doing anything to have me, I would not contradict you. In men, these kinds of desires are blind; but do you think that the force of your desire is a credit to you? Really, do you think so? If you do, why would you deny M. Moserwald an equal right to my benevolence?"

She made me suffer horribly. She was right in what she said; but wasn't I right too, to find that this cold wisdom was coming too late after three days of trust and of silent encouragement? I complained vigorously; I was outraged and ready to crush everything even if it meant crushing myself.

She was not offended by anything I said. She had experience and perhaps she was used to such scenes. "Look," she went on, after I had expressed my disappointment and my suffering, "you are unhappy right now; but I am to be pitied more than you, and it is for my whole life . . . I feel that I shall never be cured of the harm you are causing me, whereas you . . ."

"Explain yourself," I cried out, violently squeezing her hands in mine. "Why would you suffer because of me?"

"Because I have a dream, an ideal that you are upsetting and shattering terribly. As long as I have lived, I have aspired to friendship, to true love. I can use this word if you find the word *friendship* revolting. I am looking for an affection that is both ardent and pure, an absolute, exclusive preference of my soul for a being who would understand it and who would consent to fill it without destroying it. I have only been offered a pedantic and despotic friendship, or an extravagant passion, full of selfishness and offensive, painful demands. When I saw you . . . , oh, I can tell you now that you have already scorned it and forced it back in me, I felt for you a strange affinity . . . treacherous, certainly! I dreamed, I thought I felt loved; but the next morning you hated me, you insulted me. Then you repented immediately, you asked for my forgiveness with tears. I began believing again. You were so young and you seemed so naïve. Three days went by . . . and see how flirtatious and cunning I am, I felt happy and I am telling you so! It seemed that at last I had met my friend, my brother . . . , my solace in a life of suffering and bitterness such as you cannot fathom! . . . I went to sleep in peace, mad that I was. I was telling myself: it is perhaps *he* who is here! But today, I saw you somber and burdened with problems. Fear took me and I wanted to know . . . Now I know, and I am at peace, but gloomy like a sorrow without cure nor hope. The last illusion is vanishing and I am going back to the peace of death."

I felt vanquished, but I was also broken. I had not foreseen the effects of my passion, or, at least, I had only dreamt about a succession of joys or terrible sorrows to which I had valiantly submitted. Alida was showing me another future, quite unknown and more frightening still. She was imposing on me the task of comforting her broken life and of giving her a little peace and happiness at the cost of all my own happiness and peace. If she had truly wanted to drive me away, this was the cleverest means to do it. I was frightened; I kept cruelly silent, my head down.

"Well," she continued with a sweetness that was not without a mix of scorn. "You see! I understood and I did well to understand: you don't love me, and the thought of fulfilling a duty of the heart you owe me crushes you like a death penalty! I find this quite simple and quite fair," she added as she held out her hand with a sweet and cold smile. "And as you are too sincere to be pretending, I see that I can still respect you. Let us remain friends. I no longer fear you, and you can stop fearing yourself.

You will have the easy and successful life of men whose only goal is pleasure. You are in the realm of the real and the true; don't be ashamed. The *anonymous author* no longer writes poetry, you told me; he is quite right since poetry left him. He has one honest mission left: that of deceiving no one."

It was a sort of call to honor, and the idea did not cross my mind that I could be unworthy even of the cold regard given as a last resort. I made no attempt to justify myself or to apologize. I remained silent and somber. Alida left me and soon I heard her talk with Paule with apparent calm.

My heart broke all of a sudden. Was the ardent life to which I had been born so few days ago and which already seemed the normal habit, the goal, the destiny of my whole being gone forever? No, it could not be! Everything Alida had said to quash my passion, to make me ashamed of my violent aspiration only served to rekindle its intensity. "Selfish, I admit it, I said to myself. Can love be anything but an irresistible expansion of personality? If she considers it a crime, it is because she does not share my turmoil. Well, I cannot take offense. I have lacked initiative; I have been clumsy; I have been unable to speak or to be silent at the right moment. This delightful woman, indifferent to the tributes paid to her beauty, took me for a child without heart or moral strength, capable of abandoning her the day after her defeat. It is up to me to prove to her now that I am a man, a man who is practical in matters of love, it is true, but capable of being devoted, grateful, and faithful. I shall win her trust by accepting as a test all the sacrifices that she'll choose to impose on me. It is up to me to convince her gradually, to entrance her reason, to touch her heart, and to make her share the passion that possesses me.

I promised myself that I would not be hypocritical, that I would not have any promise of impossible virtue be wrested from me, and that I would simply have my submission accepted as a mark of respectful patience. I wrote a few words in pencil on a notebook page: "You are quite right; I was not worthy of you. But I shall be, if you don't let me despair."

I went to her room under the pretext that I wanted a book returned. I slid the note almost under Paule's eyes and I went back to the gallery to wait for the answer, which was not long in coming. She brought it herself, holding out her hand with an ineffable look and a smile. "We shall try!" She told me and, blushing, she ran away.

I was too young to harbor suspicions about the sincerity of this woman, and in this I was more perceptive than experience would have allowed, for this woman was sincere. She needed to love, she loved, and she was looking for a way to reconcile her sense of pride with the élan of a heart yearning for emotions. She took refuge in a *mezzo termine* where virtue would not have seen very clearly, but where alarmed modesty could be at peace for a while. She helped me to deceive her, and we deceived each other by convincing ourselves that the strictest loyalty ruled over this treacherous and lame contract. All this was leading me to an abyss. My debut in love began with a kind of betrayal, for by vowing a temporary virtue which I was eager to abandon, I was more guilty than I had been until then when I had given myself up to a passion that was unbridled but without ulterior motive.

I was not able to see it clearly enough to avoid it. From then on, Alida, who was elated with a gratitude that I was far from deserving, intoxicated me with her irresistible seductions. She become tender, naïve, trusting to the point of madness, simple to the point of childishness to compensate for the deprivations that she was imposing on me. Her charm and her abandon created for her extraordinary dangers of which she made light as if she could ignore them. No doubt, there is a great charm in the sufferings of a suppressed love that waits and hopes. She intensified for me its delights and its torments. She was passionately flirtatious with me, no longer hiding it and saying that it was allowed for a woman who loved passionately and who wanted to give her lover all the happiness compatible with her sense of modesty and her duties. This was a strange sophistry from which she actually drew for her own account all the happiness of which she was capable, but the bitter pleasures of which poisoned my soul, quashed my conscience, and withered my faith!

Two days went by without my having any signal from the mountain, or any news from Obernay. This moral concern made me ravenous for happiness, and remorse added even more to the intoxication of my guilty pleasures. At night alone in my room, I shuddered at the idea that perhaps at that very moment Obernay and Valvèdre, buried under the ice were giving forth their last breath in a final embrace! And me! I had been able to forget my friend during hours on end in the company of a woman who gazed at me with a celestial look of blissful tenderness, without an inkling of the fate hanging over her and which was perhaps making her widow at that instant! I would then feel drenched in cold sweat; I felt like dashing out into the night to look for Obernay; there were moments when, thinking that I was deceiving Valvèdre, who may have been dying, a martyr to science, I felt like a coward and a murderer.

Finally I received a letter from Obernay. "Everything is fine," he told me. "I haven't been able yet to join Valvèdre, but I know he is in B., six leagues from where I am, and that he is in good health. I am resting for a few hours and rushing after him. I hope to convince him to leave it at that and to bring him back to Saint Pierre, for the storm has swept through the high snows, and the dangers he encountered when trying to get out would be impossible to overcome now. You can now tell the truth to the ladies and urge them to be patient. We shall all be together in two or three days."

When she learned that Valvèdre had been in great danger, when she guessed, through Obernay's silence about himself, that he too must have been in serious danger, Paule, with whom I shared the letter, was seized with a rather violent fit of nervous shaking and squeezed my hand silently. "Be brave!" I told her. "They are saved! A scientist's fiancée must be a strong woman and get used to suffering."

"You are right," the courageous child answered while wiping away abundant tears that came at the right time to relieve her. "Yes, yes, one needs courage. I shall be brave! Let us think about my sister-in-law; what shall we tell her? She is not strong; for the last few days in particular, she has been very nervous and restless. She can't sleep. Leave the letter with me; I'll show it to her only after I have properly warned her."

"Is she so fond of her husband?" I asked carelessly.

"Do you have any doubt about it?" Paule replied, surprised at my exclamation.

"Of course not, but . . ."

"But you do! You doubt it! Ah, you haven't gone through Geneva without hearing some slanderous gossip about poor Alida! Well, remove it from your thoughts. Alida is good and kind-hearted. In many regards, she is like a child, but she is fair and she knows how to appreciate the best of men. He is so good to her! If you had seen them together but one moment, you would know right away what to think about their alleged lack of harmony. So many mutual attentions, such exquisite thoughtfulness and delicate tokens of respect are not found among people who have serious reasons to blame each other. There are between them differences of taste and opinion, that is certain; but if this is a real misfortune in married life, there are also sufficient compensations in the serious reasons for a mutual affection. Those who accuse my brother of being cold are unfair and poorly informed; those who accuse his wife of being ungrateful or frivolous are nasty and stupid."

Whatever Paule's optimistic ingenuity may have been, her speech made a strong impression on me. I felt torn between a nascent but violent jealousy against a husband who was so perfect, so respected, and a kind of bitter blame against the woman who was seeking affection and protection elsewhere. This was the onset of the implacable illness that was to torture me later. When I saw Alida again, the change in her face seemed to confirm her sister-in-law's assertions; she had been upset and seemed to be waiting impatiently for her husband's return. This put me in a wretched mood, and as the weather had become milder and we were walking along the stream, Paule would often walk away with the guide to look for plants and satisfy her need for movement, and I pressed Madame de Valvèdre with sharp questions and desperate comments. She then found herself compelled and almost forced to speak to me about her husband, her household, and to tell me about her life.

"I have loved M. de Valvèdre passionately," she said. "He is the only passion in my life. Paule told you that he was perfect; well, yes, she is right. He is perfect. He has only one fault; he does not love. He cannot, knows not, will not love. He is above passions, sufferings, above the storms of life. As for me, I am a woman, a true woman, weak, ignorant, worthless. I know only how to love. This ought to have been taken into account and I should not have been asked for anything else. Didn't he know, when he married me, that I had no serious knowledge of anything, nor any noticeable talents? I did not wish to disguise the truth, and such an attempt would have been rather useless with a man who knows everything. He liked me, he found me beautiful, he wanted to be my husband in order to become my lover. Here is all the mystery of these great affections to which an inexperienced young woman is doomed to fall prey. It is true that the man who misleads her thus is not guilty of dissembling. He is blinded; he deceives himself; and his mistake brings its own punishment with it, since this man is forever chained and will live to regret it later. Valvèdre had regrets, that is certain; he hid it as well as he could. But I guessed it and felt horribly humiliated. After much suffering, wounded pride has killed love in my heart. Thus neither of us has been guilty. We were the victims of fatality. We are intelligent enough, equitable enough, to have admitted it and not to have harbored bitter feelings against the other. We have remained friends, brother and sister, silent about the past, calm in the present, and resigned about the future. This is our whole story. What cause for anger or jealousy can you find in this?"

I found many as well as numerous suspicions and worries. She had passionately loved him; she declared it in front of me without appearing to realize what torture it was for a new heart to hear these words from the adored woman: "You are not the first man in my life." I wished that she had lied to me, that she had led me to believe it was a marriage of reason, a quiet affection from the beginning; or that she had made the effort to repeat this common, often naïve lie given by women who have strong passions: "I thought I loved, but what I feel for you shows me that I was wrong. You are the only one who has taught me what love is." At the same time I realized that I would have given absolutely no credence to this lie, that I would have been submerged by anger at feeling deceived from the very first words. I was prey to all the contradictions of a wild and despotic feeling. At times, I made an attempt at friendship, pure love as she understood it; but I recognized with terror that what she had told me about her husband could easily apply to me. I did not find in her the basic logic, the maturity of mind, the conscious will that are the indispensable basis for a beneficial affection and a happy intimacy. As she had indeed confessed, she was a woman from head to toe, made only for love, she said . . . made, certainly, to light a thousand flames without the possibility if anticipating whether she was capable of quelling them and of converting them someday into a long-lasting and true happiness. Besides, a question remained veiled in her brief story, and this terrible question, infidelity . . . *infidelities* which people attributed to her, I both wanted and did not want to clarify. I could not help asking questions in spite of myself, she took offence.

"You want me to give you explanations about my behavior?" she said haughtily. "What right do you have to ask questions? Why do you do me the honor of loving me if you do not respect me beforehand? Do I question you? Didn't I accept you as you are, without knowing anything about your past?"

"My past?" I cried out. "Do I have a past? I am a child whose life everyone has been able to follow in full view, and I have never had the least reason to hide any of my actions. Besides, I have told you and I can swear on my honor that I have never loved. I have thus nothing to confess, nothing to tell you, whereas you, you who are rejecting blind and trusting passion and who are demanding a disinterested affection, an ideal love, you need to impose the respect of your character and to give moral guarantees to the man whose conscience and life you are taking."

"The question is quite inappropriate," she answered, pulling out of her bosom the note that I had written her two days before. "I thought that you were asking me to make you worthy of me and not to abandon you to despair. Today, it is something else; I am the one who apparently has to implore your trust and beg you to believe that I am worthy of you. Here, poor child, you have a violent temperament with a weak head and I am neither energetic enough nor clever enough to teach you to love. I would suffer too much, and you would become mad. We invented a romance. Let's forget it..."

She tore the note into tiny pieces that she threw into the grass and the bushes; then she got up, smiled, and moved to join her sister-in-law. I should have let her do it; we would have been saved! But her smile was heartbreaking and there were tears in her yes. I stopped her, asked for her forgiveness, and promised to refrain from ever questioning her again. The next two days I broke my promise a hundred times, but she gave no more explanations, and tears were her only answer. I hated myself for making such a sweet creature suffer, for, in spite of numerous outbursts of chagrin and strong irruptions of pride, she did not know how to break off. Resentment was foreign to her, and her forgiveness was infinitely patient.

IV

I forgot everything in the middle of these storms mixed with delights, and while exerting my strength against the flow that carried me away, I felt myself weakening and turning toward a dream of happiness at all cost, when a signal from the mountain brought me the news of Obernay's likely return the next day. It was a double white flare attesting that everything was fine and that my friend was coming toward us. But was M. de Valvèdre with him? Would he be in Saint Pierre in twelve hours?

It was the first time that I thought about the attitude I would have to adopt with her husband, and I could not imagine one that did not numb me with terror. I would have given anything to deal with a brutal and violent man whom I would have paralyzed and dominated with cold disdain and quiet courage! But this Valvèdre, who had been described as so calm, so indifferent, or so merciful toward his wife, in any case, so polite, so cautious, and so scrupulous in his respect of the most delicate proprieties, how would I hold his gaze? With what demeanor would I receive his overtures? For it was quite certain that Obernay had already mentioned that I was his best friend and that because of his age and station in society, M. de Valvèdre would treat me as a young man to be encouraged, protected, or mentored if need be. I had no longer felt strong enough to question Obernay about him. Since I loved Alida, I wished that I could have forgotten the existence of her husband. From the few words that, in spite of myself, I had been forced to hear, I imagined a man who was cold, very dignified, and rather sarcastic. According to Alida, his was the type with generous intentions and the secret scorn of a conscience that is full of its own superiority.

Whether he was paternal or cutting in his benevolence, I was unhappy enough although without having the shame and the remorse to betray a man whom I perhaps would have to esteem and respect in spite of myself. I resolved not to wait for him, but Alida found me cowardly and ordered me to stay. "You are exposing me to strange suspicions on his part," she said to me. "What will he think of a young man who, after accepting the responsibility of protecting me in my isolation, runs away like a guilty man when he comes near? Obernay and Paule will also be struck by this behavior and will not have any better reason than I do to give an explanation. What! Had you not foreseen that when loving a married woman you were contracting the obligation to quietly face meeting her husband, that you would have to suffer for me, I who am going to suffer for you a hundred times more than you? Think about the role of the woman in such circumstances. If there is a need to dissemble and to lie, it is on her alone that all the weight of this odious necessity falls. It is enough if her accomplice seems calm and does not do anything foolish; but she is the one who risks everything: her honor, her peace, and her life. She must exert all the strength of her will to avoid suspicion. Believe me, for a woman who does not like to lie, it is real torture; and yet I am going to be subjected to it, and I haven't even thought of mentioning it to you. I haven't asked you to feel sorry about it; I haven't reproached you with exposing me to this. And you, when the danger that is threatening me comes nearer, you abandon me saying, 'I don't know how to dissemble. I am too proud to be subjected to such a humiliation!' And you claim that you love me, that you would like to find some terrible opportunity to prove it, to force me to believe it! Here is one that is as expected, banal, vulgar, and easy as ever there was one, and you are running away!"

She was right. I stayed. Destiny, which was leading me to my downfall, appeared to come to my rescue. Obernay came back alone. He was bringing Madame de Valvèdre a letter from her husband, which she showed me, and which contained approximately the following:

> My dear friend, do not resent me for having succumbed once again to the *temptation of the peaks*. They are not always deadly since I have come back safe and sound. Obernay has told me the reason for your excursion in these mountains. I submit without dispute to your reasons and I hold as my primary duty to grant your requests. I am going to Valvèdre to fetch my older sister. I shall attend to moving her right

away to Geneva so that you can return to your house without annoyance. At the same time, I shall arrange everything in Geneva for Paule's wedding and I shall ask you to kindly join me there with her at the beginning of next month. In this way, my older sister will be able to attend the ceremony without giving the impression that you are on bad terms with her. You will bring the children. Now is the time for Edmond to go to preparatory school. Obernay will complete my letter with any details that you may want. Rest assured of the everlasting devotion of your friend and servant,

Valvèdre

This letter, of which I am sure I rendered the content and the spirit if not the precise terms, fully confirmed everything Alida had told me about the courtesy and the politeness of her husband; at the same time it depicted the indifference of a superior soul to the disappointments and disasters of love. There was perhaps a poignant drama underneath this perfect serenity, but its impression was erased either through the force of his will or the coldness of his constitution.

I do not know why reading this letter had an effect quite opposite to what Madame de Valvèdre expected: she had asked me to read it, thinking it would quell the fire of my jealousy; it was revived and as if exacerbated. A husband who governed his family in such irreproachable manner had, before God and man, the right to demand everything in return for his prompt and generous consideration. He was quite legitimately the master and the arbiter of this woman whose servant and devoted friend he chivalrously said he was. Yes, he did have the law on his side since he had justice and reason sovereign. Nothing could ever authorize his weak companion to break a bond that he knew how to make doubly sacred. She was his forever, be it as a sister, as she claimed, because that brother, husband or not, was a support more legitimate and more serious than any lover of the past or future.

I felt my role to be a fleeting, almost ridiculous one. I flattered myself that I would dismiss it when my passion had been assuaged and my only thought was to assuage it. Alida did not see things in the same light. I began to deceive her resolutely and to make her trust me, with the firm intention of surprising her imagination or her senses.

She was to leave two days later for the Valvèdre villa. Obernay was in charge of accompanying her, but they would take the longest way in order to avoid M. de Valvèdre who was taking his old sister to Geneva. I had no more pretexts to remain near Alida for I had announced to Obernay that after a week devoted to him I would go on with my travels through Switzerland, except for a visit to him in Geneva before going to Italy. He did not help me to change my plans. "Valvèdre has set the date of my wedding on August 1," he told me. "I consider it impossible that you should refuse to attend. I myself will be with my family as early as July 15, and I will wait for you. This is the 2nd, so you have ample time to go see some of our great lakes and beautiful mountains; but don't delay your tour. I hasten your departure, as you can see, but it is to make sure that you'll come back."

Attending Henri and Mademoiselle de Valvèdre's wedding meant that I would inevitably find myself in the presence of the husband whom I was so pleased to have avoided. I did not want to see Alida again before the very eyes of this entire family with its patriarch foremost. However, I could not find any way to refuse. Having started on a path of lies, I promised to be there, but I had the firm intention of breaking a leg on my trip rather than keeping my word.

I packed and left one hour later, leaving Alida frightened by my great hurry and hurt by my resistance to her desire to have me as an escort part of her way. Leaving her worried and unhappy was part of my seduction scheme.

I smile with great sadness when I think now about my attempts at perversity: they hardly fit my age and were so far from my natural inclinations that I felt as if relieved to be able to forget them for a few days. I went deep into the high mountains while waiting for the moment when M. de Valvèdre and Obernay's return to Geneva would allow me to go to Alida's residence for a surprise visit, for which I had drawn a detailed itinerary on my road map.

I spent a week and a half tiring my legs and exalting my brain. I went across the Pennine range and went up the Alps from the Valais canton toward the Simplon pass. The vista from these grandiose regions opened up in turn on Switzerland and Italy. It is one of the largest and grandest vistas that I have ever seen. I decided to go as high as possible on the mountaintop of the Italian Sempione to see its strange and terrible ferruginous cascades which, along milky, frothy rivers, seem to line the snow with rivers of blood. I braved the cold, the danger, and the feeling of moral distress that overcomes a young soul in these terrible deserted spots. Shall I admit it? I felt the need in my own eyes to compete in courage and stoicism with M. de Valvèdre. I had been irritated to hear his wife and his sister speak incessantly of his strength and his intrepidness. It seemed as if he were a Titan, and one day when I had expressed the desire to attempt a similar excursion, Alida had smiled as if a dwarf had spoken about racing a giant. I would have felt childish practicing in her presence; but alone, and at the risk of breaking my bones or getting lost in the precipices, I was nursing my wounded pride, and I also strove to become a kind of man full of vigor and daring. I was forgetting that what made these desperate ventures worthy endeavors was having a serious goal, the hope of scientific advances. It is true that I thought I was marching toward the conquest of the poetic demon, and I struggled to improvise in the middle of glaciers and chasms. But one needs to be a demigod to find in such surroundings the expression of a personal feeling. I could hardly find in the shimmering casket of romantic epithets and images a weak equivalent to translate the sublimity around me. At night, when I attempted to write my rhymes, I became well aware that rhymes was all they were. And yet my observations, my descriptions, my translations had been well done, but precisely poetry, like painting and music, comes into being only if it is something other than an equivalent for a translation. It has to be an idealization of the ideal. I was frightened by my inadequacy and my only comfort was to attribute it to a state of physical exhaustion.

One evening, in a wretched little chalet where I had asked for shelter, I was grieved by a scene quite human, which I strove to consider coolly in order to give it later a literary form. A child was dying of convulsions. The father and the mother did not know how to relieve him and figuring that he was lost, were looking at him with tearless and gloomy eyes as he struggled on the straw. The silent despair of the woman was sublime in its expressiveness. This ugly, goitrous, half-cretin creature was becoming beautiful through maternal instinct. The father, sullen and religious, was praying without hope. Sitting on my pallet, I was looking at them and my fruitless pity found only words and comparisons! I became irritated at myself, and I thought that it would have been better at that instant to have been a simple country doctor than the best poet in the world.

When daybreak came I woke up, and only then did I realize that I had been overcome by fatigue. I got up, expecting to see the child dead and the mother prostrate; but I saw the mother sitting, and on her lap the child was smiling. By them stood a man wearing a woolen blouse and leather gaiters, whose white hands and open travel bag indicated someone who was not a peddler or a smuggler. He gave the young patient a second dose of some sedative, gave instructions to the parents in their dialect, which I did not understand well, and left, refusing the money he was offered. When he was gone, they realized that instead of accepting money, he had left some for their use in the household wooden bowl.

He had come while I was sleeping; he had been sent there in this deserted spot by Providence, he the man of goodness and rescue, the message of hope and life, the little country doctor, the antithesis of the poet full of skepticism.

There was a *subject* in all of this: I began to outline it while coming down the mountain, after adding my offering to the doctor's; but soon I forgot everything to admire the grandiose portico which I was crossing. After a half-hour's walk, I had left above the glaciers and the formidable peaks. I was entering the Rhône Valley, which I dominated still from a vertiginous height, and which opened under my feet like an abyss of greenery across which ran thousands of golden and scarlet snakelike streams. The river and the many streams which rush into its bed flared up in the fiery light of the morning. A pink mist, which was quickly lifting, gave me the impression that the snowy crenelation of the horizon and the magical depths of the amphitheater were even farther away. At every step, appearing from these depths, I could see suddenly steep ridges crowned with picturesque rocks or patches of green gilded by the morning sun; and, between these ridges which became gradually less high, there were other chasms of meadows and forests. Each of these recesses offered a magnificent vista when the eyes and the mind stopped for a moment; but if you looked around, beyond and below it, the sublime landscape was but a small asperity lost in the immensity of the view, a detail, a speck, and a kind of facet of the diamond.

Facing these Alpine basins, the painter and the poet are like drunken men who would be offered the world's empire. They do not know what small shelter to choose for cover and to escape dizziness. The eye would like to stop on some departure point to count its riches: they seem infinite for, when going down the sinuous lines of the various planes, each vista changes appearance and presents to the eye other colors and other shapes.

The sun was climbing; its warmth increasingly penetrated the layers of these deep valleys. As the High-Simplon no longer pierced my back with its icy rays, I stopped so that I would not lose too early the spectacle of the entire Valais. I sat on the moss of an isolated rock, and I ate a piece of brown bread that I had purchased at the chalet; afterward, as the shadow of the great pines was stretching obliquely on me, and the bells of invisible flocks lost under the leafy boughs lulled my reverie, I fell asleep for a few moments.

Awakening was a delicious moment. It was eight in the morning. The sun had reached down into the most mysterious depths, and everything was so beautiful, so natural, and so gracefully primitive around me that I was delighted. At that moment, I thought about Madame de Valvèdre as the ideal of beauty which was the standard for all the things I admired, and I remembered her ethereal form, her disappointing caresses, her mysterious smile. It was the first time that I found myself in a situation conducive to meditation since I had been loved by a beautiful woman, and although I did not draw from this thought the sweet and deep feeling of true happiness, at least I found all the intoxication, all the vapors of contented pride.

It was the time to be a poet, and so I was in my dreams. When looking at nature around me, I felt dazzled and moved as I had never been before. Until then, I had reflected on the beauty of things after the fact, after being intoxicated with the spectacle they offered. It seemed to me that these two mental operations were occurring within me simultaneously, and that I both felt and described at the same time. Expression seemed to me mixed with the ray of the sun, and my vision was like a poem already written. I had a feverish shiver, a burst of immense pride. "Yes, yes," I exclaimed inwardly, and I was speaking aloud without realizing it. "I am saved. I am happy. I am an artist!"

I had rarely happened to engage in these monologues, which are real outbursts of delirium, and although lately I had become accustomed to reciting my poems to the sound of the cataracts, the echo of my voice and of my prose in this peaceful place frightened me. I instinctively looked around me as if I had committed a sin, and I had a feeling of real shame when I saw that I wasn't alone. Three steps away from me, a man, leaning over a rock was drawing water in a leather cup from the trickling spring, and that man was the one I had seen two hours earlier saving the sick child at the chalet and giving alms to his hosts.

In spite of his mountain attire, which was more that of a mountaineer than of a tourist, I was struck by the elegance of his figure and his facial expression. Moreover he was remarkably handsome in type and in shape, and did not seem to be over thirty years old. He had removed his hat, and I saw his face, which I had only barely glimpsed at the chalet. His black, short, and thick hair framed a large and white forehead that was remarkably serene. His eyes, well defined, had a soft and penetrating look; his nose was delicate and the expression of his nostril was linked to that of his lip by a half-smile full of a quiet benevolence and a tasteful liveliness. His average height and broad torso suggested physical strength, while his slightly stooped shoulders revealed sedentary study or frequent meditation.

I forgot, while looking at him somewhat analytically, the kind of confusion that I had just felt, and I greeted him warmly. He returned my greeting with cordiality and offered me the cup full of water that he was going to bring to his lips, saying that this water was so pure that it deserved to be offered like a delicacy.

I accepted, obeying the attraction that led me to exchange a few words with him; but, from the way in which he was looking at me, I felt that for him I was an object of curiosity or solicitude. I remembered the strange exclamation I had let out in his presence, and I wondered if he was not taking me for a madman. I could not help laughing and, to reassure him while saving my pride, I said, "Doctor, you prescribe for me this pure water as a remedy, admit it, or you are checking to see if I am not hydrophobic; but don't worry, you won't have to treat me. I have all my wits. I am a poor traveling actor and you caught me as I was reciting a fragment of a part."

"Really?" he said doubtfully. "You don't look like an actor."

"No more than you look like a country doctor. However, you are a disciple of science, and I a disciple of art, what do you say?"

"Perhaps," he continued, "I took you neither for a naturalist nor for a painter; but, from what the people at the chalet told me about you, I was taking you for a poet?"

"What did they say about me?"

"That you were reciting aloud all alone in the mountain. That is why these good people thought you were mad."

"And were they sending you to my rescue, or is it charity that sent you looking for me?"

"No," he said with a laugh, "I am not one of these doctors who run after clients and asks for your money or your life on the edge of some woods. I was walking to Brig. I wandered on the way. I was thirsty and the murmur of the spring took me near you. You were reciting or improvising. I disturbed you . . ."

"Not at all," I cried out. "You were going to smoke a cigar, and, if you allow me, I'll smoke mine with you. Do you know, Doctor, that I am very happy to see you at leisure and to speak for a moment with you?"

"Sorry? You don't know me, do you?"

"No more than you know me; but you are for me the improvised hero of a little poem that I was tossing about in my actor's brain. A fable, a fantasy, I suppose: two scenes to depict the contrast between the two types which you and I exemplify. The first is quite to your advantage. The child was dying; I was sorry for the mother while falling asleep. You were consoling her; you saved the child when I woke up! The decor was simple and touching and you came off best. In the second scene, I would like, however, to raise the artist. As you can imagine, one doesn't give up the pride of one's vocation! But what can I imagine in order to have here more wit and more sense than you do? I can't find anything at all, for individually you seem quite superior to me in everything... You would need to be modest enough to help me prove that the artist is the doctor of the soul as the man of science is that of the body."

"Yes," my amiable doctor answered as he sat next to me and accepted one of my cigars, "there is an idea and I am laying bare my heart so that you may develop it. I don't think that I am superior of anyone, but let us suppose that I am very intelligent but weak in philosophy, that I have a great sorrow or doubt: it is up to your eloquence applied to the topic of feelings and of fervor to cure me by moving me or giving me my faith back. Let's see; improvise!"

"Oh, slow down!" I cried out. "I cannot improvise without answering something and you are not telling me anything. It is not enough to make a supposition. I can't be exalted without a warm-up. Tell me your worries; imagine some tragedy, and if there is none in your life, invent one!"

He started laughing good-heartedly at my whimsy. Yet, in the middle of his gaiety, I thought I saw a cloud troubling his handsome forehead, as if I had imprudently reopened a hidden wound. I was not mistaken. He stopped laughing and told me softly, "Dear Sir, let's not play this game or let's play it seriously. At my age, one has always had a tragedy in one's life. Here is mine: I very much loved a woman who is dead. Do you have words or ideas to console me?"

I was so struck by the simplicity of his plaint that I lost all desire to be witty. "I beg your pardon for my blunder," I said. "I should have told myself that you were not a child like me and that, in any case, this topic would not give me any advantage over you. After your departure, I will be able to find in prose or in verse some impressive speech to answer and console you; but here, faced with a figure that commands sympathy, faced with words that command respect, I feel like such a little boy that I would not even take the liberty of feeling sorry for you, certain as I am that I have much less wisdom and courage than you do."

My answer touched him; he held out his hand to me, telling me that I was a modest and good fellow, and that I had just spoken to him like a man, which was even better than to speak like a poet.

"However, it is not that I scorn poets and poetry," he added, shrugging off his melancholy with a generous effort. "Artists have always seemed to me to be as serious and useful as scientists when they are true artists, and a great mind who would be as much a scientist as an artist would seem to be the most noble prototype of the true and the beautiful in mankind."

"Ah, since you are kind enough to speak with me," I went on, "you must allow me to contradict you. Let us agree ahead of time that you will be right, but let me express my thoughts."

"Of course, please do. I may be the one who is wrong. Youth is quite the judge in these matters. Do speak."

I spoke abundantly and with conviction. I shall not repeat what I said, which I hardly remember, and which the reader will imagine without much effort by recalling the theory of art for art's sake, which was much in fashion at that time. Besides, my interlocutor's response, which I recall clearly, will be enough to give an idea of the defense I presented.

"You defend your church with energy and talent," he told me, "but I am sorry to always see superior minds willingly sink into a notion that is a disastrous impediment to the progress of human knowledge. Our fathers had a different understanding; they simultaneously cultivated all their mental faculties, all the manifestations of the beautiful and the true. It is said that knowledge has developed to such an extent that a man's life is barely long enough for one of the smallest areas of specialization. I am not quite sure that this is true. People waste so much time talking or maneuvering to make a name for themselves, not to mention those who spend most of their lives doing nothing! It is because social life has become very complicated that some waste their life working their way up and others don't want to undertake anything for fear of getting tired. And then the human mind has become overly subtle and under the pretext of intellectual analysis and inner contemplation, the powerful and unfortunate race of poets wears itself out in vagueness or emptiness, without looking for its peace, its light, and its life in the sublime spectacle of the world! Please," he said with a soft and convincing vivacity as he saw me ready to interrupt, "I know what you want to tell me. Poets and painters claim to be the privileged lovers of nature; they claim that they have its sole ownership because they have forms and colors, and a strong and deep feeling to interpret it. I don't deny it and I admire their translation when it is well done; but I myself maintain that the most skillful and the happiest, the most lasting and the most inspired among them are those who are not satisfied with the appearance of things and who go look for the raison d'être of the beautiful deep into the mysteries from whence the splendor of creation blossoms. Do not tell me that the study of natural laws and the search for causes chill the heart and hinder the development of thought; I would not believe you, for if you look ever so little at the ineffable source of eternal phenomena, I mean God's logic and magnificence, we are dazzled by its creation. You only want to take into account one of the results of this sublime logic, the beauty that strikes the eye. But, without your realizing it, you are scientists when your eyes are sharp because beauty would not exist without the wise and ingenious in its causes; but you are incomplete and dogmatic scientists who deliberately shut yourselves out of the doors of the temple while truly religious minds look for its sanctuaries and study its divine hieroglyphics. Do you think that this oak whose magnificent boughs move you to poetic reverie would lose its attraction in your mind, if you had examined the frail embryo which produced it, and if you had followed the laws of its development among the favorable conditions that universal Providence prepared for it? Do you think that the little moss upon whose cool velvet we are treading would stop pleasing you on the day you discover with a magnifying glass the marvelous polish of its structure and the ingenious singularities of its fructification? There is more: many objects that seem to you insignificant, disparate, or clumsy in the landscape would become interesting to your mind and even to your eyes, if you could read there the history of the earth written in deep and indelible characters. In general the lyric poet turns away from these thoughts, which would lead him high and far: he wants to strike some chords only, that of personality first; but consider those who are truly great! They are interested in everything and they interrogate even the innermost layers of rocks. They would be greater yet without public prejudice, without the general ignorance that rejects as too abstract what fails to flatter the passions or the instincts. Notions are distorted, as I told you, and intelligent men amuse themselves with making distinctions, camps, and sects in the pursuit of truth so that what is beautiful for some is no longer so for others. This is the unhappy outcome of the exaggerated tendency to specialize! What a surprising fatality to see that creation, spring of all light and source of all enthusiasm, can only reveal one of its facets to its privileged spectator, to man, who alone among living beings in this world has received the gift of seeing above and below, that is to supplement with calculations and reasoning the organ he is missing. What! We had broken the sapphire vault of Empyrean, we found the notion of the infinite with the presence of countless worlds. We have pierced the crust of the earth and we have discovered there the mysterious elements of all life at its surface, and poets will say to us: 'You are cold pedants, number handlers, you don't see anything, you don't appreciate anything around you!' It is as if, upon hearing a foreign language that we would understand and that they could not, they claimed they could feel its beauty better than us, under the pretext that the meaning of the words prevents us from understanding their harmony."

My new friend spoke with an extraordinary charm; his voice and his enunciation were so beautiful and his accent so soft, his eyes were so persuasive and his smile so kind that I let him scold me without rebelling. I found myself softened and as if influenced by this rare mind endowed with such charming contours. Was he a simple country doctor, or rather some famous man savoring the charms of solitude and *incognito*?

He showed so little curiosity about me that I thought I should imitate his discretion. He only asked me if I was coming down the mountain or if I intended to climb back up. I did not have any fixed plan before July 15 and it was only the tenth. I was thus tempted to accept his offer to go to Brig for dinner where he was planning to spend the night. But I thought that it would be imprudent to be seen on this road, which was the one leading to Valvèdre, and where I intended to go without leaving my name in any village. I gave as an excuse an excursion I had already planned in the opposite direction; however, to have the pleasure of his company a few more moments, I accompanied him for two miles toward his shelter. Thus we spoke again on the same topic that had occupied us and I was forced to admit that his reasoning had great merit and force upon his tongue, but I asked him to admit in turn that few minds were vast enough to embrace from all sides the notion of beauty in nature.

"The fact that the study of the most irksome classifications," I said to him, "hasn't chilled a superior soul like yours cannot be doubted when I listen to you. However, you must admit that there are things that in themselves are mutually exclusive in most human constitutions. I don't have the modesty to think that I am stupid; yet I tell you that a dry nomenclature and the more or less ingenious research that has been done to the countless modifications of divine thought diminishes it remarkably in my eyes and that I would be sorry, for example, to know how many species of flies around us are sucking the wild thyme and lavender around us at this moment. I know quite well that the absolute ignoramus thinks that he has seen everything when he has noticed the buzzing of the bee; but I myself who know that the bee has many winged sisters who modify and spread their kind, am not asking to be told where it begins and where it ends. I prefer to convince myself that it ends nowhere, that it begins nowhere, and my need for poetry finds that the word *bee* sums up everything that enlivens with its song and its work the fragrant carpets of the mountain. Thus do allow the poet to see only the synthesis of things and do not require that the bard of nature also be its historian."

"I think that here you are quite right," my doctor answered. "The poet must summarize, you are right, and the harsh and often arbitrary technology of naturalists will never belong to his domain. Let's hope so! But the poet who will sing of the bee will benefit from knowing it in all the details of its organization and of its life. He will form from it, as well as from its superiority over related species, a greater, more just, and more fruitful idea. And it is thus for everything, believe me. The close examination of everything is the key to the whole. But this is not the most important point of the thesis that you have allowed me to defend in front of you. There is a purely philosophical point that has a much greater importance: the health of the soul does not reside in the perpetual tension of lyrical fervor any more than the health of the body is to be found in the exclusive and prolonged use of stimulants. The peaceful and healthy pleasures of learning are necessary to our balance, our reason, and allow me to add, our morality!"

I was struck by the similarity of this assertion with Obernay's theories, and couldn't help telling him that I had a friend who preached the same thing to me.

"Your friend is right," he rejoined. "He probably knows through experience that civilized man is a patient who is quite fragile and who must become his own doctor for fear of becoming mad or stupid."

"Doctor, this is a statement too full of skepticism for a believer of your strength!"

"I have no strength," he answered with a melancholy good nature. "I am quite like the others, weak in the struggle of my affections against my logic, often troubled in my trust in God by the feeling of my intellectual failings. Poets may not have this feeling as much as we do. They are intoxicated with an idea of greatness and power that brings them solace, even if it leads them astray. A man devoted to reflection knows fully well that he is weak and always liable to misuse the excess of his strength and become exhausted. It is when he forgets his own misery that he finds the renewal or the conservation of his faculties; but this salutary neglect is neither found in laziness nor in intoxication; it can only be found in the study of the great book of the universe. You will see this as you move along in life. If, as I think you do, you feel strongly, you will soon be tired of being the hero of the poem of your own life, and you will ask God more than once to substitute himself for you in your concerns. God will listen to you because he is *the great listener of creation;* the one who hears everything, who answers everything according to the need that every being has to know the secret of his destiny. It is enough to think of him respectfully when contemplating the least of his works to be in direct relation and close conversation with him, like a child with his father. But I have already indoctrinated you too much, and I am sure you are making me talk to hear a summary in general language of what your brilliant imagination knows better than I do. Since you don't want to go to Brig, I shall not detain you any longer. Until we meet again and bon voyage!"

"Until we meet again? Where and when would that be, dear Doctor?"

"Until we meet again in everything and everywhere! Since we live in one of the stages of infinite life and we have the feeling we do. I don't know if plants and animals have an instinctive notion of eternity, but man, especially the one whose intelligence has practiced reflection, cannot go by another man like a ghost and wander off in eternal night. Two free souls are not annihilated one for the other: as soon as they have shared a thought, they have given something of themselves to each other, and even if they were never to meet again materially speaking, they know each other enough to find each other in the paths of memory, which are not the pure abstractions people think they are. But enough of metaphysics! Good-bye again and thank you for the nice and pleasant moment you have added to my day!"

I was sorry to leave him but I thought that I should keep the strictest incognito, as I was not far from the end of my mysterious trip. Finally the day came when I could count on Alida being at home alone with Paule and her children, and I arrived on the side of the Alps that dips into the banks of Lake Maggiore. I recognized from afar the villa that I had asked Obernay to describe for me. It was a delightful residence halfway up the hill, in a paradise of greenery and light across from the narrow and deep perspective of the lake for which the mountains provide a wonderful frame, at once austere and gracious.

As I was coming down into the valley, a terrible storm was gathering to the south and I could see it coming to meet me, invading the sky and the waters with a purplish tint veined with burning red. It was a grandiose spectacle, and soon wind and lightning multiplied by a thousand echoes, gave me a symphony worthy of the scene it was filling. I took refuge in a farm and I introduced myself to the peasants as a landscape painter; they were accustomed to guests of this kind and they welcomed me under their isolated roof.

It was a tiny farm, neatly kept and indicating a measure of comfort. The woman spoke willingly and I learned while she was preparing my meal that the small domain was part of the Valvèdre estate. Hence, I could hope for accurate information on the family. And while giving the impression of not knowing them and of only being interested in the details of my old hostess's life, I learned everything that mattered most to me personally. M. de Valvèdre had come on July 4 to fetch his older sister and his oldest son to take them to Geneva. But as Mademoiselle Juste wanted to leave the house and things in order she hadn't been able to leave the same day. Madame de Valvèdre had arrived on the 5th with Mademoiselle Paule and her fiancé. There had been an explanation. Everyone knew that Madame de Valvèdre and Mademoiselle Juste did not get along. Mademoiselle Juste was a little harsh and Madame a little quick tempered. Finally they had come to an agreement since they had kissed when they had left. The servants saw it. Mademoiselle Juste had asked to take Mademoiselle Paule to Geneva to take care of her trousseau and Madame de Valvèdre, although pressed by her family, had preferred to remain in the castle alone with her younger son M. Paolino, Mademoiselle Paule's godson; but the child had shed many tears because he did not want to be separated from his brother and his godmother, so that Madame, who could not stand to see *the gentlemen* cry, had decided that day that the boys would leave together and that she would stay at Valvèdre until the end of the month. The whole family had left on the 7th, and the people in the house were quite surprised by the notion that Madame had to stay three weeks all by herself at Valvèdre where everyone knew she was bored even when she had company. All these details had reached my hostess through her nephew, who was a gardener at the castle.

I would have liked to attempt a night walk around this enchanted castle, and nothing would have been easier than to leave my retreat without being noticed, for at ten o'clock the old couple was snoring as if they wanted to compete with thunder. But a storm was raging and I had to wait until the next day.

    The sun rose splendidly. I took my travel sketchbook with affectation, and I left for a rather eerie walk. I went around the property five or six times, always making the circle smaller in order to know as if from a bird's-eye view all the details of the area. Paths, ditches, fields, houses, brooks, and rocks, everything became as familiar to me after a few hours as if I had been born in the area. I came to know the open country and the inhabited areas where I should not go again in order to avoid drawing attention to myself, the spots which other landscape painters had taken over and where I didn't have to make their acquaintance, the shaded paths that were only trod by herds on the hillside where I was almost certain not to meet overly civilized people. Finally I secured an improbable but admirably mysterious path to go from my lodging place to the villa, a way which offered secluded refuges where I could escape distrustful or curious looks, by going deep into the woods thrown straight down along the ravines. Once this exploration was done, I ventured onto the Valvèdre grounds through a hole I had managed to discover. It was being repaired but the workers were not there. I stepped under the grove, I reached the edge of a luxuriant flower bed, and I saw across from me the white Italian-style house built on a solid mass of masonry surrounded with columns. I noticed four windows with pink silk curtains shimmering in the setting sun. I moved forward a little, and I stayed there hidden in a grove of laurel bushes for over one hour. Night was coming when I finally saw from afar a woman whom I identified as Bianca, Madame de Valvèdre's devoted servant. She pulled the curtains to let in the coolness of the evening and I soon saw lights moving. Then the bell was rung and the lights disappeared. It was the call for dinner; the windows were those of Alida's apartment.

    Thus I knew everything it was important to know. I went back to Rocca (as my little farm was called) so as not to worry my hosts. I had dinner with them and I withdrew into my little room where I rested for two hours. When I was sure that I was the only one awake in the farm, I left without a noise. The weather was in my favor: absolutely cloudless, with many stars and no revealing moon. I had counted the angles of my path and noted, I think, all the stones. When the thickness of the trees immersed me in darkness, I made my way from memory.

I had not shown sign of life to Madame de Valvèdre since I had left Saint Pierre. She probably thought she had been abandoned and must have despised and hated me; but she had not forgotten me, and she had suffered. Of that I was sure. I did not need much experience in life to know that in love the wounds of pride are harrowing and bleed for a long time. I rightly told myself that a woman who thought she had been adored or simply passionately desired is not easily cured from the insult of being quickly and easily forgotten. I was counting on the bitter feelings accumulated in this weak heart to strike boldly through my sudden appearance, and my romantic enterprise. My siege had been laid. I intended to say that I had wanted to recover and that I was coming to admit defeat. If deception was not enough to move this already troubled soul, I would be even more cruel and treacherous, I would pretend to want to go away forever and to have come only to be strengthened by a last good-bye.

There were indeed moments when the conscience of youth and love rebelled in me against this tactic befitting a vulgar rake. I wondered whether I would have the necessary cool to make her suffer without falling to my knees on the spot, if all this stack of tricks was not going to crumble in front of one of these irresistible looks of plaintive languor and sorrowful resignation that had taken hold of me and overcome me already so many times, but I endeavored to believe in my own perversity, to divert my attention, and I was moving forward quick and quivering under the soft light of the stars through bushes already covered with dew. I made my way so well that I arrived at the foot of the villa without awakening a single bird in the foliage, without having been detected from afar by a guard dog.

An elegant and vast flight of steps led from the terrace down to the flower beds but it was closed by an iron gate. I did not dare call out. In any case I wanted to take her by surprise, to appear like a deus ex machina. Madame de Valvèdre was still up; it was only eleven. Only one of her windows was lighted, open even, with the pink curtain shut.

Climbing onto the terrace was not easy, but it had to be done. The terrace was not high, but where could I find a point of support along the white marble columns that held it? I went back to the breach left open by the masons; they had not left the ladder that I had noticed there during the day. I stole into an orangery which lined one of the sides of the flower bed and I found another ladder, but it was much too small. How I still managed to reach the terrace; I could not tell. Sheer will works miracles, or rather passion gives lovers the mysterious sense that sleepwalkers have.

The open window was almost level with the flagstones of the terrace. I stepped over the edge without making a noise. I looked through the slit of the curtain. Alida was there, in a exquisite boudoir softly lit by a lamp set on a table. At this table where she appeared to have sat to write a letter, she was dreaming or dozing, her face covered by her two hands. When she looked up, I was at her feet.

She held back a scream and threw her arms around my neck. I thought she was going to faint. My passion brought her back to consciousness. "I allow your presence in my room in the middle of the night," she said, "and without any possibility of help that I could call for without ruining my reputation. It is because I have faith in you. Come the time when I think I was wrong, and that will be the last moment of my love. Francis, you may not forget it!"

"I am forgetting everything," I answered. "I don't know, I don't understand what you are telling me. I know that I am seeing you, hearing you, that you seem happy to see me, that I am at your feet, that you are threatening me, that I am dying of fright and happiness, that you can send me away and that I can die. This is all I know. Here I am! What do you want to do with me? You are everything for me; am I anything for you? Nothing shows it, and I don't know where I got the demented idea to convince myself of it and to come to you. Speak, do speak, comfort me, reassure me, erase the horror of the days I have just spent away from you, or tell me immediately that you are sending me away forever. I cannot live without a solution for I am losing my mind and my will. Have enough for the two of us, and tell me what will become of me!"

"Become my only friend!" she answered. "Become the solace, the salvation, and the joy of a lonely, careworn soul, whose long-dormant energy is turned toward an all-consuming need to love. I am hiding nothing from you. You have come at a time in my life when, after years of prostration, I felt that I must love or die. I found in you sudden, sincere but terrifying passion. I was frightened; I swore a hundred times that the remedy to my boredom was going to be worse that the illness, and when you left me, I almost blessed you as I was cursing you, but your absence was useless. I suffered more from it than from all my fears and now that you are here, I too feel that you must decide my fate, that I no longer belong to myself, and that if we part forever, I shall lose my mind and the will to live."

I was elated by her lack of restraint; hope was coming back to me, but she quickly came back to her threats. "Above all," she said, "to be happy to have your affection, I must feel respected; otherwise the future you are offering me fills me with horror. If you love me only as my husband loved me, and as many others after him have offered to love me, it is not worth it for my heart to be guilty and to lose the feeling of conjugal faithfulness. You told me over there that I was incapable of any sacrifice. Don't you see that, even in loving you as I do, I am a soul without virtue, a spouse without honor? When the heart is adulterous, duty is already betrayed, I have thus no illusion about myself. I know that I am a coward, that I am giving into a feeling that morality condemns, and that is a secret insult to my husband's dignity. Well! Who cares? Let me bear this torment. I shall know how to bear my shame before you, you of all people who will not reproach me with it. I may suffer from my dissimulation toward the others, but you will never hear me complain. I can endure everything for you. Love me as I wish, and if on your side you find my discretion painful, know how to suffer, and find in yourself the tactfulness of not reproaching me for it. Should a great passionate love be the gratification of blind appetites? Where would the merit be? And how two lofty souls could love and admire each other for the gratification of an instinct? . . . No, no, there are some tests that love cannot meet! In marriage, friendship and familial ties can compensate for the loss of enthusiasm; but in a relation that nothing sanctions, that everything offends and opposes in society, you need great strength and the consciousness that it is a lofty struggle. I believe that you can do this and I feel that I can. Do not take away this illusion if it is one. Give me some time to enjoy it. If we must succumb someday, it will be the end of everything, and at least we shall remember that we loved!"

Alida expressed herself better than I can make her speak here. She had the gift of being able to express admirably a certain range of ideas. She had read many novels, but for the exaltation or the subtlety of feelings, she could have given lessons to the most skillful of novelists. Her language sometimes bordered on the bombastic and suddenly shifted back to simplicity with a peculiar charm. Her intelligence, which had not been well cultivated, had in this regard a real force, for she was in good faith, and found for the benefit of sophistry itself arguments that were admirably sincere. She was a dangerous woman if there ever was one, but dangerous to herself more than to others. A stranger to any perversity, and stricken with a disease that was deadly for her conscience, that is the exclusive analysis of her personality.

I was less, but still much too much so, stricken with the same disease that could be called still today the poet's disease. I was wrapped up in myself, I would bring back all too easily everything to my own appreciation. I did not want to ask religion, society, sciences, or philosophy to sanction my ideas and my actions. I felt in me live forces and a rebellious spirit that was not at all reasoned. The *ego* held an inordinate place in my reflections as well as in my instincts, and because these instincts were generous and eagerly turned toward greatness, I concluded that they could not lead me astray. By flattering my pride, Alida, without schemes or calculations, was to succeed in taking possession of me. If I had been more logical and wiser, I would have thrown off the yoke of a woman who neither knew how to be a wife nor a lover, and who was seeking her rehabilitation in some dream of false virtue and false passion; but she was appealing to my strength, and strength was the dream of my ambition. Hence I became captive and I enjoyed in my sacrifice the incomplete and feverish happiness which was the ideal of this overexcited woman. By convincing me that my submission made me into a hero, almost an angel, she gently intoxicated me: flattery went to my head and I left her, if not feeling satisfied with her, at least greatly pleased with myself.

I must not and did not want to compromise Madame de Valvèdre. Thus I had resolved to leave the very next day. I would have been less cautious, less thoughtful perhaps, if she had given way to my passion: overcome by her virtue and forced to submit, I did not want to expose her reputation for nothing, but she insisted with such tenderness that I had to promise to come back the following night, and indeed I came back. She was waiting for me in the country and more out of romanticism than passion, she wanted to go on a boat ride with me on the lake. It would have been ungracious of me to refuse such a poetic whim. However, I found it rather dull to be condemned to the role of rower, instead of being at her feet and taking her into my arms. After I had taken to the middle of the lake, the pretty row boat which she had helped me find in the reeds along the shore, and which belonged to her, I let the oars float to lie down at her feet. The evening was splendidly serene, and the water so calm that you could barely see the shimmer of the stars' reflection. "Aren't we happy like this?" she said to me, "And isn't it lovely to breathe together this pure air, with the deep feeling of the purity of our love? And you wanted to deny me the charming night, you wanted to leave guilty, whereas here we are in God's presence, worthy of his benevolent pity and perhaps blessed in spite of society and its laws."

"Since you believe in God's goodness," I answered her, "why not trust it entirely? Would it be such a great crime?" She put her sweet hands to my mouth. "Hush," she said, "don't disturb my happiness with complaints and don't offend the awesome peace of this sublime night with grumbling against destiny again. Even if I was certain of divine mercy for my sin, I still would not know how long your love for me would last after my fall."

"So, you believe neither in God nor in me!" I cried out.

"If it is the case, feel sorry for me, because doubt is a great misery that I have dragged along all my life, and try to cure me, but allay my fears and give me trust, trust in God first! Tell me, do you strongly believe in the God who sees us, who hears us, and who loves us? Answer, answer! Do you have faith, do you have certainty?"

"No more than you do, alas! I only have hope. I was not long deluded by the sweet dreams of childhood. I drank at the cold spring of doubt, which flows over all things in our miserable century, but I believe in love, because I can feel it."

"I do too, I believe in the love that I feel, but I can see that we are both miserable since we only believe in ourselves."

The sad judgment that she had let slip out threw me into a dark melancholy mood. Was it to judge each other thus, to measure as skeptical poets the depth of our nothingness that we had come to enjoy the union of our souls under the starry skies? She reproached me, my silence, and my somber attitude. "It's your fault," I answered bitterly. "Love, which you want to make into something rational, is by nature a state of ecstasy. If, instead of looking toward the unknown by calculating the chances the future, which is not ours, may hold, you were submerged in the pleasures of my passion, you would not remember having suffered, and you would believe in another person for the first time in your life."

"Let us go," she said, "you are frightening me! These pleasures, these raptures about which you are speaking, that's not love, that's a fever, a daze, the forgetting of everything. It's something brutal and crazy that has no past and no tomorrow. Pick up the oars, I want to go back."

A kind of rage overtook me. I seized the oars and took her farther off. She became frightened and threatened to jump in the lake if I continued with this fiercely silent trip, which looked like an abduction. I took her back to the shore without a word. I was prey to a violent inner disturbance.

In tears, she fell onto the sand. Disarmed, I also broke into tears. We were deeply unhappy without quite knowing what the causes of our suffering were. Of course I was not so weak that the violence done to my passion seemed such a great effort and such a great misfortune, and as for her, the fright I had caused her was not so serious as she wanted to believe. What was there that was so impossible between us? What wall kept our souls apart? We remained facing this frightening problem without being able to solve it.

The only remedy to our sorrow was to suffer together, and this was really the only bond that was deeply true between us. The sorrow that I saw in her, so heartbreaking and so deeply felt, purified me, in the sense that I abjured my plans to use surprise and wile to seduce her. Unhappy through and by her, I loved her more. Who knows if success would not have made me ungrateful as she feared?

The very next day I took the direction of Saint Gothard to then go to Lake Quatre-Cantons. Alida blamed my eagerness to leave her; she thought I could spend a week in Rocca with impunity. But I could see that one day my old host's curiosity would prevent her from sleeping and my nocturnal walks would be an object of reflection and comments in the surrounding countryside.

After the first hours of walking, I stopped at an enormous rock that Alida had pointed out to me from afar as one of her favorite walks. From there, I could still see her white villa like a shining point amidst the dark woods. While my gaze was fixed on the house and my heart was sending it a sweet good-bye, I felt a light hand rest on my shoulder, and turning around, I saw Alida herself who had come ahead of me. She had ridden her horse followed by a servant who she had left behind at a distance. She was carrying a small basket filled with delicacies. She had wished to have lunch with me on the moss sheltered by her beautiful rock, in this absolutely deserted place. I was so moved by this gracious surprise that I strove to make her forget the sorrows and the storms of the previous night. I claimed my submission and I did my best with her and myself to convince her without lying that I would be happy like this.

"But when and where shall we see each other again?" she asked. "You haven't been completely willing to commit to being in Geneva for Paule's wedding, and still it is the only way to meet again without danger to myself. Our relations, such as they are, chaste and now sanctioned by true love, can be established quite properly if you make up your mind to be acquainted with my husband and be a natural part of the circle of friends who are close to me. I don't always live alone as you see me now. The unjust suspicions and the sour temper of my old sister-in-law have created a void around me recently: because of her, I was discouraged from being in friendly and neighborly relations. But since her departure, I have made a few visits, I have erased the bad impression made by her lack of civility, to which I might have seemed somewhat party. People will come back to me. I don't have many acquaintances. I have never liked that, and it is all the better. You will find me with a circle of friends large enough that we won't look as if we are trying to be alone with each other, and free enough that we will be alone often and naturally. Besides I shall discover how to go away sometimes, and we shall meet on neutral territory, far from indiscrete eyes. I am going to exert myself thence to make it possible and even easy; I shall send away the people whom I don't trust. I shall gain the affections of loyal servants. I shall invent pretexts beforehand, and as our acquaintance will be acknowledged, our encounters, if they are found out, will have nothing about which to be surprised or scandalized. See! Everything is in our favor. You have before you the freedom of the traveler, and I will have that of the neglected spouse, for M. de Valvèdre thinks too about a long trip that I shall no longer oppose. He may be gone for two years. Do accept to be introduced to him before then. He already knows that I have met you and he cannot suspect anything. Let's be in step with M. de Valvèdre and society. It will give us time, freedom, and safety. You will travel through Switzerland and Italy, you will become a great poet with the beauty of nature before your eyes and love in your heart. I, myself, have been spiritless and disaffected until now, but I am going to become active and ingenious. I shall think of nothing but this. Yes, yes, we have already two years of pure happiness ahead of us. God sent you to me, at a time when the sorrow of parting from my son was going to kill me. When I have to leave my younger son, I shall have the compensation of living for longer periods of time, perhaps always, near you, because then I will have the right to tell my husband: I am alone. I have nothing left to keep me at home. Allow me to live where I please. I shall pretend to like Rome, Paris, or London, and, both strangers, lost in the middle of a big city, we shall see each other every day. I shall be quite able to do without luxury. Mine bores me tremendously and all I dream about is a cottage in the Alps or a garret in a large town, as long as I am truly loved."

We parted on these plans, which were not too impossible. I promised to sacrifice all my reluctance to attend Obernay's wedding in Geneva, thus to be introduced to M. de Valvèdre.

I was so far from agreeing with this decision then after Alida had left, I almost ran after her to take back my word, but I was held back by the fear of appearing selfish. I could see her again only at that cost, otherwise at every encounter I ran the risk of estranging her from her husband, people, the whole of society. I continued my journey, but instead of traveling through the mountains, I took the shortest way to go to Altorf and I remained there. That is where Alida was to send me her letters. And what did all the rest matter? We wrote every day, and you could say all day, for in two weeks we exchanged volumes of effusion and enthusiasm. Never had I found in myself such an abundance of emotion in front of a sheet of paper. Her own letters were delightful. To express love, to write love, were in her supreme faculties. Quite superior to me in this regard, she had the touching simplicity not to realize it, to deny it, to admire me, and to tell me so. This was ruining me; while elevating me to the level of her sentimental theories, she was working toward convincing me that I was a great soul, a great mind, a bird of the sky the wings of which only needed to spread out to fly over his century and posterity. I did not believe it, no! Thank God, I avoided this folly, but under the pen of this woman, flattery was so sweet that I would have paid for it at the price of public ridicule and I no longer understood how to live without it.

She also succeeded in destroying my rebellions regarding the life plan she had adopted for both of us. I agreed to see her husband, and I was looking forward to the time of going to Geneva. Finally this month of fever and giddiness, which was the term of my burning aspirations, was reaching its last day.

I had promised Obernay that I would come knock on his door the day before his wedding. On July 31 at five in the morning, I went aboard a steamboat to cross Lake Geneva from Lausanne to Geneva.

I had not slept all night, so afraid was I to miss the time of departure. Exhausted, I took a few moments of rest on a bench, draped in my coat. When I opened my eyes, you could already feel the sun. A man, who also seemed to be asleep, was sitting on the same bench. I recognized at first glance my anonymous friend from the Simplon.

This meeting at the gates of Geneva was somewhat worrisome; I had made the mistake of writing to Obernay from Altdorf and giving him a false itinerary of my excursion. This excess of caution was becoming an unfortunate blunder if the person who had seen me on the road to Valvèdre was from Geneva and acquainted with the Valvèdres or the Obernays. I thus wanted to hide from his sight; but the boat was quite small, and after a few moments, I found myself face to face with my amiable philosopher. He was looking at me closely as if he was not sure he recognized me; but his doubts soon dissipated and he came up to me with the grace of a man belonging to the best society. He spoke to me as if we had just parted, and out of great tactfulness, refraining from expressing any surprise and any curiosity, he took up the conversation where we had left it when we were on the road to Brig. I fell again under his charm, and without thinking further about contradicting him, I sought to profit from the serene and pleasant wisdom that he carried modestly within himself, like a treasure of which he thought to be the guardian rather than its master or inventor.

I could not resist the urge to question him, and yet several times my meditation let the conversation drop. I felt the need to summarize inwardly and to savor his words. During these moments, thinking that I preferred to be left alone and having no desire to impose himself, he would try to leave; but I followed him and took him up again, condemned by an invisible power to follow this man's footsteps, a man whom I had decided to avoid. When we neared Geneva, the passengers who irrupted from the cabin unto the deck separated us. My new friend was approached by several of them and I had to move away. I noticed that everyone seemed to speak to him with the highest deference; however, as he had had the tact of not inquiring after my name, I felt bound to respect his own incognito.

Half an hour later I was at Obernay's door. My heart was beating so violently that I stopped a moment to compose myself. Obernay himself came to open the door; from the terrace of his garden, he had seen me arrive. "I was counting on you," he told me, "and yet here I am in a transport of delight as if I had given up hope of seeing you. Come, come! The whole family is gathered and we are expecting Valvèdre shortly."

I found Alida among a dozen people who only allowed us to exchange customary greetings. Besides Obernay's father, Henri's mother and his fiancée were present, as well as Valvèdre's older sister Mademoiselle Juste—a person less old and less unpleasant than I had imagined, and an amazingly beautiful young woman. Although I was absorbed by thoughts of Alida, I was struck by this splendor of gracefulness, youth, and poetry, and in spite of myself I asked Henri, after a few moments, if this beautiful person was a relative of his.

"Good gracious!" he exclaimed with a laugh, "she is my sister Adélaïde! And here is another whom you did not know as a child, as you did this one; here is our little Demon," he added as he kissed his sister Rosa who was coming in.

Rosa was also gorgeous, but less ideally so than her sister and more pleasant, or, more exactly, less imposing. She was barely fourteen and her demeanor was not yet that of a reasonable young lady; but there was so much innocence in her exuberant gaiety that one was not ready to forget how close the child was to becoming a young woman.

"As for the oldest," Obernay went on, "she is your mother's godchild and my student, an accomplished botanist, I warn you, and one who does not appreciate the superior jests of people like you. Mind your wit, if you want her to acknowledge your presence. However, thanks to your mother, who does her the honor of writing her every year in answer to her New Year's wishes, and whom she still holds in great reverence, I hope that she won't react badly to your disheveled poet's face; but my mother is the one who must introduce her."

"Later," I replied when seeing that Alida was looking at me. "Let me recover from my surprise and dazzle."

"You find her beautiful? You are not the only one; but don't let her see it, if you don't want to upset her. Her beauty is like a curse for her. She cannot go out of the Old Town without having people gathering to look at her; and she is not only intimidated by their greedy gaze; she is also hurt and offended. She really suffers from it and becomes sad and withdrawn outside of her circle of friends and relatives. For her, tomorrow will be a day of forced exhibition, thus a day of torture. If you want to be among her friends, look at her as if she were fifty."

"Speaking of fifty," I continued in order to change the subject, "it seems to me that Mademoiselle Juste is not much older than that. I thought she would be a real duenna."

"Speak to her for fifteen minutes, and you will see that the duenna is a woman of great merit. Here! I want to introduce you to her because I like this sister-in-law and I want her to like you too."

He did not allow me to hesitate and pushed me toward Mademoiselle Juste whose dignified and kind welcome led me naturally to begin a conversation with her. She was an old maid, somewhat skinny and with strongly marked features, but who must have been almost as beautiful as Obernay's sister, and whose spinsterhood seemed to me to hide some mystery, for she was rich, of good breeding, and endowed with a very independent mind. When I listened to her talk, I found in her a rare distinction and even a kind of serious and deep charm that filled me with respect and fear. She, however, showed interest and asked me questions about my family, which she seemed to know quite well, without, however, alluding to or explaining the circumstances in which she had known them.

People had already had lunch but a light meal had been kept for myself and M. de Valvèdre. While waiting for his arrival, Henri took me to my room. On our way upstairs, we met Madame Obernay and her two daughters who were attending to some household duties. Henri stopped his mother so that she could introduce me to her eldest daughter in particular. "Yes, yes," she answered with a warm liveliness, "you are going to make deep bows to each other as is the custom; but don't forget that you were childhood companions for a year in Paris. Then M. Valigny was a boy who treated you quite gently and kindly, my daughter, and you took advantage of it without scruples. Now that you are all too reasonable, thank him for the past and talk to him about your godmother who has been and still is so good to you."

Adélaïde was quite self-conscious, but I was so careful about the danger of frightening her that she felt reassured with a marvelous tactfulness. In one moment, I saw her transformed. This dreamy and proud beauty became animated with a splendid smile, and she held out her hand to me with a kind of charming awkwardness that added to her natural gracefulness. I was not moved when I touched her pure hand, and, as if she had felt it, she broke into a large smile and seemed to me even more beautiful.

She was a type very different from Obernay and Rosa, who both looked like their mother. Adélaïde had also gotten from her the pallor and the glow of her complexion but she had the black and pensive eyes, the high forehead, the thin waist and the fine extremities of her father, who had been one of the most handsome men of the country. Madame Obernay remained graceful and youthful under her graying hair and like Paule de Valvèdre was, without being pretty, quite attractive. It was said in town that when the Obernays and the Valvèdres were together, it was like going into a museum of human forms who were more or less beautiful, but all full of nobility and worthy of a statuary or a painter's brush.

I had hardly changed when Obernay came to call me. "Valvèdre is downstairs," he said to me. "He is waiting to make your acquaintance and have lunch with you."

I went down in great haste but on the last step of the stairs a strange terror seized me. A vague apprehension, which for the last two weeks had often crossed my mind and which had visited me often during the day, overtook me to such an extent that, seeing the door of the house open, I felt like running away; but Obernay was at my heels, cutting off my retreat. I went into the dining room. The meal was served. A voice that was both soft and masculine was coming from the drawing room. No more uncertainty, no more refuge; my stranger from the Simplon was M. de Valvèdre himself.

A world of lies, each more extravagant than the other, a century of anxieties filled the few moments left before the inevitable meeting. What was I going to tell M. de Valvèdre, Henri, Paule, and both families to explain my presence in the vicinity of the Valvèdre estate, when I was thought to be in northern Switzerland at that very time? This fear was accompanied by a feeling of extraordinary sorrow that I found impossible to fight with the vulgar arguments of selfish motives. I loved, loved by instinct, impulse, conviction, by fate perhaps, this accomplished man whom I had come with the intent to deceive and thus to make him unhappy or ridiculous.

My head was spinning when Obernay introduced me to Valvèdre and I don't know if I succeeded in putting on a bold front. As for him, he had a very strong feeling of surprise which was immediately repressed. "Is it your friend?" he said to Henri, "Well, I already know him. I went across the lake with him this morning and we philosophized together for more than an hour."

He held out his hand and shook mine cordially. Adélaïde called us for lunch, and we sat across from each other, he peaceful and without any suspicions since he was not aware of my lie, I eating as if I was awaiting torture. To top it all, Alida came to sit next to her husband with a look of interest and deference, and attempted while speaking to guess what impression we had made on each other. "I met M. Valigny before you did," she said to him. "I have told you that he was our protector, Paule and me, in Saint Pierre, while Obernay was looking for you in those terrible glaciers."

"I had not forgotten," Valvèdre answered, "and I am glad to be indebted to a person whom I liked when I first saw him."

As she saw us getting on so well, Alida went back to the drawing room, and Adélaïde came to take her place. I noticed between her and Valvèdre an affection in which it was certainly impossible to see any harm unless one had a brute mind and vulgar judgment, but which was nonetheless striking. He had known her since she was a young child, and as he was forty years old, he still said *tu* to her, whereas she addressed him in the formal *vous* form with a mix of respect and tenderness which reinstated family decorum in their close relations. She waited upon him attentively, and he let her wait on him, saying, *"Thank you, my dear girl,"* with a very paternal tone. But she was so grown-up and so beautiful, and he himself was still so young and so charming! I did my best to imagine that this husband who had been deceived would willingly agree not to notice, as he was such a happy father!

We soon parted to meet again at dinner. The family was busy with a thousand preparations for the big event of the next day. The men went out together. I remained in the drawing room with Madame de Valvèdre and her two sisters-in-law. This was a new phase of torture. I was worriedly waiting for the opportunity to exchange a few words with Alida. Paule, who was called by Madame Obernay to try on her wedding gown, soon left; but Mademoiselle Juste appeared riveted to her armchair. Was she thus carrying on as the guardian of her brother's honor in spite of the measures taken to release her from it? I carefully watched her austere profile, and I could feel in her something different from the desire to annoy. She was fulfilling a duty that weighed heavily on her. Her lucid gaze, which caught Alida's blushing impatience and detected my horrible discomfort, seemed to say to both of us, "Do you think I find this amusing?"

After one hour of very difficult conversation, which Mademoiselle Juste and myself kept going on our own, Alida being too irritated to be able to hide it, I finally learned by chance that instead of accompanying his sisters and children to Geneva on the eighth of July, M. de Valvèdre had entrusted their care to Obernay in order to stop at the Simplon. I hastened to anticipate the discovery that was threatening me by saying that it was there that I had met M. de Valvèdre and had become acquainted with him without knowing who he was.

"It is strange," Mademoiselle Juste remarked, "M. Obernay did not think you were in those parts."

I answered coolly that when I had wanted to reach the Rhône Valley through the Matterhorn peak, I had gone the wrong way, and that I had taken advantage of my mistake to see the Simplon, but that, fearing Obernay's jokes about my lack of care in orienting myself in spite of his instructions, I had not mentioned it in my letter.

"Since you were so close to Valvèdre," said Alida with the same composure, "you should have come visit me."

"You had not given me permission to do so," I answered, "and I did not dare."

Mademoiselle Juste looked at us both, and it seemed to me that she had not been fooled.

As soon as I was alone with Alida, I spoke to her with terror of this fateful meeting and asked her whether she did not think that her husband could suspect something. "He, jealous?" she answered with a shrug. "He does not dignify me thus! Come, collect yourself, be calm. I must warn you that you are not, and that here you have given the impression that you were particularly shy. People have already noticed that you were not like this when you first came to the house."

"I can't hide from you," I continued, "that I am on pins and needles. It seems that at any moment people are going to ask for explanations about this trip near Valvèdre and to crush me under the ridiculous pretext

I have just found. M. de Valvèdre must resent my having made a fool of him by pretending that I was an actor. It is true that he allowed himself to be called a doctor; I took him for a physician but I initiated my mistake and he did nothing to confirm or deny it, whereas I . . ."

"Has he mentioned it again?" Alida added somewhat worriedly.

"No, not a word. It is quite strange!"

"Then it is quite natural. Valvèdre does not know how to pretend. He has forgotten the whole incident; let's put it out of our minds, and let's speak about the pleasure of being together."

She was holding out her hand to me. I did not have the time to press it against my lips. Her two children were coming back from their walk. They were coming in like a tornado into the house and the drawing room.

The oldest was handsome like his father and looked strikingly like him. Paolino resembled Alida, but like a caricature; he was ugly. I remembered that Obernays had told me about a marked preference that Madame de Valvèdre had for Edmond, and instinctively I watched for the first gestures of affection that welcomed each of them. Tender kisses were given to the oldest and she introduced him and asked if I found him handsome. She barely touched the other's cheeks, adding, "As for that one, he is not, I know!"

The poor child started laughing and he said, holding his mother's head in his arms, "*All the same*, you must kiss your monkey!" She kissed him while scolding him about his roughness of manners. He had bruised her cheeks with his kisses, in which some mischief and revenge seemed to be mixed with his display of affection.

I don't know why I found this little scene quite painful. The children started playing. Alida asked me what I was thinking about while I was looking at her so somberly. And as I did not answer, she added in a whisper: "Are you jealous of them? It would be cruel. I need you to comfort me, for I am going to be apart from both of them unless I stay in this hateful town of Geneva. And it is not at all certain that I would be allowed to do so."

She told me that M. de Valvèdre had decided to entrust the education of his two sons to the excellent Professor Karl Obernay, Henri's father. Brought up in that happy and wholesome household, they would be cared for with great affection by the women and seriously educated by the men. Alida was thus to be happy about this decision which spared her children the harsh experiences of boarding school, and indeed she was delighted but with tears that were visibly meant for Edmond, although she did her best to consider as equally painful the departure of little Paul. She was also suffering from a circumstance that was quite personal; I mean, the increasing power that Juste was going to have on her children. She had hoped to remove them from it, but she saw them falling even more under this influence since Juste was settling in Geneva in the house next door.

I was going to tell her that this persistent bias against Juste did not seem quite fair when Juste came in and kissed the children with equal affection. I noticed the trust and happiness with which both of them climbed on her lap and played with her cap, the lace of which she allowed them to crumple. The mischievous Paolino even removed it completely and the old maid made no fuss about in showing her gray hair tousled by these wild little hands. At that moment I saw on that rigid face a motherhood that was so real and a good nature so touching that I forgave her for the irritation that she had caused me.

Dinner brought everyone together, except for M. de Valvèdre who came only afterward during the evening. I thus had two to three hours of respite, and I was able to get back in step. There was in this household an atmosphere of charming congeniality, and I thought that Alida was wrong when she said she was condemned to live with oracles. It is true that one could feel, in each of the persons present, a fundamental depth and an element of maturity and calm that reveals studiousness or at least a respect for studies, but one could also feel in them, with the essential qualities of everyday life, all the charm of a life full of happiness and dignity. In several respects, it seemed to me that I was at home with my family; but the home of my Geneva friends was more lively and as if warmed by the rays of youth and beauty shining in Adélaïde's and Rosa's eyes. Their mother seemed in a religious rapture when looking at Paule and thinking about Henri's happiness. Paule had the peacefulness of innocence, the trust of honesty. She was not given to much effusiveness, but each word, each look addressed to her fiancé, her parents, and her sisters was like an inexhaustible fund of devotion and admiration.

The three girls had been friends since they were children; they used the familiar *tu* form to address each other, and they waited on each other. All three loved Mademoiselle Juste, and although Paule had not taken her side during the disagreements with Alida, you could tell that she loved her more. Was Alida loved by these three girls? Obviously Paule knew she was unhappy and loved her naïvely to comfort her. As for the Obernay sisters, they did their best to like her, and both treated her with great consideration and attention; but Alida did nothing to encourage them and responded to their quiet overtures with a cool and slightly mocking grace. In a whisper, she called them "bluestocking," and according to her, little Rosa was already full of pedantry.

"It does not appear to be so at all," I said to her. "The child is a gorgeous girl and Adélaïde seems to be an excellent person."

"Oh, I was sure you'd make allowances for those beautiful eyes!" Alida went on with irritation.

I did not dare answer: the state of nervous tension in which I could see her made me fear that she would betray herself.

Other young ladies, cousins, friends arrived with their parents. We moved to the garden which, without being very large, was quite beautiful with many flowers and large trees, with a superb view from the edge of the terrace. The children asked for a game, and everyone joined in, except for the old people and Alida who, seated apart from the others, signaled to me to come to her. I did not dare obey. Juste was watching me, and Rosa, who had become much bolder with me during dinner, came to firmly take my arm, claiming that all the *young crowd* had to play; her dad had said so. I did try to pass as one of the old people, but she did not pay any attention. Her brother was starting the game of tag and he was older than I was. She claimed me for her camp because Henri was in the opposite one and I must be as good a runner as he was. Henri also called me. I had to remove my coat and get sweaty. Adélaïde was running after me as swiftly as an arrow. I could barely escape this young Atalanta, and I was surprised to see such strength combined with such litheness and grace. The beautiful girl was laughing; she revealed dazzling teeth. At ease among her relatives, she forgot the tormenting gaze of strangers; she was happy, like a child; she shone in the fiery glow of the sunset, like the roses seemingly set ablaze in the crimson fire of the evening.

Still I only looked at her with the eyes of a brother. God is my witness that I only thought of escaping this whirl of races, cries, and laughter to go to Alida. When I finally managed to do so, through marvels of determination and stratagems, I found her somber and haughty. She was repelled by my weakness, my childishness; she wanted to speak to me, and I had been unable to make an effort to leave these stupid games and to come to her! I was a coward; I was afraid of what people would say, or I was already under the charm of Adélaïde's eighteen years and pink cheeks. In a word, she was indignant; she was jealous; she cursed the day for which she had waited with such fervor as the most wonderful day in her life.

I was despairing of being able to comfort her; but M. de Valvèdre had just arrived, and I didn't dare say a word as I could feel his presence. It seemed to me that he could hear what I said before words had come through my lips. Alida, who was more daring and as if scornful of danger, was reproaching me for being too young, for lacking presence of mind and being more compromising with my terror than I would be with boldness. My lack of experience made me blush; I made great efforts to find a remedy to it. The rest of the evening, I succeeded in appearing very lively; then Alida found me too joyful.

As one can see, we were condemned to meet in the most painful and irksome circumstances. At night, after returning to my room I wrote to her:

"You are displeased with me and you showed it angrily. Poor angel, you are suffering and I am the cause of it! You are cursing this long-awaited day which failed to give us a single moment of safety to read in each other's eyes! Here I am distraught, angry at myself, and not knowing what to do to avoid the anguish and impatience that consume me too, but that I would bear with resignation if I could carry their full weight on my shoulders alone. I am too young, you say! Well, forgive my lack of experience, and make allowances for the naïveté and the novelty of my emotions. See, youth is a force and support for great things. You'll see if, for perils of another kind, I am below your ideal. Do I have to violently pull you away from all the bonds that weigh on you? Do I have to face the world and seize your destiny at any cost? I am ready, just say a word. I can break everything around us two... But you don't want me to; you order me to wait, to put myself to the test against which the honesty of my youth rebels! What greater sacrifice could I make for you? I am doing my best. Take pity on me, cruel woman! And you too, have patience.

"Why aggravate these sorrows with your injustice? Why tell me that Adélaïde... No! I don't want to remember what you said to me. It was irrational; it was most unfair! Another woman! But are there other women on this earth besides you? Let's forget this madness and never go back to it. Let's speak about a circumstance that struck me much more forcefully. Your two children are going to live here... And you, what are you going to do? Won't your husband's decision change your life? Are you planning to go back to the solitude of Valvèdre, where I would have so little right to live near you, under the eyes of your provincial neighbors, and surrounded by people who will record all of your movements? You had mentioned going to a big city... Do you realize! You can do it now. Tell me, when are you leaving? Where are we going? I cannot accept your hesitation. Answer, dear soul, answer! One word, and I'll bear everything in order to keep up appearances, or rather, no, I'll leave tomorrow night. I'll say that my parents called me back. I shall remove myself from all this horrible dissembling that aggravates me as much as it does you. I'll rush to wait for you wherever you want. Ah, come, let us run away! My life belongs to you."

The next day went by without my being able to slip the letter to her. Whatever Madame de Valvèdre had said to me, I did not quite dare trust Bianca who seemed to me too young and alert for the role of guardian of the greatest secret of my life. Besides, Juste de Valvèdre mounted guard so well that I was losing my mind.

I shall not describe the ceremony of the Protestant wedding. The church was so close to the house that we walked there under the eyes of the townspeople, roused, so to speak, to see the charming bride, but especially the beautiful Adélaïde in her fresh and modest attire. She was giving her arm to M. de Valvèdre whose consideration seemed, above all, the means to provide respect to protect her from the brutality of admiration. Nonetheless she was hurt by the offensive curiosity of the crowds and was walking sadly, her eyes lowered, beautiful in her suffering dignity like a queen being taken to the executioner.

After her, Alida was also a subject of emotion. Her beauty was not striking at first sight, but its charm was so deep that people admired her especially after she had gone by. I heard comparisons and comments, more or less silly. It seemed to me that they were mixed with suspicions about her behavior. I felt like finding an excuse for a quarrel; but if, in Geneva, people are quite small-town, they are generally good-natured so my anger would have been ridiculous.

In the evening, there was a little ball, including about fifty people who were relatives or close friends of the two families. Alida appeared in exquisite dress, and at my request she danced. Her indolent grace had its usual magical effect; people gathered around her, the young men vied with each other for her attention and were all the more feverish that she seemed to care for none of them in particular. I had hoped that the dance would give me the opportunity to speak to her. The contrary happened, and in turn I resented her. I was observing her, and sulked, quite ready to pick a quarrel with her, if I was to catch the least sign of flirtatiousness on her part. It was impossible: she wanted to charm no one, but she could feel, she knew that she was charming all the men and there was in her indifference a kind of bored monarchy, but still absolute, which irritated me. I thought that she spoke to these young men, not as if they had some rights on her, but as if she had rights over them, and it was, to my taste, to do them too much of an honor. She had the complete self-confidence of high-society women, and I thought I saw again in the way she looked at strangers the dominance which had overpowered and ravished my soul.

Indeed, next to her, Adélaïde and her young friends were simple bourgeoises, quite unaware of the power of their charms and quite incapable, in spite of the radiance of their youth, of vying with her for the most humble conquest; but how pure their modesty was, and what safeguard against familiarity their extreme politesse provided! A small circumstance made me insist in my own mind on this remark. When getting up Alida dropped her fan; ten admirers rushed to pick it up; they all but fought. She took it from the triumphant hand that presented it to her without a word of thanks, without a smile of civility, as if she was too much the mistress of this stranger's will to be the least grateful for his enslavement. He was a good little provincial man who seemed happy at such a familiarity. In fact, it was a mistake on his part; in theory he was nonetheless right. When a woman treats a man with disdain, she provokes him more than she rejects him, and whatever people may say, there is always some encouragement behind these regal forms of *pierciflage*.

To avenge myself of the secret vexation that I felt, I looked for some favor I could do Adélaïde who was dancing near me. I saw that she had almost fallen when slipping over some rose leaves that had separated from her bouquet, and as she was coming back to her spot, I quickly and skillfully removed them. She seemed somewhat taken aback by such great zeal, and that very surprise was an expression of modesty. I did not look at her, afraid that I would appear to be begging for thanks; but she did thank me a moment later, when the step of the quadrille placed her again beside me. "You saved me from a fall," she said aloud with a smile. "You are always good to me, as *before*!"

Good to her! It was too much gratefulness certainly, and it could induce a declaration from an impertinent fellow; but one would have been so to the point of imbecility not to feel in the extreme politeness of this pure girl a self-doubt which inspired in others a respect without bounds.

I did not wait until the end of the ball. I was suffering too much. As I was going to reach my little room, Valvèdre happened to be in front of me and signaled to follow him to the side. Here is the explanation, I thought: let him finally resolve to pick a quarrel, this mysterious character! This will relieve me of a mountain that oppresses me! But it was about a very different matter. "Some relatives from Lausanne arrived unexpectedly this afternoon. We have to offer them hospitality and to give them your room. They are both quite old and naturally they must have your room; but the Obernays do not want to send you to the inn; they are entrusting you to me. I have my pied-à-terre in town, quite nearby; would you allow me to be your host?"

I made my thanks and accepted determinedly. If he wants to wait for an explanation at his place, I said to myself, all the better! I prefer it that way.

He called his servant who took away my slim luggage and he himself took my arm to lead me to his residence. It was a house in the neighborhood where he led me through several rooms cluttered with boxes and strange instruments, some of which were quite large and vaguely glowed in the dark with a dull and metallic gleam.

"It is my scientific equipment," he told me with a laugh. "It looks somewhat like an alchemist laboratory, doesn't it? You understand why," he added with an indefinable tone, "Madame de Valvèdre does not like this house and she prefers the pleasant hospitality offered by the Obernays. But you will sleep here very peacefully. Here is the door to your room and the key to the house, for the ball is not finished over there, and if you want to go back..."

"Why would I go back," I answered, pretending to be indifferent, "I don't like balls!"

"Isn't there anyone in this ball who interests you?"

"All of Obernays interest me; but dances are the most unpleasant way of enjoying the company of people one likes."

"Ah, not always! It brings a certain liveliness... When I was young, I did not hate that noise."

"It is because you had the wit to be young, M. de Valvèdre. Nowadays, people don't have it. They are old at twenty."

"I don't believe this at all," he said while lighting his cigar, for he had followed me into my room as if to check that there was everything needed for my comfort. "I think that is a pose."

"On my part?" I answered, somewhat hurt by the lesson.

"Perhaps also on your part, and without your being necessarily guilty or ridiculous. It is a fad and youth cannot avoid its dictates. Young people submit to it in good faith because the latest fad always seems to be the best one, but if you believe me, you will examine with some seriousness the dangers of the fashion and you won't be too taken by it."

His tone was so gentle and so kind that I no longer thought there was a trap set by his suspicion against my lack of experience, and, falling again under his spell, I suddenly felt more than ever the need to open up my heart to him. There was something horrible in this, something that I could not even today explain to myself. I wished for his respect and I was seeking his affection without being able to give up inflicting upon him the most severe blow against his dignity!

He said a few more words which were like an illumination on what was in the back of his mind. It seemed to me that by inviting me to go back to the dance, that is inviting me to be young, naïve, and trusting, he was trying to find out what impression Adélaïde had made on me and whether I had the capacity to love, for the name of this charming girl landed, I don't remember how, on his lips.

I talked about her in the most glowing terms, as much to appear free of heart and mind in relation to his wife as to see if he felt some hidden sorrow about his adoptive daughter. I would have given anything to discover that he loved her unbeknownst to himself and that Alida's unfaithfulness would not upset the peace of his generous soul! But if he loved Adélaïde, it was with a selflessness so true or with a self-sacrifice so heroic that I could not detect any embarrassment either in his eyes or his words.

"I have nothing to add to your praise," he said, "and if you knew her as I do, I who have known her since she was born, you would know that nothing can express the honesty and the goodness of this soul. Happy be the man who will deserve to be her companion and her support in life. It is such a great honor and a great happiness to consider, that he will have to work at it seriously, and will never have the right to describe himself as skeptical and disenchanted."

"M. de Valvèdre," I cried out unwittingly, "you seem to say that I could aspire..."

"To gain her trust? No, I cannot say that; I have no idea. She knows you too little yet, and none can predict the future; but you are not without knowing that, in case it should happen, your parents and hers would be quite pleased."

"Henri may not be so pleased!" I answered.

"Henri? Who loves you so? Be careful not to be ungrateful, my dear child!"

"No, no, don't think that I am ungrateful! I know he loves me; I know it all the more that he loves me in spite of our differences of opinion and personality; but these differences, which he forgives on his account, would make him hesitate, if it was a matter of entrusting me with the fate of one of his sisters."

"What are these differences? He did not mention them when he spoke of you effusively. Come! Are you loath to tell me? I am the friend of the Obernay family, and there was in your own family a man for whom I had the greatest love and respect. I am not speaking about your father who also deserves these feelings, but whom I hardly know; I am speaking about your uncle Antonin, a scientist to whom I owe the first and best notions of my intellectual and moral life. There was, between him and me, about the same age difference that exists today between you and me. You can see that I have the right to take great interest in you, and that I would like to honor his memory by becoming your mentor and friend as he was mine. Speak to me quite openly and tell me what the good Henri Obernay blames you for."

I was about to open my heart to Valvèdre like a child who confesses, and not like a proud man who defends himself. Why didn't I give in to a salutary impulse? He would probably have pulled out of my chest, without knowing it and only through the power of his high morality, the poisoned arrow that was to turn against him; but I held my wound too dear and I was afraid to see it heal. I also felt an instinctive horror of such openness with the man whose rival I was. I had to resolve to no longer be so or to become the worst hypocrite. I avoided the explanation.

"Henri precisely reproaches me for my skepticism, this malady of the soul of which you want to cure me; but this would lead us too far for tonight and, if you allow me, we'll discuss it another time."

"Well," he said, "I can see that you want to go back to the dance, and it might be a better remedy to your angst than all my reasoning. Just a question before saying good night. Why did you tell me when we first met that you were an actor?"

"To avoid being mortified! You had caught me speaking to myself!"

"And also, when one travels, one likes to mystify the people one meets, isn't it true?"

"Yes, one does what is pleasant for oneself; one thinks one is quite witty, and all of a sudden, one realizes that one is in bad taste and impertinent in the presence of a man of merit."

"Well, well," Valvèdre went on with a laugh, "the poor man of merit forgives you with all his heart and won't tell a word of it to the good Adélaïde."

I was quite embarrassed by the role I was playing and, at times, I convinced myself that, notwithstanding the free spirit of M. de Valvèdre, if he had in spite of himself a touch of jealousy, it was much more about Adélaïde than about his wife. I thus cursed myself for being still obliged to cause him suffering. However, I remembered the words he had said to me at the Simplon peak: "I loved very much a woman who is dead." He thus loved in memory, and that is how he probably took the strength to be neither jealous of his wife nor in love with another woman.

In any case, I at least wanted to free him from a possible confusion by telling him that I thought I was still too young to think about marriage and that, if I came to consider it, it would be when Rosa was old enough to leave her dolls. "Rosa!" he answered with some intensity. "Ah, but! Yes . . . your ages may be a better match then! I know her as well as I do the other and this child is also a dear. But go and make my little pink rascal dance. Come on, you are not yet as old as you were saying."

He held out his hand to me, his loyal hand which burned mine and I ran away like a guilty man while he disappeared in the midst of his telescopes and test tubes.

VI

I went back to the Obernays'. People were still dancing; but Alida, secretly hurt by my departure, had gone to her room. The garden was lighted; clusters of dancers were walking in between quadrilles and waltzes. There was no way to have any secret meeting in this modest good-natured party filled with honest relaxation. I did not see Valvèdre there again and I pretended to be quite happy and free-spirited in front of Mademoiselle Juste who was hanging on until the end. Someone suggested we dance a cotillion and the girls decided that everyone would be part of it. I went over to ask Mademoiselle Juste for the dance as Henri had invited his mother.

"What!" the old maid said with a smile. "You want me to dance, too? Well, why not! I'll go around the room once with you; after that I shall be free to find you a partner whom I'll secure ahead of time to replace me."

I could not see the person to whom she was speaking; there was some confusion at the start. I found myself with her across from M. Obernay senior and Adélaïde. After they had opened the step, the two solemn characters signaled to each other and disappeared. I was becoming Adélaïde's partner, with whom I had not dared dance in Alida's presence and who held out her beautiful hand trustingly. Mademoiselle Juste meant no harm by it but she knew exactly what she was doing. She was whispering to Obernay senior while looking at us with a half-benevolent, half-mocking gaze. The candid face of the old man seemed to answer her: "Do you think so? As for myself, I don't know, but it is possible."

Yes, as I learned later, they were speaking of a marriage that had vaguely been planned with my parents a long time ago. Juste, without knowing anything about my love for Alida, could sense that some spell had already been cast on me by the enchantress, and she was attempting to make it fail by bringing me closer to my fiancée. My fiancée. This splendid and perfect creature could have been mine! And I preferred over an excellent life full of heavenly happiness the storms of passion and the destruction of my life! I was telling myself these things while holding her hand in mine, facing her magnificently divine smile, gazing upon the perfection of her whole pure and sweet being! And I was proud of myself because she sparked in me no instincts, no seed of unfaithfulness toward my dangerous and terrible sovereign! Ah, if she could have read in my soul, the one who possessed it entirely! But she was misreading it, and her irritated gaze was condemning me at the time of my greatest self-control, for there she was, this breathless and jealous magician: she was spying on me with eyes blurry with fever. What a victory for Juste if she could have guessed!

Madame de Valvèdre's apartment was above the room where we were dancing. From a powder room on the mezzanine you could see everything happening below through a rose window hidden by garlands. Alida had wanted to have a last instinctive glance at the little party; she had pushed the leaves apart, and, seeing me there, had remained rooted to the spot. And I, feeling Juste's eyes on me, thought I was quite the diplomat and that I skillfully served the cause of my love by taking care of Adélaïde and playing the part of the little young man intoxicated by movement and joy.

So the next day, after I had succeeded in having a letter taken to Madame de Valvèdre, I received a devastating answer. She was breaking everything up; she was giving me my freedom back. During the morning, Juste and Paule had spoken in front of her of the plans for my marriage to Adélaïde and about a recent letter my mother had sent to Madame Obernay where this wish was delicately expressed.

"I did not know any of this," Alida said, "you had left me unaware of it. When learning that your trip to Switzerland had no other motive than seeking this marriage, and, last night, seeing with my own eyes how smitten you were by the beauty of your future wife, I came to understand your behavior of the last three days. As soon as you entered this house, as soon as you saw the woman they mean for you to marry, you completely changed the way you treat me. You haven't found one single moment to speak to me in secret; you haven't been able to invent the least scheme when you know quite well how to climb above walls to enter into fortresses, when desire comes to the help of your ability. You have been vanquished by the brilliance of youth, and I have paled, I have disappeared like a star of the night in front of the rising sun. It is quite simple. Child, I don't bear you a grudge; but why not be honest? Why did you make me endure a thousand tortures? Why, knowing that I rightly hated a certain old maid, did you treat her with a ridiculous respect? Didn't you already feel some movements of bad will, of loathing almost, against the unfortunate Alida? It seems to me that at the moment, the single moment when your eyes, if not your words, could reassure me, you let me know that you thought me a bad mother. Yes, yes, you had already been told that I preferred my handsome Edmond over my poor Paul, that Paul was a victim of my preference, of my injustice: this is Mademoiselle Juste's favorite theme; and she had succeeded in convincing my husband, who respects me; she must have succeeded faster to prove it to my lover, who doesn't respect me!

"Well, one must rise above all these misfortunes! I must scorn all this and teach you that I may be a hateful person but at least I have my pride. Spare me your useless lies; you love Adélaïde and you will be her husband. I will help you with all my might. Return my letters and take back your own. I forgive you with all my heart as one must forgive children. More difficult will be the task of absolving myself from my folly and credulousness."

So the terrible situation in which we were vis-à-vis family and society was not enough: despair, jealousy, and anger had to reduce to ashes our poor hearts already so battered.

I was taken by a fit of rage against fate, against Alida, and against myself. I went to say good-bye to the Obernays and left for my so-called pleasure trip; but I stopped within two miles of Geneva, in prey to a terrible sorrow. I had not taken my leave of Madame de Valvèdre; she was out when I had said my good-byes. Upon returning and learning about my abrupt decision, she was the kind of woman capable of betraying herself; my departure, instead of saving her, could ruin her... I retraced my steps, unable to bear the thought of her suffering. I pretended that I had forgotten something at the Obernays and I arrived before Alida's return. Where had she been all morning? Adélaïde and Rosa were alone at home. I ventured to ask them whether Madame de Valvèdre had also left Geneva. I was sorry I had not said my good-byes to her. Adélaïde answered me with a blessed peacefulness that Madame de Valvèdre was at the Catholic chapel down the street. And as she mistook my confusion for surprise, she added, "Are you surprised? She is a fervent Papist, and we heretics respect all sincerity. Tomorrow, she told us, is the anniversary of her mother's death, and she blames herself for having made for us the sacrifice of dancing last night. She wants to confess, order a mass, I think... Well, if you wanted to say your good-byes, wait for her."

"No," I answered, "you'll be kind enough to give her my regrets."

The two sisters attempted to convince me to stay, they said, as a pleasant surprise for Henri who would be back soon. Adélaïde was quite insistent; but as I was not giving in and as, without resentment, she said cordially good-bye and "bon voyage," quite gaily, I saw that this simplicity and kindness of manners was not concealing any piercing regrets.

I was hardly outside when I turned toward the little church. I went in; it was deserted. I went around the nave; in a dark and cold corner, I saw, between a confessional and the corner of the wall, a woman dressed in black, kneeling on the flagstone, as if she were overcome under the weight of an ecstatic grief. She was covered with so many veils that I had hardly recognized her. Finally, I recognized her delicate features under her black mourning crepe and I ventured to touch her arm. This stiff and ice-cold arm felt nothing. I rushed toward her, lifted her up, I pulled her away. She revived somewhat and attempted to push me away. "Where are you taking me?" she said confusedly.

"I don't know! Outside! In the sun! You are lifeless."

"Ah! You should have left me to die. It felt so good!"

I pushed a side door that I happened to see in front of me and I found myself in a narrow, quiet street. I saw a garden with an open gate. Alida, without knowing where she was, found the strength to walk there. I took her inside the garden and had her sit on a bench in the sun. We were in the garden of strangers, vegetable growers; the owners were absent. A day laborer who was working in a patch of vegetables looked at us when we came in, and supposing that we were part of the household, went back to his work without paying us any further attention.

Chance was thus finally bringing about this impossible tête-à-tête! When Alida felt revived by the heat, I led her to the back of the garden, which was fairly deep, and went back up the hill of the old town, and I sat by her under a vine arbor.

She listened to me for a long time without saying anything; then, letting me take her warm and trembling hands into mine, she admitted that she was yielding. "I am exhausted," she said to me, "and I am listening to you as if this were a dream. I prayed and cried all day, and I wanted to go back to my children only when God had given me back the strength to go on living; but God is abandoning me; he crushed me with shame and remorse without sending me the true repentance that inspires good resolutions. I invoked my mother's soul; she has answered me. Peace can only be found in death. I felt the chill of the last moments, and far from fighting it, I gave in with a bitter pleasure. It seemed to me that by dying there, at the feet of Christ, not redeemed enough by my faith, but purified by my grief, I would at least have eternal peace, and nothingness as a refuge. God has rejected my destruction as he did my tears. He brought you here to force me to love, to burn, to suffer again. Well, let his will be done! I am less frightened by the future now that I know that I can die of exhaustion and grief when the burden is too heavy."

Alida was so striking and so beautiful in her voluptuous prostration that I found the eloquence of a deeply moved heart to convince her and to bring her back to life, love, and hope. She saw me so distressed by her grief that in turn she took pity on me and blamed herself for my tears. We swore to each other most enthusiastically to belong to each other forever, whatever might happen to us; but upon parting, what were we going to do? For everyone in Geneva, I was supposed to be gone. It was getting late; Madame de Valvèdre's absence could be a cause of worry and they could look for her. "Go back," I said. "I must leave this town where we are surrounded by danger and bitterness. I'll stay close by; I shall hide and write to you. We must definitely find a way to meet safely and arrange our future decisively.

"Write to Bianca," she said. "I will have your letters faster than with the poste restante. I shall stay in Geneva to receive them, and, for my part, I will think about ways to make it possible to see each other soon."

She went down the garden, and I stayed there after her so that we would not be seen leaving together. After ten minutes, I was going to withdraw when I heard someone calling me with a whisper. I turned around; a small door had just opened in the wall behind me. No one could be seen; I had not recognized the voice. I had been called by my first name. Was it Obernays? I stepped forward and saw Moserwald who was signaling me to come to him with a mysterious look.

As soon as I entered, he closed the door behind us, and I found myself in another garden, deserted, landscaped like a wildflower field, or rather abandoned to natural vegetation, where two goats and a cow were grazing. A grapevine arbor supported by a narrow diamond-shaped trellis which seemed quite new ran along the perimeter of this neglected enclosure. It was under this shelter that Moserwald was inviting me to follow him. He put a finger to his lips and led me under the canopy of a sort of shed located at one end of the field. There he told me:

"First, be careful, my dear fellow. Everything said under the arbor can be heard to the left and right through the walls, which are neither thick nor high. To the left, you have the garden of Manassé, one of my poor fellow Jews, who is quite devoted to me; that is where you were a while ago with *her*. I heard everything. To the right, the wall is even more treacherous. I had it thinned and drilled with invisible openings that let you see and hear everything happening in the Obernays garden. Here, between the two lots, you are on my property. I bought this plot of land to be near *her*, to look at her, to listen to her, to find out her secrets, if possible. I was on the watch without results for the last few days, but today, when I happened to listen on the other side, I learned more than I wished. No matter; it is done. She loves you; I hope no more, but I remain her friend and yours. I had promised you I would be, and I am a man of my word. I can see that you are both quite distressed and tormented. I shall be your providence. Stay hidden here; the cabin is not pretty, but it is clean enough inside. I had it fixed in secret and silence, without letting anyone know I was doing it, already six months ago, when I hoped that one day or another *she* would be moved by my attentions and would do me the honor to come and rest here . . . I must no longer think of it! She will come for you. Well, my money and my know-how will not be quite wasted since they will serve for her happiness and yours. Good-bye, my dear fellow. Don't show yourself during the day; don't walk in areas that are exposed; someone could see you from the neighboring houses. Write love letters as long as the sun shines, or go out only under the arbor. In full night, you will be able to venture in the countryside, which starts a few feet away. Manassé will be at your service. He will do your cooking fairly well; he will dismiss the workers who might talk. If need be, he will carry your letters and deliver them with an unequaled skill. Trust him; he owes me everything; and in a moment he will learn that he belongs to you for three days. Three days is quite sufficient to devise something, for I see that you are looking for a way to be together. It will end with an elopement! I am expecting it! However, be careful; don't do anything without consulting me first. It is possible to ensure one's happiness without destroying the social position of a woman. Don't act foolishly; behave like a man of honor, or else, well! I think that I'll turn against you and that, despite my distaste for duels, we'd have to cut each other's throats . . . Good-bye, good-bye; don't thank me! What I am doing,

I am doing out of selfishness; it is still love! But hopeless love. Good-bye! . . . Ah, by the way, I need to take away some papers; let's go in."

Astounded and indecisive, I followed him inside this dilapidated barn covered with ivy and tufts of Jupiter's beard. A small new building was encased in the barn and opened on the other side of the garden onto a small flower bed resplendent with roses. The mysterious apartment comprised three small, incredibly luxurious, rooms.

"See!" Moserwald said pointing out a chiseled gold cup filled to the brim with very large pearls on a Turkey-red console. "I am leaving it here. It is the necklace that I intended for her on her first visit, and at every visit the cup would have contained some other treasure; but at that time, you know, she did not even deign to notice me! No matter; you will offer her these pearls as a gift from me . . . No, she would refuse them; you'll give them to her as if they came from you. If she despises them; she can make a necklace for her dog! If she doesn't want them, she can throw them in the nettles! As for me, I don't want to see them again, these pearls that I had chosen one by one in the best collections of the Middle East. No, no, it would hurt me to look at them. This is not what I wanted to remove. I wanted a pack of letter drafts that I wished to send to her. She must not find them here and make fun of them. Ah, see, the packet is big! I used to write to her every day when she was here; but when it came to seal and send them, I no longer dared do it. I could feel that my style was clumsy; my French incorrect. I would have given anything to be able to write as you probably know how to! But nobody taught me and I was afraid to be laughed at, when I felt so passionate while writing. Well, I'll take back my poetry and I am leaving. Don't speak to me. No, no, not a word, good-bye. My heart is heavy. If you were to prevent me from devoting myself to her, I would kill you and then I would kill myself. Ah, now that I think of it. When you have a rendezvous with a woman, you must not be caught by surprise and murdered. Here are some pistols in their box. They are good! They were made for me, and no king has better ones. Listen, one more word! If you want to see me, Manassé will give you a disguise and will lead you to my mansion in the evening. He will let you in without having anyone notice. I will see you even if it is in the middle of the night. You will need my advice, you'll see! Good-bye, good-bye. Be happy but make her happy."

It was impossible for me to interrupt this flow of words in which the vulgarity and the ridiculousness of the details were swept away by the force of an intense and sincere passion. He avoided my refusals, thanks, denials, which besides I knew to be useless. He had my secret, and I had to let him exert his devotion or else fear his spite. He pushed me back into the house and locked me in the garden; and I let him and liked him in spite of everything, for he was crying his eyes out, and I was also crying like a child crushed by feelings beyond his strength.

After I had somewhat come back to my senses and reviewed my situation, I was horrified by my weakness. "No," I exclaimed to myself, "I shall not lure Alida to this place where her image was desecrated by offensive hopes. She would only feel disgust for this luxury and those gifts meant for her by a love unworthy of her. And I myself suffer here as if in an unhealthy atmosphere charged with revolting ideas. I will not write to Alida from this place. I shall leave this impure refuge tonight and will never go back to it!"

Night was coming. As soon as it was dark, I asked Manassé, who had come to take my orders, to take me to Moserwald's; but Moserwald was coming at the very moment to find out how I was, and we went back to the house together where, at his master's request, Manassé served us a very elegant meal.

"Let's eat first," Moserwald was saying. "I would not have come in if I risked meeting a person who is not supposed to see me here; but since you tell me that she won't come, and since you wanted to talk to me, we'll be more quiet here than at my house. You hadn't thought about dinner; I knew it. I, myself, only thought about it for your sake, but now I feel very hungry; I cried so much! I see that people are right to say that crying makes you hungry."

He ate like a horse, after which, Spanish wines helping with the digestion of his thoughts, he naïvely said to me: "My dear man, believe it or not, this is the first meal I have had in six months. You saw that in Saint Pierre I had no appetite. Beyond my usual melancholia, I had love in mind. Well! Today's shock has healed my body by calming my imagination. Truly, I feel quite different, and the idea that I am finally doing something good and great raises me above my daily life. Don't laugh! Would you do as much if you were in my shoes? It is not certain at all! You witty men, you have eloquence on your side. It must wear out the heart in the end! But we are alone now. Manassé will come back only when I ring him, for as you can see, there is over here a cord that slides under the vines and ends up at his cottage in the fenced-in garden next door. Speak: What did you want to tell me? And why are you claiming that Madame de Valvèdre cannot come here?"

I explained it to him frankly. He listened to me with the utmost attention as if he had wanted to reflect and learn about the subtleties of love; then he spoke again:

"You are mistaken about my expectations; I did not have any."

"You did not have any, and you were having this house decorated, you were choosing one by one the finest pearls in the Orient? . . ."

"I did not hope anything from these, especially since the ring incident. Do I need to repeat that for me these were only disinterested tributes, proofs of my devotion, the joy of giving a little feminine pleasure to a fashionable woman? You don't understand that, do you? You said to yourself: 'I shall deserve and obtain love through my talent and my rhetoric.' I myself do not have any talent. All my worth is in my money. Each offers what he has, by God! The thought of buying such a worthy woman has never crossed my mind; but if through my passion I had been able to convince her, what offense would there have been if I had put my treasures at her feet? Everyday, love expresses its gratefulness through gifts, and when a millionaire offers bouquets of jewels, it is as if you offered a sonnet in a handful of wildflowers."

"I see," I said, "that we won't agree on this point. Admit, if you will, that I have unreasonable scruples, but know that my reluctance is indestructible. Never, I say, never will Alida ever come here."

"You are ungrateful!" Moserwald said shrugging his shoulders.

"No," I cried out, "I don't want to be ungrateful! I can see that you did not mislead me when you told me that you had a wealth of goodness in you. That wealth, I accept it. You know the secret of my life. You discovered it; thus I did not have the merit to tell it to you, and yet I feel it is safe with you. You want to advise me about the material means that can ensure or compromise the happiness and the dignity of the woman I love? I believe in your experience, as you know more than I do about real life. I shall consult you, and, if you advise me well, I shall be eternally grateful. All my feelings of repulsion against some aspects of your nature will be strongly opposed and perhaps erased in me through friendship. It is already so: yes, I feel for you a real affection. I respect in you some qualities all the more precious since they are innate and spontaneous. Don't ask me for anything else; never attempt to make me accept favors that have a material value. You are only rich, you say, and each offers what he can! You are maligning yourself: you can see that you have a moral value, and that it is because of it that you have gained my gratitude and my affection."

The poor Moserwald hugged me and started to cry again.

"At last, I have a friend," he cried out, "a real friend who does not cost me money! Well, he is the first and he will be the only one. I know human nature well enough to know that much. Well, I shall keep him like the apple of my eye and you, as my friend, take my heart, my blood, and my soul: Nephtali Moserwald is yours for life and death."

After these outbursts of feelings, in which he managed to be both comical and touching, he told me that we had to talk reasonably on the crucial point, the future of Madame de Valvèdre. I told him how I had become acquainted with the husband without knowing it, and, without sharing with him anything about the upheavals of my love, I let him understand that normal relations protected by the hypocrisy of social proprieties were impossible between two strong-willed, passionate personalities. I had to have Alida's soul in solitude; I was unable to deceive her husband and her close circle.

"You are quite wrong to be this way," Moserwald answered. "This puritanism will make things quite difficult; but if you are curt and clumsy, the smartest thing to do is to disappear. Well, let's look for the means to do it. M. de Valvèdre is rich, and his wife has nothing: I obtained my information from good sources and I know things which you probably don't know. You called my love for her offensive and yet in fact yours will be more harmful to her. Do you know that one can marry this charming woman, and that my fortune would allow me to aspire to it?"

"To marry her! What are you saying? Is she not married? . . ."

"She is a Catholic; Valvèdre is a Protestant, and they married according to the rite of the Augsburg denomination, which allows divorce. Although M. de Valvèdre is, from what people say, a great philosopher, he did not want to submit to the Catholic act, and although Alida and her mother were quite orthodox, this marriage was so good for a girl without dowry, that they did not insist on having it ratified by your church and by the civil laws that confirm the indissolubility of marriage. People claim that Madame de Valvèdre later regretted this kind of union which did not seem to her to be legitimate enough, but that nothing has been able to convince her husband to denationalize himself, legally and religiously speaking. So the day when Valvèdre is displeased with his wife, he will be able to repudiate her, whether she agrees to it or not, and leave her to live more or less in poverty. Don't take the situation lightly, Francis! You have nothing and this woman has lived in comfort for ten years. Poverty kills love."

"She won't live in poverty; I shall work."

"You won't work long; you are too much in love. Love washes away genius; I know it from experience, I who only had a solid common sense and who nonetheless became mad! I did not make a single good business deal since I had this madness in mind. Fortunately, I did some before; but let's go back to your case, and, let's suppose, if you want, that in spite of love, you'll write superb poetry. Do you know how much you make with that? Nothing when you are unknown, and very little when you are famous. It is also the case that very often, to begin, you have to be your own publisher, even if you do sell half a dozen copies. Trust me, poetry is a prince's pleasure. Think about it only in your spare time. I'll find you a job but you'll have to attend to it and to keep at it. Numbers, you won't enjoy them, and if Alida is bored in the town where you will settle! . . . I told you the first time I saw you; you should go into business. You don't know anything about it, but you can learn it faster than Greek or Latin, and with good advice you can succeed, as long as you don't have excessive scruples and wrong ideas about the workings of society."

"Don't talk to me about this, Moserwald !" I answered sharply. "You are considered an honest man; don't tell me anything about the transactions that have made you a rich man. Let me think that the source of your money is pure. I either might not understand or find myself in a terrible disagreement with you. Besides my opinion about this is of no importance; there is a first and insurmountable obstacle, which is that I haven't the least capital to invest."

"But, I myself want to invest for you . . . I'll only associate you to the profits!"

"Let's drop the subject; it is impossible!"

"You don't like me!"

"I want to like you regardless of questions of interest, I have told you. Do I need to explain? . . . The causes and circumstances of our friendship are exceptional; what an ordinary friend might accept quite naturally from you, I must refuse."

"Of course, yes, I understand. You think that in fact Alida would owe her well-being to me! . . . Then let's speak about it no more; but I'll be damned if I know what will happen to you! To give you good advice, we'd need to know the husband's frame of mind."

"It is impossible. The man is inscrutable."

"Inscrutable! . . . Well, if I were to get involved . . ."

"You?"

"Yes, me, indeed, and without seeming to at all."

"What do you mean?"

"He must trust someone, that husband of hers?"

"I don't know."

"But I do! He sometimes opens the lock of his brain for your friend Obernay . . . I heard him speak, and as he mixed in some science to his conversation, I did not understand too well; but he seemed to me to be morose or preoccupied. However, he did not give any name. He might have been speaking about a woman other than his wife; he may be in love with the marvelous Adélaïde . . ."

"Ah! Hush, Moserwald! Obernay's sister! A married man!"

"A married man who can get a divorce."

"Oh, God, it is true! Was he speaking of divorcing?"

"Well, I can see that this matter is of more interest to you than to me, and by the way, to you alone now. If Alida had had the good sense to love me, I would not worry much about her husband, I wouldn't. I would have made her sever all ties; I would have provided for her a life ninety percent nicer than what she has now and I would have married her, for I am a free and honest man. As you can see, my thoughts do not degrade her; but love is whimsical and it is you she is choosing: let's forget about it. Therefore it is important for you and it behooves you to explore the heart and conscience of the husband. Don't leave this precious house, dear fellow; lie in wait often at the end of the wall, under the arbor of yoke-elm that you can see from here and which is like the one at the corner of the Obernay garden. That's where I had a well-hidden hole made. The wall is not long, and even when the characters are talking as they stroll from one end to the other, you will hear almost everything if you have a good ear. Do this job patiently five to six times every twenty-four hours, if need be, and I bet you'll find out what you want to know."

"Your idea is certainly clever, but I won't take advantage of it. I think that discovering the secrets of the Obernay family in this manner is contemptible!"

"Here you go again with your exaggerations! This does not involve the Obernays! If your friend gives his sister in marriage to Valvèdre, you'll find out a little earlier than other people; that's all. And you can, I imagine, keep to yourself the secrets that you'll discover. What is of immense importance for Alida is to know whether Valvèdre still loves her or if he loves another woman. In the first case, he is jealous, angry, he gets his revenge by putting a stop to everything, and things are not going well for you; we'll have to rack our brains to get out of that one. In the second case, you are saved: you have got the Valvèdre fellow. Eager to break his chain, he gives his wife a quite respectable settlement that she'll even be able to negotiate, and they separate very quietly; for if a divorce can be obtained in spite of the opposition of one of the spouses, there is a scandal in these cases, whereas, by mutual agreement, none of the parties is discredited. Valvèdre will sacrifice much for his reputation. It will be up to his wife to take advantage of the moment. Then you marry her; you won't be very well-off but you'll have the bare necessities, and you can devote yourself to literature. Otherwise . . ."

I interrupted Moserwald with irritation. I did my best to like him, but he always found a way to offend me with his positivism.

"You would make of my passion," I said to him, "a matter of interest. You would cure me of it if I let you gain influence on me. Look, I am sorry, but everything you have advised today is detestable. I want neither to lure Alida here nor take from you the means to have her live with me, nor overhear behind walls—one might as well eavesdrop—nor worry about money, nor want a divorce that would allow me to make a financially advantageous marriage. I want to love, to believe, I want to remain sincere and enthusiastic. I shall brave destiny, whatever it may be, as there are no irreproachable means to get the better of it."

"Quite well, my poor Don Quixote!" answered Moserwald as he was taking his hat. You easily speak of risking everything! But if you love, you'll think it over before plunging Alida into shame and poverty. I am leaving; sleep on it, and you'll spend the night here because you don't have your belongings, and you need to give me the time to have them brought to you. Where are they?"

I had left them near Geneva, in a country inn that I mentioned. "You will have them tomorrow morning," he said, "and if you want to leave for the realm of the unknown, you'll leave; but the God of love will first inspire you with something more reasonable and above all something more delicate. Tomorrow night, I'll come back to see if you are still here and have dinner with you . . . that is if you are by yourself."

I wrote to Madame de Valvèdre summarizing everything that had happened, to wit that I was very near her and could catch a glimpse of her if she walked in the garden. I slept for a few hours, and first thing in the morning I had my letter delivered by the clever and devoted Manassé who brought me the reply and my traveling bag. "Stay where you are," Madame de Valvèdre was telling me, "I trust this Moserwald, and I am not opposed to going in this garden. Arrange to have the one across the chapel opened, and don't go anywhere all day."

At three o'clock in the afternoon, she slipped into my garden. I was reluctant to let her in the house. She made light of my scruples. "How can I," she said to me, "be offended by the marriage plans of this fellow Moserwald? He wanted to win my heart with rings and necklaces! He was reasoning according to his point of view, which is not ours. A Jew is a sui generis animal, as M. de Valvèdre would say: there is no reasoning with these people, and nothing coming from them can affect us."

"You hate Jews that much?" I asked.

"Not at all; I just despise them!"

I was shocked by this prejudice so unjust in so many regards; I saw in it another proof of the leaven of bitterness and real unfairness that was part of Alida's character; but it was not the time to pay attention to an incident, whatever that might be; we had much to say to each other.

She came into the house; she criticized its lavishness disdainfully and did not even look at the pearls. "In all of Moserwald's nonsense," she said, "there is a good idea I am taking for myself. He wants us to discover my husband's secrets. You may find this repulsive but it is my right, and I came here to attempt to do it."

"Alida," I replied, filled with apprehension, "you are worried about your husband's resolve?"

"I have children," she answered, "and it matters to me to know what woman will claim to become their mother. If it is Adélaïde . . . But why are you blushing?"

I don't know if indeed I had blushed, but it is certain that I felt offended to see Obernay's immaculate sister be mixed in with our preoccupations. I had not shared with Madame de Valvèdre Moserwald's comments in this regard. I would have felt it was a betrayal of the cult of family and friendship; but some remaining jealousy made Alida cruel toward this young woman, me, Valvèdre, and all the others.

"You don't think that I am dim-witted enough," she said, "not to have noticed for the last week that the beautiful among the beautiful finds my husband quite nice, that she almost faints with admiration at every word coming out of his eloquent mouth, that Mademoiselle Juste already treats her like a sister, that one acts as a little mother with my sons, finally that as early as yesterday the whole family, surprised by your abrupt departure, definitively turned their eyes toward the pole, that is toward the name and the wealth! These Obernays are quite positivist, such reasonable people! As for the young person, she was extremely happy when she told me that you had left. I would have noticed many other things if I had not been exhausted and forced to withdraw early in the evening. Today I feel more alive; you are here and I imagine that I will learn something that will give me back the freedom and peace of my conscience. And to think that I felt remorse and took my husband for a Greek philosopher of antiquity! Really! He is still young and handsome, and burning like a volcano under the ice!"

"Alida!" I exclaimed, struck by a ray of light, "you are not jealous about me, but about your husband!"

"It would be about you both," she continued, "because I am horribly jealous about you; I cannot hide it. It started again this morning when I felt alive again."

"It may be about both of us! Who knows! You loved him so!"

She did not answer. She was worried, upset; it seemed that she regretted our reconciliation and our oath of the day before, or that a preoccupation greater than our love finally showed her the dangers of this love and the obstacles contained in the situation. It was obvious that my letter had upset her and she pressed me with questions about the revelations made by Moserwald. "In turn," I said, "let me ask you questions. How is it that, seeing me so unhappy with all that comes between us, you have never told me: 'All this does not exist; I can invoke a law more human and kinder than ours. My marriage vows were Protestant?'"

"It is possible that I assumed you knew," she answered, "and that your opinion on that was like mine."

"What is your opinion? I don't know what it is."

"I am a Catholic . . . as much as a person who is unfortunate enough to have doubts about everything and about God himself can be. I believe at least that the best possible society is one that recognizes the absolute authority of the church and the indissolubility of marriage. I have thus bitterly suffered from what is lacking and irregular in mine. Wasn't it one more reason to add to it through faith and my will, the sanction that Valvèdre denied it? My conscience has never accepted and will never accept that he or I have the right to break it off."

"Well," I answered, "I love you more this way: it is more worthy of you, but what if your husband forces you to take back your freedom?"

"He can take his own back, as far as he ever lost it; but as for me, nothing will convince me to remarry. That is why I never told you that it was possible."

Would you believe that such a strong resolve hurt me deeply? An hour before, I was still dreading the idea of becoming the husband of a thirty-year-old woman who had two children and her former husband's charity as her only fortune. All my passion was weakening in the face of such a formidable prospect, and I had said to myself that if Alida, repudiated because of me, demanded of me this solemn reparation, I would if need be become naturalized as a foreigner in order to give it to her; but I was hoping that it would not ever occur to her, and now I was questioning her; now I found myself humiliated and as if offended by her faithfulness, even if it was to the ungrateful husband! It was in the destiny and also in the nature of our love to be steeped in worries at every turn, at all times, to make each other distrustful, easily offended. We exchanged some harsh words, and we parted more enamored than ever, for we needed a stormy atmosphere and enthusiasm mounted in us only after the excitement of anger and pain.

What was remarkable is that we were never able to make a decision. It seemed to me that a mystery was hidden behind Alida's reserve and her hesitations. She claimed that there was one in me too, that I still had some thoughts of marrying Adélaïde, or that I liked my freedom as an artist too much to devote myself to our love. And when I offered her my life, my name, my religion, my honor, she would refuse everything and invoke her own conscience and dignity. What inextricable labyrinth, what frightening chaos surrounded us!

After she had left, saying as usual that she would think it over and that I should wait for a solution, I walked restlessly under the arbor and found myself without thinking at the corner of the wall behind the Obernay's arbor. Adélaïde and Rose were there chatting.

"I can see that I must work to please our parents, my brother, and you," the little one was saying, and also to please my good friend Valvèdre, and Paule, well, everyone! "However, since I feel a little lazy by nature, I would like you to tell me yet other reasons to force me to conquer myself."

"I already told you," the angelic voice of the older sister answered, "that work pleases God."

"Yes, yes because my courage will show him the love that I feel for my family and my friends; but why is it that I am the only one who doesn't enjoy the difficulty of learning?"

"Because you don't think. Do you figure that you would enjoy being lazy? You are quite mistaken! As soon as what satisfies us pains those who love us, we are in the wrong, with remorse and unhappiness as a result. Do you understand this? Do you?"

"Yes, I understand. So will I be bad if I am lazy?"

"Well, I can assure you of that!" said Adélaïde with a tone that seemed full of unspoken allusions.

It seemed as if the child had guessed the object of these allusions, for she added after a pause: "Tell me, sister, is our friend Alida bad?"

"Why would she be?"

"Well, she does not do a thing all day and she openly says that she has never wanted to learn anything."

"She is not bad for all that. It must be because her parents did not want her to be educated, but since you are speaking about her, do you think she is very happy doing nothing? It seems to me that she is often bored."

"I don't know if she is bored, but she is always yawning or crying. You know our friend is not cheerful. What does she think about from morning till night? Maybe she does not think?"

"You are mistaken. She has much wit, and she does think quite a bit; on the contrary, perhaps she even thinks too much."

"To think too much! Papa always tells me: 'Think, think, you silly head! Think about what you are doing.'"

"Father is right. You must always think about what you are doing and never about what you should not do."

"What is Alida thinking about? Come! Can you guess?"

"Yes, and I am going to tell you."

Adélaïde was instinctively lowering her voice: I stuck my ear against the opening in the wall, without remembering in the least that I had vowed never to eavesdrop.

"She thinks about everything," Adélaïde was saying. "She is like you and me, and perhaps much more intelligent than we are; but her thoughts are without order or direction. You can understand this; you often tell me your dreams of the night. Well, when you are dreaming, are you thinking?"

"I do since I see plenty of people and things, birds and flowers..."

"But is it in your power to see or not see these ghosts?"

"Of course not, since I am sleeping!"

"So you have no will, and consequently no reason, and no purpose of mind when you are dreaming. Well, there are people who dream almost all the time, even when they are awake."

"Is it an illness?"

"Yes, it is, a very painful illness and from which you could be cured by studying true things because one doesn't always, like you, have good dreams. People have sad and scary dreams when their brains are empty, and they come to the point of not believing in their own visions. That is why you see our friend cry without any apparent reason."

"Ah, that's it! And, now that I think of it, we never cry, the two of us! I only saw you cry once when mommy was sick; as for me, I sometimes yawn but it is when the clock shows 10:00 P.M. Poor Alida! I can see that we are more reasonable than she is."

"Don't think that we are better than other people. We are much happier because we have parents who give us good advice. For this, you can thank God, little Rose. Give me a kiss, and let's go and see if mother needs us for housework."

This simple and quick morality and philosophy lesson given by an eighteen-year-old girl gave me much to think about. Hadn't she put her finger on the wound with an extreme wisdom when lecturing her sister? Did Alida have a really lucid mind? Didn't her imagination lead her judgment to a painful and continuous dizziness? Her indecisions, her inconsequential desires for religion and skepticism, her jealousy directed sometimes at her husband, sometimes at her lover, her stubborn dislikes, her racial prejudices, her quick enthusiasms, her very passion for me, a passion both so austere and so ardent, what to think of all this? I felt so frightened by her that for one moment I thought I had been freed from the fatal spell by the simple and saintly conversation of the two children.

But could I be so easily saved, I who carried, like Alida, heaven and hell in my troubled mind, I who had devoted myself to the dream of poetry and passion, without being willing to admit that there was, above my own visions and my inner free creative impulses, a world of research sanctioned by the labor of others and the investigations of great minds? No, I was too arrogant and too feverish to understand the deep and simple words of Adélaïde to her sister: *"the study of true things."* The child had understood, and I was shrugging my shoulders while wiping the sweat from my burning forehead.

The following days had their share of happy hours, terrible moments of elation, and palpitations in the midst of their distress and discouragements. I stayed in the house and I attempted to sketch out a book, precisely on the question that was burning my soul, about love! It seemed that fate had thrown me into my topic in full light, and that chance had given me for writing room the haven poets dream about. I was between four walls, it is true, in a kind of prison regularly framed by a bower of monotonous greenery; but in this enclosed field, left untended, grew masses of thickets and festoons of brambles which provided like a velvet frame for the beautiful cow and the graceful goats shining in the sun. Grass grew so thick that in the morning it had repaired the damage done by the grazing of the day before. Behind the house, I had the scent of roses and a curtain of a most brilliant red honeysuckle. The little swallows drew in the sky supple figures below the larger and bolder curves of the dark-feathered swifts. From the garret of the house, above the houses leaning off the steep slopes, I could catch a glimpse of a corner of the lake and few mountain peaks. The weather was hot, oppressive, the mornings and nights were splendid.

Alida would come every day and spend one or two hours with me. She was supposed to be praying in the church; she would escape through the side door. Manassé helped her by a signal given the moment when the street was empty. I did not appear; I never left my enclosure; no one could know that I was there.

Moserwald showed an extreme discretion in his relations with me when he learned that Madame de Valvèdre was my guest. He only came when I called him. He no longer asked me questions. He lavished attention and treats on me; and they were probably secretly meant for the woman he loved, but they did not shock her. She laughed about it and claimed that this Jew was handsomely rewarded for his efforts by the trust she showed him in coming to his house and by the friendship that with him I took seriously.

I had accepted this strange situation and I imperceptibly got accustomed to it when seeing how little importance Madame de Valvèdre accorded to it. Our plans were not moving forward; they were constantly questioned and became ever more questionable. Alida was beginning to think that Moserwald had been right; that is, that Valvèdre, who was extraordinarily preoccupied, was hatching some mysterious decision. But what was this decision? It could be an exploration of the South Seas as well as a petition for legal separation. He was still as mild mannered and polite as ever with his wife; he never made the least allusion to our meeting near his villa. No one seemed to have heard him mention it; there wasn't the least indication of any suspicion. Alida wasn't watched at all; on the opposite, her freedom grew daily. The Obernays had resumed their peaceful and hard-working life. They saw each other at meal time and in the evening. Far from making her feel that they doubted or blamed her, Madame de Valvèdre's hosts showed her a cordial solicitude and were urging her to extend her stay in their home. It was necessary, they argued, in order to accustom the children to a change in their environment under their parents' eyes. Valvèdre came every day to the Obernays and seemed entirely absorbed in setting up his sons, arranging their first studies, and seeing the first joys of his sister Paule's married life. Mademoiselle Juste kept increasingly to herself and seemed at last to have really given her resignation. All was thus for the best, and we had to ask the heavens to prolong this situation, Madame de Valvèdre would say; yet she admitted having moments of terror. She had seen or dreamed of a dark cloud, an unknown sadness, without precedent, deep into the placid eyes of her husband.

But although love may be quick to fear, it is even quicker in its daring, and as nothing new had happened by the end of the week, we were beginning to breathe more easily, to forget danger and to speak of the future as if we only had to bend down to make a carpet of it under our feet.

Alida detested practical things; she would arch her beautifully black eyebrow whenever I attempted to speak of a trip, of a temporary settling in whatever place, of reasons to find so that she would have the right to disappear for a few weeks. "Ah," she would say, "I don't want to know yet! These questions of inns and stage coaches must be decided on the spur of the moment. Opportunity is always the only advice one may follow. Don't you like it here? Are you bored with seeing me between four walls? Let's wait till fate drives us out this nest found on a branch. Inspiration will come to me when we have to take refuge elsewhere."

You see that we were no longer speaking of being together forever and even for a long time. Alida, worried about her husband's plans, did not admit the possibility of her creating a scandal that would give him public grounds against her.

No longer hoping to change her destiny and realizing quite well that I should not, I endeavored to live like her one day at a time, and to enjoy the happiness which her presence and my own work should have brought me in this charming and safe haven. I was still consumed by an anxious and unsatisfied love in her presence, but, in her absence, I had poetry as an outlet for the feelings of overexcitation in which she left me. I felt this firing up of all my faculties so powerfully that I was almost thankful to my inflexible lover for having made me experience it and for maintaining me in this state; but she was for my brain like an all-consuming liquor that revives you only at the price of exhausting you. I thought that I was embracing the world in my aspirations as a lover and an artist, and after hours of daydreams full of divine ecstasy and immense aspirations, I would fall back in prostration and unable to hold my dream. In spite of myself then, I would remember Adélaïde's modest definition: "Dreaming is not thinking."

VII

I had resolved to stop spying on the secrets of our neighbors and I had spoken so severely to Madame de Valvèdre that she herself had given up listening; but, walking under the trellis, I would unintentionally stop at the sound of Adélaïde's or Rosa's voice and I would sometimes remain riveted, not to their conversation, which I no longer wished to overhear by stopping under the arbor or coming too close to the wall, but to the music of their sweet exchange. They came at regular hours, from eight to nine in the morning and from five to six in the evening. These must have been the hours of recess of the little one. One morning, I remained under the charm of a melody sung by the older sister. Yet, she was singing in a low voice as if she wanted to be heard by Rosa only, to whom she appeared to be teaching the song. It was in Italian; words full of freshness, somewhat unusual, on a melody of exquisite sweetness, which has remained in my memory like a breath of spring. Here is the meaning of the words which they repeated several times alternately.

"*Rose of roses, my beautiful patron, you neither have a throne in the heavens, nor a starry dress; but you are queen on earth, unrivaled queen in my garden, queen in the air and the sun, in the paradise of my gaiety.*

Roses of the brambles, my sweet godmother, you are not very proud but you are so pretty. Nothing bothers you; you spread your garlands like arms to bless freedom, to bless the paradise of my strength.

Rose of the waters, white nymphaea of the fountain, dear sister, you only ask for coolness and shade; but you smell good and you seem so happy! I shall sit by you to think about modesty, the paradise of my wisdom . . ."

"One more time!" said Rosa. "I can't remember the last line."

"It is the word *wisdom* that you find difficult to say, isn't it, you naughty girl?" Adélaïde replied with a laugh.

"Perhaps! I understand gaiety, freedom, ... strength even better! Do you want me to climb this old yew tree?"

"I don't! It is bad manners to look in the neighbors's property!"

"Pooh! The neighbors! Over there we can only hear animals bleating!"

"And you want to talk to them?"

"You are not nice! Let's listen to your last verse again! It is pretty too and it is good that you put the water lily with the roses ... although botany forbids it completely! But poetry means you have the right to lie!"

"If I took this liberty it is because you wanted it! When falling asleep last night, you asked me to write you three verses for this morning, one for the mossy rose, one for the wild rose, and one for your nymphaea that just bloomed. That's all I could find when falling asleep too."

"You fell asleep when you got to the word *wisdom*? No matter, here I know your word and your tune too. Listen!" She sang the tune, and right away she wanted to sing it in a duo with her sister.

"All right," answered Adélaïde, "but you will do the second part, right now, by ear!"

"Oh, by ear, I like that; but watch out for wrong notes!"

"Yes, watch out! And sing in a low voice, like me; we shouldn't wake up Alida. She goes to bed so late!"

"And then you are afraid someone will hear your songs! Tell me, do you think Mother would scold us if she knew that you are composing poetry and music for me?"

"No, but she would if we mentioned it to people."

"Why?"

"Because she'd think it is not something to boast about, and she would be right!"

"I do find it quite beautiful, though, what you are doing!"

"Because you are a child."

"That is to say, a little goose! Well, I feel like asking ... Let's see, no one from our family, as parents always say that their children are silly; but I'll ask my friend Valvèdre!"

"If you tell and if you sing to anyone the silly things that you have me do, you know our bargain? I won't do it anymore."

"Oh, then not a word! Let's sing!"

The child sang her part with much precision. Adélaïde found the harmony correct but vulgar, and she suggested changes that the other discussed, understood, and did right away. This short and joyful lesson was enough to prove to trained ears that the little girl was wonderfully gifted, and that the other was already an accomplished musician guided by the true creative spirit. She was also a poet, for the next day I also heard other verses in several languages that she recited or sang with her sister, whom she asked to summarize, through play, several of the notions she had acquired; and in spite of the care she had taken in her compositions to always be at the level of the child and even to her taste, I was struck by an extraordinary purity of form and high intelligence. First, I thought I was under the spell of these two youthful voices; and their mysterious whisper stroked my ear like that of water and wind over the grass and the leaves. But when they were gone, I began to write everything my memory had been able to retain, and I was soon surprised, perturbed, almost oppressed. This eighteen-year-old virgin, for whom the word *love* appeared to have only a sublime metaphysical sense, was more inspired than I was, I the king of storms, the future herald of passion! I reread what I had written for the last three days and I angrily destroyed it. And yet, I said to myself, trying to recover from my failure, I have a "subject," a focus, and this contemplative, innocent girl does not have any. She sings empty nature, stars, plants, rocks; man is absent from this dull creation, which she symbolizes in an original way, it is true, but that cannot ignite ... Shall I allow myself to abandon my vocation because of a schoolgirl's rhyming exercises? I wanted to burn Adélaïde's ruminations on the ashes of my own. I reread them first and I was taken with them, quite taken. They seemed to me more original than anything renowned poets were writing, and the great charm of the monologues of this young soul facing God and nature stemmed precisely from the complete absence of any active personality. Nothing suggested it was a girl who knows she is beautiful and who seeks, solely with the intention of finding her own image, the mirror of water and clouds. The young muse was not a visible form; it was a spirit of light soaring over the world, a voice which sang in the heavens, and when she said "I," it was Rosa, it was childhood to which she gave voice. It seemed that this blue-eyed cherub above had the right to be heard in the great concert of creation. It was an unimaginable limpidity of expression, an astonishing greatness of appreciation and feeling accompanied by a complete self-effacement ... a natural or a conscious one? Had this quiet flame already devoured the vitality of youth? Or did it keep it dormant, restrained? Was this angelic adoration for the "author of beauty," which is what she called God, a way to put off a womanly passion that was still dormant?

I was getting lost in this analysis, and some religious élans, some lines expressing the ecstasy of intelligent contemplation clung to my memory to the point of obsession. I attempted to change some of their expressions to make them mine; I could not find better. I could not even find something else to express such a deep and pure emotion. "Ah, virginity!" I cried out with terror, "are you the acme of intellectual power as you are that of physical beauty?"

The poet's heart is jealous. This admiration, which overtook me with such power, made me morose and inspired in me a respect mixed with aversion for Adédaïde. In vain did I try to fight this bad instinct; I found myself, that very evening, listening to the lessons she gave her sister with the need to discover that she was vain or pedantic. It would have been quite easy if her modesty had not been genuine and total. The conversation was like a review of nomenclature that she had Rosa do. While walking with her along the garden, she had her name all the plants of the border, all the rocks of the paths, all the insects which came before their eyes. I could hear them coming back toward the wall and carry on rapidly, both always very cheerfully, one who, already quite knowledgeable out of natural aptitude, was trying to rebel against the attention required of her by substituting pleasantly ingenious names of her invention to the scientific names that she had forgotten; the other who, through the strength of a devoted will, kept an unfailing patience and a persuasive playfulness. I was amazed by the coherence and the order of her teaching. At that moment, she was no longer poet or musician; she was the true daughter, the eminent student of the scholar Obernay, the most lucid and pleasant professor, according to my father and to those who had heard him and who were capable of appreciating him. Adélaïde resembled him in spirit and personality as well as in facial characteristics. She was not only the most beautiful creature who may have lived at that time, but she was also the most learned and the most pleasant, the wisest and the happiest creature.

Did she love Valvèdre? No, this serene and studious girl did not know unhappy and impossible love. To become convinced of this, you only had to see with what freedom of mind, with what maternal solicitude she taught her younger sister. It was a charming struggle between this precocious maturity and this childlike exuberance. Rosa always wanted to escape the method and relished interrupting and confusing everything with gibes and inopportune questions, mixing all the kingdoms of nature, speaking of the butterfly passing by in the same breath as the algae in the fountain, and of the grain of sand with the wasp. Adélaïde reacted to the jibe with stronger mockery and described all things without allowing herself to be distracted. She also enjoyed confusing the child's memory and wisdom when the latter, feeling sure of herself, would recite her lesson with disdainful volubility. Last, to unexpected and irrelevant questions, she had sudden, surprisingly simple answers with a surprising depth of vision, and the younger girl, awed, convinced, because she too was admirably intelligent, forgot her mischievousness and her need to rebel in order to listen and make her explain further.

Victory thus rested with the teacher, and the little girl went back home with a renewed knowledge of her previous studies, her mind opened to worthy interests, kissing her sister and thanking her after putting her patience to the test, looking forward to being able to have a good lesson with her father, who was the supreme master of one and the other, or with Henri, the beloved tutor. Last, she would conclude: "I hope you have tormented me enough for today, my beautiful Adélaïde! I must be a marvel of wit and reason to have endured all that. If you don't write me a ballad tonight, you must have neither head nor heart!"

Thus Adélaïde wrote in her spare time at night, when falling asleep, the verses that had thrilled my spirit, the melodies that sung in my soul and that gave me something like a furious envy to take out my oboe, doomed to silence! She was an artist *on top of all that*, when she had a free moment, and without desiring any other audience than Rosa, or any other confidante than her pillow! And she did not torment it for long, that virginal pillow, for her cheeks had the velvety freshness which is the result of peaceful sleep and joie de vivre in full bloom. And I! I rejected any technical study, so afraid was I to dampen my creativity and to slow down my inspiration! I did not think that life could be divided by a series of varied preoccupations; I had always thought it was too bad that poets reasoned or philosophized and that women should have any other preoccupation besides being beautiful. I was careful for my part to keep inactive the various faculties that my first education had developed in me up to a point; I was jealous because I only had one lyre for expression and only one string to this resounding lyre that was supposed to shake the world . . . and which had not said anything yet!

Let's admit, I thought to myself, *that Adélaïde is a superior woman, that is, a kind of man. She won't remain beautiful for long; she'll grow a beard. If she gets married, it will be to an idiot who, unaware of his own inferiority, will not be afraid of her. One can admire, respect, esteem such exceptions; but don't they always scare love away?*

And I recalled the voluptuous charms of Alida, her exclusive preoccupation with love, the feminine art which allowed her faded and tired beauty to rival the most luxuriant youths, her tender idolatry for the object of her predilection, her ingenious and intoxicating blandishments, finally, the cult she had for me during her good moments, the incense of which I found so delicious that it made me forget the wretchedness of our situation and the bitterness of our moments of discouragement. "Yes," I would say to myself, "she knows herself quite well! She declares herself to be a true woman, and she is the womanly type. The other is but a hybrid perverted by education, a schoolboy who knows his lesson well and who will die of old age while repeating it, without having loved, without having inspired love, without having lived. Therefore, let us love and let us sing but of love and women! Alida will be the priestess; she is the one who will light the sacred fire; my genius—still captive—will break loose of its prison when I have loved more, suffered more! The true poet is made for disturbances as the bird amid storms, and for suffering as the martyr of inspirations. He cannot order expression and cannot bear the restrictions of vulgar logic. He does not find a stanza every night while putting on its night cap; he is condemned to frightening barrenness as well as to miraculous births. Give me some more time, and we'll see if Adélaïde is a master and if I must go to her school like little Rosa!"

And then I vaguely remembered my childhood and the kindness I had shown Adélaïde when she was a child. I could see her again with her brown hair and her large peaceful eyes, an active and sweet nature, never noisy, already polite and easy to please, without being tiresome when no one was paying attention to her. I thought, in this mirage from the past, I could hear my mother exclaim, "What a well-behaved and pretty girl! I wish she were mine!" and Madame Obernay answering her "Who knows? It could be possible someday!"

And the day when it could have been possible, indeed, the day when I could have led into my mother's embrace this accomplished creature, the pride of the town and the joy of her family, the ideal of a poet certainly, that day, the poet, indecisive and morose, sterile and unhappy with himself, strove to put her down and could hardly refrain from envy!

These slightly monstrous peculiarities in my moral situation were motivated all too much by the idleness of my reasoning faculties and the morbid activity of my fancy. After burning my manuscript, I thought that I could start it over to my new satisfaction, but it was not so. I kept being attracted toward the garden where the secret of my life was perhaps moving a few steps away from me without my having any desire to know it. When I felt Valvèdre or one of his sisters approach with M. Obernay or with Henri, I always thought I heard my name. I strained my ears in spite of myself, and when I was reassured that they were not speaking about me, I would move away without realizing the inconsistency of my behavior.

Everything seemed peaceful there; Alida never came close to the wall, so fearful was she that I would do something rash or that her reconciliation with the place she had proscribed as having too much exposure to the sun would arouse suspicions. I often heard the boisterous games of her sons and the steady voice of the older relatives who encouraged or moderated their impetuousness. Alida tenderly bestowed caresses on the oldest, but never spoke to either of them.

Without being able to see her, as the front of the house was hidden by clumps of shrubbery, I could feel the loneliness of her life in this assiduously and saintly industrious household. I could see her from afar sometimes reading a novel or a poem between two planters of myrtle, or, from my window, I could see her at hers, looking in my direction and folding a letter she had written to me. She was a stranger, it is true, to the happiness of others; she scorned and failed to appreciated their deep and lasting satisfactions. But she was constantly preoccupied with me exclusively, or with herself for my sake only. All of her thoughts were mine; she forgot to be a friend or a sister, and almost even to be a mother; all this for me, her torment, her God, her enemy, her idol! How could I find blame in my heart? And had not this exclusive love been my ideal?

Every day, a little before dawn, we would exchange letters by means of a rock that Bianca would come to throw over the wall and which I would throw back with my message. Impunity had made us reckless. One morning, awakened as usual with the larks, I received my accustomed treasure and I threw my anticipated answer; but I immediately realized that someone was walking on the path and that it was no longer the stealthy, light step of the young confident: it was a firm and steady tread, a man's step. I went to look through the crack in the wall; I thought, in the twilight, I recognized Valvèdre. It was he, indeed. What was he doing at the Obernay's at such an early hour, he who had his separate residence near them? A terrible jealousy swept over me, to the point that I instinctively moved away from the wall, as if he could have heard my heartbeat.

I came back immediately. I spied, I listened eagerly. It seemed that he had disappeared. Had he heard the rock fall? Had he caught sight of Bianca? Had he taken hold of my letter? In a cold sweat, I waited. He came back ten minutes later with Henri Obernay. They walked silently until Obernay said, "Well, my friend, what is the matter? I am at our disposal."

"Don't you think," answered Valvèdre aloud, "that people could hear from the other side of the wall what is said here?"

"I wouldn't swear it was not possible if someone lived there but no one does."

"Does it still belong to the Jew Manassé?"

"Who, by the way never agreed to sell it to my father; but he lives much farther away. However, if you fear being overheard, let's leave; let's go to your house."

"No, let's stay here," said Valvèdre rather firmly and as if, master of my secret and assured of my presence, he had wanted to condemn me to hear him. He added, "Let's sit here under the arbor. I have a long story to tell you, and I feel I must tell it. If I took the time to think it over, my usual patience and resignation might lead me again to keep silent, and perhaps one needs to talk under the influence of an intense emotion."

"Be careful!" Obernay said as he sat beside him. "What if you were to regret what you are going to do? What if, after confiding in me, you were to feel less affection for me?"

"I am not capricious, and I am not afraid it will happen," Valvèdre answered, speaking with a clarity of enunciation such that it seemed intended to let me to hear every word of his speech. "You are my son and my brother, Henri Obernay! The child whose development I have cherished and encouraged, the man to whom I have entrusted and given my beloved sister. What I have to tell you after years of silence will be useful to you at this time because it is the story of my marriage that I want to confide in you; you will be able to compare our lives and reach conclusions about marriage and love on good grounds. Paule will be made happier yet by you when you know how a woman without intellectual direction or moral restraint may be pitied and can cause the unhappiness of the man who has devoted himself to her. Besides, I need to speak about myself once in my life! I hold, it is true, that emotion held back is worthier of a courageous man; but you know that I don't favor decisions without appeal, rules without exception. I think that on a given day one must open the door to sorrow so that it can come plead its cause in the court of consciousness. I have finished my preamble. Listen."

"I am listening," Obernay said. "I am listening with all my heart, which belongs to you."

Valvèdre spoke thus:

"Alida was beautiful and intelligent, but altogether without serious focus and convictions. This should have frightened me. I was already a mature man of twenty-eight years and, if I believed in the ineffable sweetness of her eyes, if I was vain enough to convince myself that she would accept my ideas, my beliefs, my religious philosophy, it is because at one time I was rash, intoxicated with love, controlled without my knowing it by the terrible force that has been placed in nature in order to create or to destroy all things in order to reach universal equilibrium.

"He knew what he was doing, he, *the author of goodness*, when he threw on the torpid principles of life the devouring fire that exalts this life to make it fecund, but as the character of infinite power is limitless effusion, this admirable force of love is not always proportionate with that of human reason. We are blinded, inebriated, we drink with too much ardor and too much delight at the inexhaustible spring, and the more experienced our faculties of comprehension and comparison are, the more enthusiasm leads us beyond caution and reflection. It is not love's fault; it is not love that is too vast and too ardent, it is us who are its all too fragile and too narrow sanctuary.

"I am thus not looking for excuses. I was the one who committed the sin in looking for the infinite in the disappointing eyes of a woman who did not understand it. I forgot that, if boundless love can open its wings and sustain its flight without peril, it is at the condition of looking for God, its restorative center, and of going with every élan to immerse and purify one's self in Him. Yes, great love, the love that does not tire of adoring and burning is possible; but one must believe, and one must have two believers, two souls merged into one single thought in a similar flame. If one of these souls falls back into the darkness, the other, caught between the duty to save it and the desire not to lose its way, floats forever in a cold pallid dawn, like the ghosts whom Dante saw at the borders of heaven and hell: such is my life!

"Alida was pure and sincere; she loved me. She also felt enthusiasm, but a sort of atheistic enthusiasm, if I may say so. I was her God, she would say. There were no other Gods but me.

"This kind of folly intoxicated me for a brief moment and quickly frightened me. If I was capable of smiling now, I would ask you if you can imagine a serious man playing the role of divinity! I was indeed taken by the idea for a day, for an hour perhaps! And straight away I understood that the minute I would no longer be a God, I would be nothing. And hadn't that moment already come? Could I conceive of the possibility of being taken seriously if I accepted the least whiff of this idolatrous incense?

"I don't know if there are men who are sufficiently vain, silly, or childlike to sit thus on an altar and to pose perfection in front of the feverish woman who has draped it over their shoulders. What atrocious disappointments, what bitter humiliations they have in store! How the lover, disappointed at the first sign of weakness given by her false God, must despise him and blame him for having accepted a cult he did not deserve!

"At least my wife cannot blame me for this absurdity. After gently mocking her, I spoke to her seriously. I wanted more than her infatuation; I wanted her respect. I was proud to appear to her the most loving and the most worthy of men, and I intended to devote my life to deserve her preference; but I was neither the foremost genius of the century nor a being above the human race. She had to realize that I needed her, her love, her encouragement, and her forbearance sometimes, to remain worthy of her. She was my companion, my life, my joy, my support, and my reward; thus I was not God, but a poor servant of God who was giving himself to her.

"This expression, I remember, seemed to fill her with joy and led her to say strange things that I want to repeat to you because they contain her entire way of looking at things, of approaching them.

" 'Since you are giving yourself to me,' she exclaimed, 'you are mine only and you no longer belong to the admirable architect of the universe whom I thought you were turning too much into a tangible being capable of inspiring love. Well, I must tell you now; I hated him, your God of scientists! I was jealous of him. Don't think me blasphemous. I know that there is a great soul, a principle, a law that has presided over creation; but it is so vague that I don't want to trouble myself with it. As for the traditional, personal God who speaks and writes, he is not great enough to my taste. I cannot enclose him in a burning bush, and even less in a chalice of blood. So I tell myself that the true God is too far for us and quite inaccessible to my inquiry and my prayers. Imagine my suffering when, to apologize for admiring for so long the crack of a rock or the wing of a fly, you tell me that loving animals and rocks is to love God! I see in this a systematic idea, a kind of obsession which bothers and offends me. The man who is mine may amuse himself with the curiosities of nature, but he may not be passionate about any other idea but my love or about any creature but me.'

"I was not able to make her understand that this kind of passion for nature was the most powerful adjuvant of my faith, my love, my moral health, that to immerse oneself in studies was to come as close as possible to the vivifying source necessary for the activity of the soul, and to become more worthy of appreciating beauty, tenderness, the sublime pleasures of love, the most precious gifts of the Divinity.

"This word *Divinity* meant nothing to her, even though she had applied it to me in her excitation. She was offended by my obstinacy. She became alarmed when she could not separate me from what she called a religion of dreamers. She tried to argue by bringing up books that she had not read, theological arguments that she did not understand; then, frustrated with her incompetence, she would cry, and I was left astonished at her childishness, unable to guess what she was feeling, unhappy to have caused her suffering, when I would have given my life for her.

"I searched in vain: what mystery can one discover in emptiness? Her soul only held vertigoes and vague aspirations toward some ill-defined, extravagant ideal which I have never been able to imagine.

"This was taking place very soon after our wedding. I did not worry about it enough. I thought it was the nervous excitement that follows the great crises of one's life. Soon I saw that she was pregnant and her constitution was somewhat too delicate to go through the formidable and divine drama of maternity without weakening. I attempted to treat her excessive sensibility with gentleness, to never contradict her, to anticipate all her desires. I became her slave, I became a child with her, I hid my books; I almost gave up my studies. I admitted all her heresies so to speak, since I left her with all her errors. I postponed until a more favorable moment the education of the soul that she so needed. I also flattered myself that seeing her child would reveal to her God's presence and truth much better than my lessons could.

"Was I wrong not to attempt to enlighten her more quickly? I felt greatly perplexed; I could see that she was wearing herself out in the dream of a childish and impossibly lasting love made of ecstasy and of *love speak*, of caresses and exclamations without anything for the life of the mind and the true intimacy of the heart. I was young and I loved her: thus I shared all her ecstasies and I let myself be swept away by her exaltation; but afterward, feeling that I loved her more, I was frightened to see that she loved me less, that each fit of enthusiasm made her then more suspicious, more jealous of what she called my *idée fixe*, more bitter when faced with my silence, more sarcastic about my definitions.

"I was enough of a doctor to know that pregnancy sometimes comes with a kind of mental imbalance. I increased my submission, my self-effacement, my cares. Her illness made her dearer to my heart and my heart was overflowing with a compassion as loving as that of a mother for the suffering child. I also adored in her the child of my own flesh and blood that she was going to give me; I thought that I could hear his little soul talking to me already in my dreams and telling me, 'Don't upset my mother.'

"And indeed she was delighted during the first few days: she insisted on breast-feeding our dear little Edmund; but she was too weak, too unwilling to submit to the prescriptions of hygiene, too irritated by the least worry; very soon she had to entrust the care of the child to a nurse of whom she became immediately so jealous that it made her even more unwell. She was making of life a continual drama; she rationalized about the filial instinct that turned ardently toward the breast of the first woman it met. And hadn't God, this intelligent God full of goodness, and in whom I pretended to believe, she would say, given to man as early as the cradle an instinct superior to that of animals? At other times, she wanted her child's preference for the nurse to be a symptom of his future ungratefulness, the sign that terrible misfortunes were in store for her.

"Nonetheless she recovered; she calmed down; she came to trust me when she saw that I was giving up all my habits and all my projects in order to please her. She had two years of this triumph and her exaltation appeared to dissipate with the resistance she had expected on my part. She wanted to make me into an *artist and society man*, she would say, and to get rid of my scientist's seriousness which frightened her. She wanted to travel like a princess, stop wherever she wished, see the world, change and move on ceaselessly. I gave in. And why wouldn't I have given in? I am not a misanthrope; the company of my fellow human beings could not be hurtful or prejudicial to me. I did not think that I was above them in my appreciation. If I had studied more than they did some specific questions, I could still receive from all of them, even from those who seemed the most superficial of men, a number of notions that I had left incomplete, like the knowledge of the human heart, which I had perhaps turned into an abstraction all too easy to solve. I thus do not resent my wife for having forced me to enlarge the circle of my acquaintances and to remove the dust off my study. On the contrary, I have always been grateful to her for it. Scientists are cutting instruments whose blades need to be dulled on occasion. I don't know if I wouldn't have become sociable by inclination with time; but Alida hastened my experience of life and the development of my benevolence.

"This, however, could not be my sole care and goal, and neither could her own future consist in having at her beck and call a perfect *gentleman* to escort her to a ball, a hunting party, to the waters, the theater, or the preach. I thought that I had in myself a man who was more serious, more worthy to be loved, more capable of bringing her and her son a consideration based on more solid grounds. I did not aspire to fame, but I meant to be a helpful servant, bringing his contingent of patient and courageous research to the edifice of science that is for him the altar of truth. I was hoping that Alida would manage to understand my duty, and that once the first thrill of domination had been satisfied, she would return to his true vocation the man who had showed his boundless love through an unconditional submissiveness.

"Having this hope in mind, I occasionally ventured to give her a sense of the emptiness of our so-called artistic life. We liked and appreciated the arts; but since neither of us was a creative artist, we had no claim to the eternal series of assessments and comparisons which make of the role of the dilettante, when it is exclusive, a life of boredom, surliness, or skepticism. The productions of art are stimulating; herein lies their splendid benefit. By elevating the soul, they communicate to it a divine emulation, and I don't believe much in the true ecstasies of admirers who are systematically unproductive. I did not speak yet of removing myself from the sweet *far niente* in which my wife was delighting, but I endeavored to bring her to make her own conclusions in this regard.

"She was gifted enough, and besides she had had enough of an introduction to music, painting, and poetry since she was a child to have the desire and the need to occupy her leisure with some study. She was infatuated with melodies, colors, or images, but wasn't she young enough, free enough, and encouraged enough by my affection to want to, perhaps not create, but at least, to practice, in turn? Had she had a specific inclination, one would have been enough, a favorite occupation, and I would have seen her saved from her idle dreams. I could understand the goal of her need to live in an atmosphere warmed, and, so to speak, redolent of art and literature: there she was becoming the bee making her honey after running from flower to flower: otherwise she was neither satisfied nor really moved as her life was neither active nor restful. She wanted to see and to touch nutritious elements with the greed of a sick child; but, having neither strength nor appetite, she was not getting nourishment.

"At first she pretended not to hear and finally presented me one day with rather specious arguments that seemed disinterested:

" 'We are not speaking about me,' she said, 'don't worry. I am of a languid disposition, in no hurry to open out to life as you understand it. I am like the coral reefs which you have mentioned to me and which quietly cling to their rock. And you are my rock, my shelter, my harbor! But alas! You now want to change all the circumstances of our common existence! Well, so be it, but don't rush so much; you still have much to gain in the so-called idleness in which I hold you. You are certainly destined to write about science, if only to give accounts of your discoveries from day to day; you will have the content, but will you have the form? And don't you think that science would be more widespread if an easy demonstration, a pleasant and vivid description made it more accessible to artists? I can see your stubbornness: you want to be positive and work only for your peers. You claim, I remember it well, that a true scientist must go straight to the fact, write in Latin, be within reach of all the scholars of Europe, and leave to minds of a less elevated level, to translators and popularizers, the task of clarifying and spreading science's majestic enigmas. This is lazy and selfish in the extreme, if you allow me to say so. You, who claim that there is a time for everything, and that it is only a question of knowing how to spend it methodically, you should improve as a speaker and as a writer; you should not dismiss drawing room successes, and you should study in the life that we lead the art of expressing yourself well and of embellishing science with a feeling for all beauties. Then you would be a complete genius, the God that I dream in you in spite of you; and me, poor woman that I am, I would be able to avoid living two thousand feet below your level, to understand your research, to enjoy it, and thus to profit from it. Come, must we remain isolated as we hold hands? Does your love want to make a part for you and one for me in this life that we are to spend together?'

" 'My dear heart,' I would answer, 'your thesis is excellent and contains its own answer. You are quite right. I need a good instrument to celebrate nature but this instrument is ready and in tune; it can't remain silent any longer.'

" 'Every tender and charming thing that you tell me about the pleasure you feel in hearing it gives me a generous impatience to give it voice; but in science subjects are not improvised: if they sometimes burst like light into discoveries, it is through facts that you need to establish quite steadily and conscientiously before you can trust them or, through ideas resulting from a meditative logic to which facts do not always submit spontaneously. All this requires, not hours and days, as when one writes a novel, but months and years; still one is never sure that one won't be led to admit one was on the wrong track and that one would have wasted one's time and one's life without the compensation, almost certain in the natural sciences, of having made other discoveries aside and sometimes across the one pursued. Time can solve everything, you claim that I say. Perhaps, but only if we no longer waste it, and it is not in our life, interrupted by a thousand unforeseen diversions that I can put this time to good use.'

" 'Ah, there we are!' My wife exclaimed impetuously. 'You want to leave me, to travel by yourself in impossible countries!'

" 'No, I shall work near you. I shall give up some investigations that would need to be pursued too far away; but you will also make some sacrifices for my sake: we shall see fewer idle acquaintances. We'll settle somewhere for a time. It will be where you want, and if you don't like it there, we'll try another environment. But from time to time, you will allow me a phase of sedentary work . . . '

" 'Yes, yes,' she continued, 'you want to live for yourself; you have lived enough for me. I understand: love is satiated, therefore it is ended!'

"Nothing could make her reconsider the prejudice that work was her rival, and that love was only possible in idleness. 'Love is everything,' she would say, 'and the man who loves has no time to do anything else. When the husband revels in the marvels of science, the wife languishes and dies. That is the fate awaiting me, and since I am a burden to you, I might as well die right away.'

"My answers further irritated her. I tried to invoke the devotion to my future about which she had first spoken. She threw aside the light mask with which she had tried to cover her ardent personality. 'I was lying, yes I was!' she exclaimed. 'Does your future exist apart from mine? Can you and should you forget that when taking my whole life, you have given me yours? Are you keeping your word when you condemn me to the intolerable boredom of being alone?'

"Boredom! It was her bane and her dread. That is what I wished I could have cured by convincing her of becoming an artist since she had such a strong aversion against science. She claimed that I scorned art and artists and that I wanted to confine her to the lowest level in my opinion. This was insulting to me and lowering me to the level of idiots. I strove to prove to her that the search for beauty is not divided in competing studies or in antagonistic manifestations, that Rossini and Newton, Mozart and Shakespeare, Rubens and Leibniz, and Michelangelo and Molière, and all true geniuses, had all walked directly toward eternal light where the harmony of sublime inspirations is completed. She mocked me and proclaimed her hate of work as a sacred right of her nature and position. 'I was not taught how to work,' she said, 'and I did not get married with the promise that I would start over with the ABC of things. What I know, I learned by intuition, by random and haphazard readings. I am a woman: my destiny is to love my husband and to bring up my children. It is quite peculiar that it is my husband who advises me to think of something better.'

" 'Then,' I answered somewhat impatiently, 'love your husband and allow him to keep his self-esteem; bring up your son and don't jeopardize your health, the future of a new maternity by living without rules, without goals, without rest, without a home, and without a desire to know this ABC of things that your duty will be to teach your children. If you cannot bring yourself to live the life of an ordinary woman without dying of boredom, then you are not an ordinary woman; and I was suggesting some course of study to connect you to your inner nature, which the vagaries and the contingencies of your current life are not likely to make worthy of either of us.'

"And as she was losing her temper, I thought I should add, 'Look, my poor darling child, you are consumed by your imagination and you consume everything around you. If you go on like this, you will manage to absorb in yourself all the life of others without giving them anything in return, not a light, not a true comfort, not a long-lasting solace. You have been taught the profession of idol, and you wish you could have taught it to me as well; but idols are good for nothing. No matter how much we decorate them and implore them, they don't bring fertility to anything and they don't save anyone. Open your eyes, look at the nothingness where you allow a splendid intelligence to drift away; look at the continual storm through which you allow even your peerless beauty to fade, the suffering that you remorselessly impose on all my aspirations as an honest and hardworking man, forsaking everything around us . . . , starting with our most cherished treasure, our child whom you consume with kisses, and in whom you smother in advance the generous and strong instincts by obeying his most harmful whims. You are a charming woman whom society admires and sweeps along; but up till now you have not been a devoted wife or an intelligent mother. Beware and think it over.'

"Instead of thinking about it, she attempted to kill herself. Hours and days were spent in wretched arguments in which all my patience, my affection, my reason, and pity came crashing against an invincible and forever bleeding wounded pride.

"Yes, this is the vice of such a seductive organization. Her pride is immense and casts like a paralysis of stupidity over reasoning. It is as impossible for my wife to follow a basic deduction, even within the logic of her own feelings, as it would be for a bird to lift a mountain. And I had guessed, I had established the cause of this: a kind of atheism drains her. Now she spends her life in churches; she tries to believe in miracles; she really does not believe in anything. To believe, you have to think, and she does not even think. She invents and raves; she admires and loathes herself; she constructs in her brain strange edifices which she hastens to destroy: she is constantly speaking about beauty and she has not the least notion of what it is. She does not feel it; she does not even know that it exists. She babbles wonderfully about love, but she has never known what it was and will never know it. She will not devote herself to anyone, but she will be able to kill herself to pretend that she loves, for she needs this game, this drama, this melodrama of passion that moves her when she is at the theater and that she would like to perform in her drawing room. A jaded despot, she is bored with submission and resistance aggravates her. Cold of heart and ardent in imagination, she never finds an expression strong enough to depict her transports and her ecstasies of love; and when she grants a kiss, she does so turning away her exhausted face and already thinking about something else.

"You know her now. Do not despise her; rather take pity on her. She was a flower of heaven whose development was stunted in a stifling greenhouse by a deplorable education. She was encouraged to become vain and morbidly sensitive. She did not once see the sun. She was not taught to admire anything through the bell-glass of her flower bed. She convinced herself that she was the thing to be admired par excellence, and that a woman should only look at the universe in her own mirror. Never looking for her ideal outside herself, seeing above her no God, no ideas, no art, no men, no things, she thought that she was beautiful and that her destiny was to be served and worshiped, that the world owed her everything, and that to nothingness, she owed nothing. She has never moved beyond this although she speaks in such a way that she could enervate the most resolute will. She has lived in isolation, believing only in her beauty, ignoring her soul, denying it on occasion, doubting her own heart, questioning it and tearing it apart with her fingernails to bring it back to life and to feel its beat, making the world parade in front of her in an attempt to entertain her, but enjoying nothing and sealing her shell rather than breathing the air that others are breathing.

"That said, she is good, in the sense that she is disinterested, tolerant, and that she feels sorry for the poor and throws them her purse through the window. She is loyal in intentions and thinks that she never lies because she has deceived herself so much that she has lost the notion of what truth is. She is chaste and dignified in her behavior; at least she has been for a long time. Meek in action, too languid and too proud for premeditated revenge, she only kills with words, only to forget them or take them back the next day.

"It took me many days of struggle against her magic to get to know her this way. For a long time she was a problem that I could not solve because I could not bring myself to see the weak and incurable side of her soul. I think that I tried everything to cure her or to change her: I have failed and I have asked God for the strength to accept without anger or blasphemy the most bitter of all disillusions.

"A second pregnancy had made me her slave once again. Her delivery was my deliverance because at that time our household witnessed events that were truly painful and intolerable for me. Our second son was sickly and homely. She reproached me with it; she claimed that he was born out of my contempt and aversion for her, that he resembled her in an ugly version, that he was her caricature, and that it was the way I had seen her when I made her pregnant the second time.

"Alida's eccentricities are not the kinds that one can remonstrate lightly and treat as something childish. Any contradiction of this kind offends her greatly. I answered her that, if the child had suffered in her bosom, it was because she had mistrusted me and everything: he was the result of her skepticism but that all was not lost. A man's beauty resides in his health and we had to strengthen the poor little creature through persistent and intelligent care. We also had to follow attentively the development of his soul and never hurt him with the thought that he might be less loved and less pleasant to look at than his brother.

"Alas! I was condemning this child while attempting to save him. Alida's mind is quite weak: she felt guilty toward her son before actually being so, and she became so for fear of being unable to escape destiny. Thus all my efforts made the matter worse and everything I said was given a fatal meaning. She was bent on finding that she did not love the poor Paul, that I had predicted to her that it would happen, that she could not avert this destiny, that she shuddered while trying to caress this horrible creature, her curse, her punishment and mine, and so on. I thought she was mad. I took her traveling again and took the child away; but she blamed herself; maternal instinct spoke louder than prejudice, or womanly pride rebelled. She wanted to be finished with hope as she said. This meant that, no longer loved by me, she gave up keeping me at her side. She asked me to have Valvèdre readied for her. She had seen it once in passing and had declared it sad and vulgar. She now wished to live there with my sisters who had settled there. I took her to the place; I turned the little manor into an opulent residence and I settled there with her.

"My friend, you can understand it now, there was no enthusiasm, no hope, no illusion, no flame left in my affection for her, but a true friendship, a devotion that was still absolute, a great respect of my word and my dignity, a fatherly compassion for this weak and violent nature, an immense love for my children with an affection perhaps more tender for the one whom my wife did not love; all this was quite enough to keep me in Valvèdre. There I spent a year which was not lost for my youngest sister and for my sons. I gave Paule a direction for her ideas and tastes that she has religiously followed. I taught my older sister the science of motherhood, which my wife did not have and did not want to learn. I also worked for myself, and, sad as a man who has lost half of his soul, I attempted to save the rest to avoid suffering selfishly, to serve humanity as far as I could by devoting myself to the progress of human knowledge, and to my family by sheltering it under the deep affection and the apparent serenity of the paterfamilias.

"Everything went well around me except for my wife who was consumed by boredom and who, refusing my ever loyal affection, took pleasure in claiming she was a widow deprived of any happiness. One day, I realized she hated me and I confined myself to the role of a friend who had no rancor and no susceptibility, the only role which hence could suit me. Another day, I found out that she loved or thought she loved a man unworthy of her. I enlightened her without letting her suspect that I had observed her deplorable infatuation. She was frightened, humiliated; she abruptly broke her chimera but she was not the least grateful for my tactfulness. Far from it, she was offended by my apparent trust in her. She would have forgotten her disappointment if she had seen me jealous. Indignant that she could no longer make me suffer or that she could not manage to make me admit to it, she looked for other mental distractions. She became enamored of several men in turn to whom she did not give herself anymore than she had to the first one, but whose attentions, even from a distance, flattered her vanity. She maintained many correspondences with admirers more or less respectable; she took pleasure in firing their imagination or her own with feigned friendships where she was extremely flirtatious. I knew everything. It is possible to betray me but more difficult to deceive me. I saw that she respected our bonds in her own way and that intervening in her way of understanding duty and feeling would only result in having her make some unfortunate decision and engage in a relationship more compromising than she herself wished. I observed and systematically practiced caution. I acted as if I was deaf and blind. She called me a *scholar* in every sense of the word; she almost came to despise me... and I let myself be despised! Hadn't I promised my firstborn child, when he was still in his mother's bosom, that his mother would never suffer because of me?

"You know, my dear Henri, how I have lived for the six years that we have been close friends. I only had one refuge, research, and, guessing the emptiness of my home, you sometimes expressed surprise at seeing me sacrifice the thought of long trips to the fear of seeming to be abandoning my wife. You now understand that what kept me or brought me back to her after moderately long absences was the need to ascertain first that my sister governed my children according to my heart and my mind, and then the desire to remove any pretext of scandal in my house. I could no longer hope for or want love; friendship itself was forbidden to me. But I wanted this terrible feminine imagination to know or feel some restraint as long as my children and my younger sister lived with her. I never hindered her freedom outside the home, and I must say that she did not ostensibly abuse it. She did hate me for this cold pressure on her, which her pride could not attribute to jealousy; but she ended up respecting me a little... during her moments of lucidity!

"At present, my children are here; my younger sister is yours; my older sister is happy and lives nearby; my wife is free!"

Valvèdre stopped. I don't know what Obernay answered. Pulled away for an instant from the violent attention with which I had listened, I became aware of Alida's presence. She was behind me, holding my opened letter, which her husband had read. She had come to announce the event and to urge me to flee, but, riveted by what we had just heard, she could only think of listening for his verdict.

I attempted to take her away. She signaled that she would stay to the end. I was so overcome by everything that had just been said that I did not feel the strength to take her hand and to reassure her with a silent caress. Thus we remained listening, gloomy like two criminals awaiting their conviction.

When the words that were being said on the other side of the wall and that had briefly escaped my preoccupation regained meaning for me, I heard Obernay plead Madame de Valvèdre's cause up to a certain point.

"She only seems to me," he was saying, "to be greatly pitied. She has never understood you and does not understand herself any better. It is sufficient reason for your being unable to make each other happy; but since in the midst of her mental aberrations she has remained chaste, it would be too severe to restrain or constrain her relations with her children. My father, I am sure, would be extremely reluctant to play this part with her, and I would not even guarantee that he would agree to it, whatever his devotion to you may be."

"I'll only need to explain myself," Valvèdre answered, "for you to understand my fears. The person about whom we are talking is currently madly in love with a young man who has no more character or reason than she does. In a flurry of excitement and illogical plans, he was writing to her... recently... in a letter that I found under my feet and which was not even sealed, proof of the derision in which my trust is held. 'If you want, we'll kidnap your sons; I shall work for them. I'll act as their tutor... everything you want, as long as you can be mine and nothing keeps us apart, etc....' I know that these are just words, mere *words*! I am quite at ease about the sincere desire that this enthusiastic lover, a child himself, can have to take into his care the children of another; but their mother may, some day of madness, take his offer seriously, if only to test his devotion! This would probably boil down to a country outing. Tired of the little ones, they would bring them back the very evening; but do you think that these poor lambs should be exposed to hear, if only for a day, these strange dithyrambs?"

"Then," Obernay answered, "we shall keep a good watch; but the best would be for you not to leave yet."

"I shall not leave without settling all things for the present and the future."

"The future, don't worry too much about it! The passing fancy that threatens will soon be gone."

"This is not certain," Valvèdre continued. "Until now, she had only encouraged men who were not to be feared, society people too well mannered to expose themselves to a scandal. Today she has met an intelligent and honest man, but one who is quite excited, inexperienced, and I am afraid, without principles strong enough to allow his good instincts to prevail; her kindred spirit, her ideal in a word. If she carefully hides this intrigue, I shall pretend I am indifferent; but if she makes the extreme decisions which this imprudent man is inviting her to, he must expect repression on my part, or she will have to stop using my name. I do not want her to degrade me; but as long as she is my wife, I shall not allow her to be degraded by another man either. There is my conclusion."

VIII

After Valvèdre and Obernay had walked away and I could no longer hear them, I turned toward Alida who had remained behind me; I saw her on her knees in the grass, livid, her eyes set, her arms stiff, unconscious, nearly dead, like the day when I had found her in the church. Valvèdre's last words, which I had been on the verge of interrupting many times, had given me back my energy. I carried Alida to the cottage, and in spite of the revelations that had crushed me for a moment, I helped her and comforted her tenderly. "Well, the gauntlet is thrown down." I said to her when she was able to hear me. "It is up to us to take it up! The great philosopher has mapped out our duty; it will be a pleasure for me to fulfill it. Let us write to him our intentions immediately."

"What intentions? What?" she answered, distraught.

"Didn't you understand, didn't you hear M. de Valvèdre? He challenged you to be sincere, and he refused me the strength to be devoted: let us show him that we love each other more seriously than he thinks. Allow me to prove to him that I think I am more capable than he is to make you happy and to keep you faithful. That is all the revenge I want to draw from his disdain!"

"And my children!" she exclaimed. "My children! Who will have them?"

"You will share them."

"Ah, yes, he will give me Paolino!"

"He won't since he is his favorite."

"No, he is not! Valvèdre loves them equally; he will never give his children away!"

"But you have rights over them. You haven't committed any breach that the law can reach?"

"No, I swear it on my children and on you; but it will mean a trial, a scandal, instead of a formality that mutual consent would make very easy. Besides, their Protestant law may give the children to the husband. I don't know anything; I never inquired. My principles forbid me from accepting a divorce and I never thought that Valvèdre would come to this!"

"But what do you want to do with your children?" I asked her, impatient with her maternal exaltation which was awakening before my eyes only to hurt me. "Be sincere with yourself; you only love one of them, your oldest, and he is precisely the one who, under all legal systems, belongs to the father unless there is a moral danger to put him in his custody. And that is not the case here. Besides, why are you tormenting yourself since while remaining Valvèdre's wife, you nonetheless have lost in his eyes the right to bring them up . . . and even to take them out for an outing. Divorce will change nothing to your situation, for no human law will take away from you the right to see them."

"It is true," Alida said as she stood up, pale, her hair disheveled, her eyes shining and dry. "Well, what shall we do?"

"You write to your husband to tell him that you are requesting a divorce and we go away; we wait for the legal period after the dissolution to be over and you agree to be my wife."

"Your wife, I cannot. It's a crime! I am married and I am a Catholic!"

"You stopped being a Catholic the day you married a Protestant. Besides, my pretty one, you don't believe in God and this point is bound to remove many scruples due to questions of orthodoxy."

"Oh, you are mocking me!" she cried out, "you can't be speaking seriously!"

"I am mocking your devotion; it is true. But, for the rest I am speaking so seriously that right now I am giving you my word as a man of honor . . ."

"No, don't promise! You want to do it out of pride; not out of love. You hate my husband so much that you are willing to marry me; that's all."

"Unjust heart! Is it the first time that I have offered you my life?"

"If I were to accept," she said looking at me doubtfully, "it would be on one condition."

"Tell me, quickly!"

"I don't want to accept anything from M. de Valvèdre. He is generous. He is going to offer me half of his income; I don't even want the alimony to which I am entitled. He is repudiating me; he is scorning me. I want nothing from him! Nothing, nothing!"

"It was precisely the condition that I was going to put to you," I exclaimed. "Ah, my dear Alida! Bless you for reading my mind!"

There was more wit than sincerity in these last few words. I had noticed that Alida had her doubts about my disinterestedness. It was horrible that at every instant she put everything into doubt; but at that moment, as there was in me more pride wounded by the husband than a real inclination toward the wife, I was determined to take offense at nothing, to convince her, to have her at any price.

"So," she said, not yet convinced but dazed by my resolve, "you would take me as I am, with my thirty years of age, my heart already spent in part, my name probably sullied by the divorce, my regrets for the past, my constant aspirations for my children, and poverty on top of all this? Tell me, you want this, you ask for it? Aren't you mistaken? Aren't you self-deceived?"

"Alida," I said to her as I knelt down at her feet, "I am poor, and my parents may be frightened by my decision, but I know them. I am their only child, the only creature they love in this world, and I assure you that you will come to be loved by them. They are as respectable as they are affectionate; they are intelligent, educated, respected. I am thus offering you a name less aristocratic and less famous than that of Valvèdre, but also as pure as the purest ones... The little that my dear parents have, they will now share with us, and as for the future, I shall die toiling or you will have a life worthy of you. If I am not gifted as a poet, I'll become a manager, a financier, a manufacturer, a civil servant, anything that you want me to be. That's all that I can tell you about the positive life that is awaiting us and which is the thing you have been the least worried about until now."

"Of course!" she exclaimed, "obscurity, isolation, poverty, dire poverty even, anything rather than Valvèdre's pity!... the man whom I saw for so long at my feet won't see me at his, neither to thank him nor to implore him! But it is not a question of me, but of you, my poor child! Will you be happy with me? Will you love me enough to accept me with the horrible character and absurd behavior that are attributed to me?"

"This behavior, whatever it may be, I don't want to know about it; let's never mention it again! As for this terrible character... I know it, and I don't think I am any better since I am your *kindred* spirit M. de Valvèdre says. So what! We are both passionate natures, hot-headed, impossible for others but necessary for each other as lightning is to thunder. We shall devour each other on the same blazing fire: such is our life!

Apart, we would not be any more peaceful or wiser. Come! We belong to the race of poets, that is to say we are born to suffer and to be scorched by the desire for an ideal that is not of this world. We shall not catch hold of it at all times, but we shall not cease to aspire to it; it will be our constant dream and sometimes we'll embrace it. What do you want that would be better elsewhere, you tormented soul? Do you prefer the nothingness of disillusion or the easy liaisons of society life, the retreat to your Valvèdre estate or the dubious life of a wife without a husband or a lover? Know that I care very little about M. de Valvèdre's opinions of you! He may be a great man whom you did not understand; but he did not understand you any better; he, who was incapable of doing anything with your individuality and who decreed his moral impotence the day he stopped loving you. If only I had been in front of him and alone with him a while ago! Do you know what I would have told him? You know nothing about Woman, you want to lay down for her a role in conformity with your systems, your tastes, and your habits. You have no idea about the mission of an exquisite creature and in this you are a pitiful naturalist. You are a Leibnitzian; I can see it, and you claim that virtue consists in participating in the improvement of human matters through knowledge of divine entities. Very well then; you take God as absolute type and, as he produces and controls eternal activity, you want man to create or order ceaselessly the prosperity of his environment through unremitting work. You marvel at the bee making honey, at the flower working for the bee; but you forget the role of the elements, which, without doing anything logical in appearance, give life and the exchange of life to all things. Be somewhat less of a pedant and more ingenious! Compare, logic requires it, passionate souls to the sea swelling and to the storm breaking to clear the atmosphere and maintain the equilibrium of the planet. Compare the charming woman who only knows how to dream and to speak of love to the insouciant breeze carrying the fragrant scents of life from horizon to horizon! Yes, this woman, so frivolous in your eyes, is, to mine, more active and more benevolent than you are. She carries with her grace and light; her very presence is an enchantment, her gaze is the sun of poetry, her smile is the inspiration or the reward of the poet. She is content to simply be, and around her people live and love! It is too bad for you if you haven't felt this ray within you and give your being new power and new joys!"

I was speaking out of spite. I thought that I was speaking to Valvèdre and I found solace from my wound by defying reason and truth. Alida was struck by what she took for true eloquence. She threw herself in my arms; sensitive to praise, eager for rehabilitation, she shed tears of relief.

"Ah, you win," she exclaimed, "and from this moment on, I am yours. Until this moment, oh, forgive me, feel sorry for me, you can tell that I am sincere, I kept for Valvèdre a vexed affection mixed with hate and regret; but from now on, yes, I swear to God and to you, you are the only one I love and to whom I want to belong forever. It is you the generous heart, the sublime spouse, the man of genius! What is Valvèdre compared to you? Ah, I had always said, always believed that poets are the only ones who know how to love, and that they are the only ones who have a sense of great things! My husband rejects me and abandons me for a peccadillo after ten years of real faithfulness, and you who hardly know me, you to whom I have given no satisfaction, no guarantee, you understand me, you set me on my feet again and you save me! Listen, let us go away! Go wait for me at the border; as for me, I am off to kiss my children and inform M. de Valvèdre that I accept his conditions."

Filled with joy and pride, relieved for the time being of suffering and apprehension, we parted after agreeing on the means to hasten our flight.

Alida went to meet M. de Valvèdre at the Obernays where, in Henri's presence, she was to speak to him while I would leave the summer cottage, never to return. I too wanted to talk to Henri, but not in an inn, for I was not to let his family know that I had stayed or had come back to Geneva; and the day of the wedding I had been seen by too many people of the Obernay circle not to risk meeting some of them. I ordered a cab in which I shut myself up, I went to ask Moserwald for shelter, and he hid me in his own apartment. From there, I wrote a note to Henri who came to me almost immediately.

My sudden presence in Geneva and the mysterious tone of my note were indications sufficiently striking for him to now recognize in me the rival whose name Valvèdre had tactfully held back. Thus the explanation of facts was alluded to but indirectly so. He held back as best he could his sadness and his blame, and spoke to me with a cold abruptness. "You probably know," he told me, "what has just happened between M. de Valvèdre and his wife?"

"I believe I do," I replied, "but it is very important for me to know the details and I beg you to tell them to me."

"There are no details," he continued, "Madame de Valvèdre left our house half an hour ago, telling us that one of her friends who is dying, a Polish woman on a journey, was asking for her in Vevey, and that she would come back as soon as possible. Her husband was no longer there. She seemed to want to see him; but when I was going to fetch him, she stopped me and told me that she preferred to write him. She quickly wrote a few lines which she gave me. I took them to Valvèdre who immediately rushed to speak to her. She was already gone, alone and on foot, probably leaving her instructions to Bianca, who has been inscrutable; but Valvèdre won't let his wife leave like this without having had an explanation from her. He is looking for her. I was going to join him when I received your note. I understood, I thought, I still think that Madame de Valvèdre is here..."

"On my honor," I interrupted Obernay, "she is not!"

"Oh, don't worry. I won't try to find her, now that I see that you have the main role in this regrettable affair! You two are going so fast that I would fear an unfortunate meeting between M. de Valvèdre and you. A man of his kind may be wise and patient, but one may be surprised by an outburst of anger. Thus you did right not to show yourself. I hid your letter from Valvèdre; and he will not think of finding you here."

"Ah," I burst out full of rage, "you think that I am hiding!"

"If you did not have this prudence and this dignity," Henri continued with authority, "you would be led by bad feelings to commit a bad action!"

"Yes, I know. I do not want my taking possession to begin with a scandal. It is to discuss these things that I wanted to see you; but I must entreat you, whatever your opinion may be, to treat me gently. I am not in control of myself as I would be if it was a matter of botanical analysis!"

"Me neither," Obernay went on, "but I'll nonetheless try not to lose my composure. Why did you call me? Speak; I am listening."

"Yes, I am going to speak; but I want to know what was in the note Madame de Valvèdre had you take to her husband. He must have shown it to you."

"He did. It said verbatim: I accept the *ultimatum*. I am leaving! In agreement with you, I am asking for a divorce, and, according to your wishes, I intend to remarry."

"Good, very good," I cried out, relieved of a great apprehension: I had feared for an instant that Alida had already changed her mind and broken the promises made in a moment of enthusiasm. "Now," I resumed, "as you can see, everything is over. I am going to abduct this woman, and as soon as she is free before the law, she will be my wife. You can see that the matter is quite settled."

"The issue cannot be resolved this way," Henri said coldly. "As long as the divorce has not been pronounced, M. de Valvèdre does not want her to be compromised. She must go back to Valvèdre or you must go away. It is only a matter of having some patience since the realization of your whim cannot be prevented. Are you already afraid, either of you, of changing your mind if you don't burn your bridges with an impulsive act?"

"Spare me your witticisms, please. M. de Valvèdre's opinion is certainly quite reasonable; but it is impossible for me to follow it. He himself has created the obstacle by presenting me with his scorn, his sarcasm, and his threats."

"Where? When?"

"Under the arbor of your garden, an hour ago."

"Ah, you were there; you were listening?"

"M. de Valvèdre had no doubt about it."

"Well, . . . yes, I remember. He insisted on speaking there. I should have guessed why. So what? He spoke about his rival, not as a reasonable man, which would have been quite impossible, but as an honest man, and indeed . . ."

"It is more than I deserve, according to you?"

"According to me? Maybe! We'll see! If you behave foolishly, I'll say that you are still too immature to really understand what honor is. What do you intend to do? Come on! To take vengeance for your own folly by defying Valvèdre? And thus to prove him right?"

"I want to defy him," I cried out. "I promised marriage to his wife and to my own conscience; so I shall keep my word; but until then I shall be her only protector because M. de Valvèdre predicted that I would deceive myself and I want him to be wrong, because he promised to kill me if I did not do as he wanted, because I am waiting for him resolutely to know which one of us will kill the other, and finally because I don't want him to think that he has intimidated me and that I am the kind of man who submits to the conditions given by a husband who abdicates and who still wants to come off in the best light."

"You are speaking like a madman!" said Obernay with a shrug of his shoulders. "If Valvèdre wanted to have public opinion on his side, he would let his wife seek a scandal."

"Valvèdre may fear not so much blame as ridicule."

"What about you?"

"It is my right more than it is his. He provoked my resentment; he should have foreseen the consequences."

"So it is settled. You are carrying her off?"

"Yes, I am and with all the secrecy possible because I don't want Alida to witness a tragedy which she does not know to be imminent; and this secrecy, you won't betray it because you don't want to be Valvèdre's witness against me, your best friend."

"My best friend? No, you would no longer be; you can resign if you persist!"

"At the cost of friendship, and of life, I shall persist; but as soon as I have put Alida in a safe place, I shall come back here, and I shall go to M. de Valvèdre to repeat to him everything that I have just said and that I am charging you to tell him as soon as I have left, that is in an hour."

Obernay could see that my will was exacerbated and that his admonishments only resulted in irritating me further. All of a sudden he made up his mind. "Well," he said, "when you come back you will find Valvèdre ready to carry on your remarkable conversation, and until tomorrow he will not know that I saw you. Leave as soon as possible; I'll try to help him not to find his wife. Good-bye. I don't wish you much happiness, for if you could be happy in the midst of such a triumph, I would despise you. I am still counting on your reflections and your remorse to bring you back to the respect of common decency. Good-bye, my poor Francis. I am leaving you on the verge of the abyss. God alone can prevent you from falling in."

He left. His voice was choked with tears that broke my heart. He retraced his steps. I tried to throw my arms around his neck. He pushed me back and asked me if I persisted, and when I answered in the affirmative, he continued coldly: "I was coming back to tell you that if you need any money, I have some at your disposal. It is not that I am not reproaching myself with giving you the means to head for disaster, but I prefer this to having you seek that Moserwald fellow's help . . . He is your rival; you are aware of it, I believe?"

I could not talk. Blood was choking me with a convulsive cough. I signaled to him that I did not need anything and he withdrew without accepting to shake my hand.

A few moments later, I was conferring with my host: "Nephtali," I said to him, "I need twenty thousand francs, and I am asking you for it."

"Ah, at last," he exclaimed with a sincere joy; "so you are my true friend!"

"Yes, I am, but listen. My parents have, in all, twice that amount invested in my name. I have no debts and am an only son. As long as my parents are alive, I won't cede this capital, the interest of which they receive. You will give me time; I shall give you an acknowledgment of debt for the amount and interest."

He did not want this guarantee. I forced him to accept, threatening, if he refused, to go ask Obernay, who had opened his purse strings to me. "Am I not already sufficiently obligated to you?" I said to him. "You who are accepting as evidence of my solvency the only proof I can give here, that is, my word?"

After fifteen minutes I was with him in his closed carriage. We were leaving Geneva and he was taking me to one of his country houses, from which I came out in post chaise to reach the French border.

I was quite worried about Alida who was supposed to join me in the evening and who, it seemed to me, had left the Obernay house with too much precipitation not to risk coming upon some obstacle, but when I arrived at our meeting place, I found that she had arrived there ahead of me. She dashed from her carriage into mine and we swiftly went on our way. At that time there were no railroads and it was not easy to reach us. It would not, however, have been impossible for Valvèdre to do so. We shall see shortly what protected us from his pursuit.

At that time Paris was still the place in the civilized world where it was the easiest thing to remain in hiding. That is where I established my companion in a comfortable and hidden apartment while awaiting further developments. I shall place here several letters written to me poste restante by Moserwald. The first letter was from him:

My child, I did what we had agreed. I wrote M. Henri Obernay to tell him that I knew where you were, that I had given you my word not to tell anyone, but that I was able to have sent to you any letter he would see fit to entrust in my care. That very day, he sent to my house the package herewith that I am transmitting faithfully to you.

> You have crossed the Rubicon, like the late Caesar. I won't mention again the admixture of satisfaction, pain, and worry that this is putting on my digestive system ... Digestion, it is quite vulgar, and *someone* will laugh at it mercilessly; but I must make the best of it. For me, the time for poetry has gone with the time of hope. Still I have felt some inclinations for a few days. *The* god is abandoning me and I shall only think about my health. The event which I expected and in which I did not want to believe, your sudden departure with *her*, upset me and I still felt some bilious movements; but it will pass and

the position of a Don Quixote, which you have given me, will give me courage. I can hear from afar that *someone* is still laughing; *someone* may even compare me to Sancho! No matter, I am *yours* (singular and plural), at your service, at your discretion in life and death.

Nephtali

The letter enclosed in this one contained a third letter. Here they are both, Henri's letter first.

I hope that when reading the letter that I am sending you, you will open your eyes on your true predicament. In order for you to understand it, you must know how I acted with respect to you.

You are naïve if you thought that I was inclined to transmit to M. de Valvèdre your provocative offers. I merely told him, in order to protect your honor, that a third party was in charge of sending to you all kinds of communication, and that the day he deemed necessary to have an explanation with you, I was personally instructed to let you know, and that finally, in that case, you would accept any meeting.

That established, I took the liberty of supposing that you were going to Brussels to talk to your parents about your future plans. As for *Madame*, I said, without much scruple, an enormous lie. I claimed I knew she was going to Valvèdre, and from there to Italy, to lock herself in a convent until the time when her husband would grant a divorce, that until then, the third party could also apprise her of any decisions made about her.

As a result of my action, M. de V...., who wished to speak to *Madame*, went immediately to Valvèdre where, for his dignity's sake and for my moral safety, I preferred to see him go rather than on the tracks of the *amiable* fugitives. From Valvèdre then, he has just written me, and if, when *Madame* and you have read this, you both persist in failing to appreciate such a character, I feel sorry for you and don't envy your way of looking at things.

I won't plead here for the good cause; I consider as a great happiness for my friend to no longer have in his life this bond that confers him *responsibility without possible repression*: a problem without solution in which his soul is consumed without profit for science. Less moral and more positive than he is in matters that affect him, I pray that the peace and freedom to travel be finally given back to him. This is not gentlemanly and you may demand satisfaction for this. I would not accept the challenge, but I must warn you about something: if you per chance persisted in asking reparation of M. de Valvèdre... for *"the affront he did to you in not contending with you for his wife"* (for it was the theme of your letter), you would find in me, no longer the friend who feels sorry for you, but the avenger of the friend whom you would have made me lose. Valvèdre is brave like a lion but he may not know how to fight. As for me, I am learning to, at the great surprise of my wife and parents, who send you their best. Good souls that they are, they don't know anything about this.

From M. de Valvèdre to Henri Obernay:

I did not find her here; she did not come here, and even, according to the information that I gathered along the way, she must have taken, to go to Italy, a completely different direction. But is she really there and did she seriously decide to lock herself in a convent if only for a few weeks?

Whatever the case may be, it is not right for me to look for her further; it would look as if I were in her pursuit, and this is not my intention at all. I wished to speak to her: a conversation is always more conclusive than written words; but the care with which she has avoided it and with which she has hidden her refuge reveals a more complete determination than I thought I could attribute to her.

According to the few words with which she has thought sufficient to end a life of reciprocal duties, I can see that she feared an outburst on my part. It was to know me little. It was enough for me that she should know my opinion about her, my compassion for her sufferings, the limits of my forgiveness for her faults; but, as she has not deemed it so, I think it is necessary for her to think again about my behavior and about the behavior she should adopt. You will therefore share my letter with her. I don't know if, when speaking to you, I have pronounced the word divorce, the premeditation of which she attributes to me. I am certain I considered this possibility only in the case when, trampling public opinion, she would give me no alternative but to either restrain her freedom or to give it back to her entirely. I cannot waver between these two options. The spirit of the law that I acknowledged when marrying her declares in favor of a mutual freedom when a long-lasting and mutually ascertained incompatibility has come to the point of compromising the dignity of the conjugal bond and the future of the children. Never, whatever may happen, will I invoke against the woman whom I had chosen and whom I loved very much, the pretext of her being unfaithful. Thanks to the spirit of the Reformation, we are not condemned to do each other harm in order to break loose. Other reasons would be enough; but we are not at that point, and I don't have motives that are evident enough to demand that *she* agree to a legal separation.

She thought, however, in a moment of irritation, that she could give me this motive by writing me that she intended to remarry. I am not the kind of man who takes advantage of an hour of spite; I shall wait for a calm and thoughtful insistence.

But she probably would like to know if I want the result that she is provoking, and if, for my part, I have wished for the freedom of contracting into a new union. She would like to know in order to reassure her conscience or satisfy her pride. I thus owe her the truth. I have never considered another marriage, and if I had done so, I would regard as cowardly the fact of not having sacrificed my desire to the duty of respecting, as far as possible, the sincerity of my first vow.

This limit of the possible is the case in which Madame de V. . . . would make a show of her new relations. It is also the case in which she would request of me, composedly and after careful consideration, the right to contract new bonds.

I shall thus do nothing to upset her current situation and carry out to their extreme determinations that I have no right to think are final. I shall not seek and shall not accept any negotiations with the person who offered to come before me. I do not anticipate on that side any more than on the other any guarantee of a lasting association, but I shall only pass judgment after a testing and waiting period.

If I am not called within a month in front of a court with the jurisdiction to grant a divorce, I shall absent myself for a time the duration of which I do not need to specify. Upon my return, I shall be the judge of this delicate and serious question, which engages us, and I shall decide but without departing from the principles of action which I have just explained.

Also tell Madame de V. . . . that she'll be able to cash at the Moserwald and Co. Bank an annuity of 50,000 francs which was previously paid to her and of which she had personally set the amount. If she wishes to live in Valvèdre or in my house in Geneva in the absence of any relationship that would compromise her, tell her that I don't see any objection. Tell her even that my wish would be to see her come here during the few days that I still have to spend here. I have no pride or at least I don't put any in my relations with her. I have had for a long time to avoid explanations that could have only resulted in irritating her and in causing her pain. Now that the ice is broken, I don't think that I am likely to be wounded by any ridicule if she wants to hear what I have to tell her now. I shall not mention the past; I shall speak to her like a father who does not hope to convince, but who wants to touch the heart. Having absolutely no selfish interest in my own cause, since we are, de facto and without any need for solemnity, separating, I feel that I myself still need to let her have a life that is, if not happy, as that cannot be, at least as acceptable as possible to her. She could still enjoy some inmost joy in the glory of sacrificing a fancy and its frightening consequences for the future of her children and her own reputation, for the affection of your family, for the faithful devotion of Paule, and for the respect of all serious people . . . If she accepts to hear me, she will find again the ever indulgent and never intrusive friend whom she knows well despite her customary misapprehension . . . If she does not want to, my duty is done and I shall go away, perhaps not reassured about her but at least in peace with myself.

The comic goodness of Moserwald had made me smile, the aggrieved and mocking harshness of Obernay had incensed me, the gentle generosity of Valvèdre crushed me. I felt so small compared to him that I experienced a moment of terror and shame before having his wife read this request both humble and lofty; but I did not have the right to refuse to do it, and I sent it to her through Bianca, who had joined us in Paris.

I did not want to witness the effect that reading the letter would have on Alida. I had learned to fear the unforeseeable nature of her emotions and to handle its repercussions on myself.

For eight days alone together, we had, through a miracle of the utmost determination of our will, succeeded in both maintaining a tone of heroic trust. We wanted to believe in each other, we wanted to overcome fate, to be stronger than ourselves, to prove wrong the somber predictions of those who had judged us so unfavorably. Like two wounded birds, we snuggled against each other to hide the blood that would have betrayed our tracks.

Alida acted with greatness at that time. She came to see me. She was smiling, beautiful like the angel of the shipwreck who supports and directs the ship in distress. "You haven't read everything," she said to me, "here are some letters given to Bianca for me at the time when she left Geneva. I had hidden them from you; now I want you to read them."

The first of these letters was from Juste de Valvèdre: "My sister," she was saying, "where are you? This Polish friend left Vevey; is she cured then? She is going to Italy and you are following her precipitously, without saying good-bye to anyone! It must be then a question of a great favor to do for her, a great help to bring her? This is none of my business, you will tell me; but will you allow me to tell you that I am worried about you, about your health altered for some time now, about Obernay's agitated look, my brother's downcast face, Bianca's mysterious air. She does not look at all like she is going to Italy... Dear, I am not asking you any questions; you denied me the right to do so, taking my concern for idle curiosity. Ah, my sister, you have never understood me; you haven't wished to read in my heart and I haven't known how to open it for you. I am a clumsy old maid, alternatively abrupt and fearful. You were right not to find me lovable, but you were wrong to think that I was not loving and that I did not love you!

"Alida, come back, or if you are still near us, don't leave! Many dangers surround an attractive woman. There is strength and safety only within the family. Yours sometimes seems too serious to you; we know it, and we shall attempt to correct it... And then, I am perhaps the one you dislike most... Well, I shall move away if I have to. You reproached me with putting myself between you and your children and with capturing their affection. Ah, take my place; don't leave them, and you won't have to see me again; but no, you are not heartless, and such resentments are not worthy of you. You could not believe that I hated you, I who would give my life for your happiness and who beg for your forgiveness if I have had some moments of unfairness or impatience against you. Come back, please, come back! Edmund cried much after your departure, which was so unexpected. Paolino has a fanciful idea, which is that you are in the garden near theirs; he claims he has seen you there once, and he can't be prevented from climbing the trellis to look behind the wall where he dreamed of your presence, where he is still waiting for you. Paule, who is so fond of you, is very sad; her husband is jealous of her sadness.

Adélaïde, who sees that I am writing you, wants to say a few words. She tells you, like me, that you must believe in us and not abandon us."

Adélaïde's letter, more shy and less tender, was even more moving in its simplicity.

Dear Madame,

You left so quickly that I did not have time to ask you a serious question. Should we trim the shirts of the *gentlemen* (Edmund and Paul) with lace, embroidery, or with a plain hem? I was in favor of quite crisp, plain white collars and cuffs; but I think I heard you say that it looked too much like paper and that it framed too sternly those sweet and dear little round faces. Rosa, who always gives her opinion, especially when nobody asks her, wants lace. Paule is in favor of embroidery, but I, please notice how wise I am, I claim that their pretty faces must please their little mother first, and that besides, she has much more taste that mere provincial girls like us. So dear Madame, please answer quickly. Everyone agrees in wanting to please you and obey you in everything. You took a piece of our heart with you, and without warning. It is wrong of you not to have given us the time to kiss your beautiful hands and to tell you what I am saying here: bring your friend back to health; don't get too tired, and come back quickly because I am at the end of my stories to make Edmund wait patiently and to put Paolino to sleep. Paule is writing to you. My father and my mother send you their most affectionate regards, and Rosa wants me to tell you that she is taking very good care of the large myrtle that you like and she wants to put one of its flowers in my letter with a kiss for you.

"What trust in my return!" said Alida when I had finished reading, "and what a contrast between the cares of this happy child and the lightning of our Sinai! Well, what is the matter with you? Are you lacking in courage? Don't you see that the more courage I need, the more comes to me? You must think that I have been quite unfair to my husband, the older sister, and the innocent Adélaïde? Do think so! You won't blame me any more that I do myself! I mistrusted those excellent and pure hearts; I denied them in order to try to forget my criminal love! Well, now that I am opening my eyes, that I see what friends I have sacrificed for you, I am reconciled with my sin and I am raising myself from my humiliation. I am glad to tell myself that you did not pick me up like a bird pushed out of the nest and thought unworthy of returning to it. Nevertheless the pity you felt is to your credit and you found in your generous heart the strength to take me in, a day when I felt degraded and when you had seen me humiliated. But today Valvèdre is taking back his word and calling me; Juste is receiving me with open arms and begging me to return, and the sweet Adélaïde is showing me my children, telling me that they are crying and waiting for me! I can go back to them and live independently, waited upon, indulged, thanked, forgiven, blessed! Now you are free, dear angel. You can leave me without remorse and without worry; you have spoiled nothing, destroyed nothing in my life. On the contrary, this very wise husband of mine, those friends so fearful of what people may say will treat me with all the more consideration since they saw me ready to sever all my ties. As you can see, we can break off our relationship without people ridiculing our short-lived love. Henri himself, this uncouth Genevan, will apologize if he sees me willingly give up what he calls my whim . . . Well! What do you want to do? Answer me! What are you thinking about?"

There are moments in the most fatal destinies when Providence offers us a way to safety and seems to tell us: "Take it or you are lost." I could hear this mysterious voice above this abyss, but the vortex of the abyss was stronger and pulled me down.

"Alida," I cried out, "you are not making me this offer in order for me to accept it, are you? You don't want it; you are not counting on it, isn't it true?"

"You understand me," she said kneeling before me, her hands in mine and in the position of someone making an oath. "I belong to you and the rest of the world is nothing for me! You are everything for me: my father and my mother who left me, my husband whom I am leaving, my friends who will curse me, and my children who will forget me. 'You are my brothers and my sisters,' as the poet says, 'and Ilion, the fatherland that I have lost!' No! I shall not retrace my steps, and since it is in my destiny to misunderstand the duties of family and society, at least I will have devoted my destiny to love! Is it nothing, and won't the one who inspires it be satisfied with it? If it is so, if in your eyes I am the first among women, what does it matter if I am the last one in the eyes of all the others? If the wrongs I have done them are virtues for you, what can I complain about? If they are suffering over there and if I am suffering from causing suffering, I am proud of it; it is an expiation of the faults in my past for which you blamed me. It is my crown of martyrdom which I am laying at your feet."

One thing only can excuse my having accepted the sacrifice of this passionate woman; it is the passion she inspired in me from that moment on, and which never wavered. I am quite guilty enough without adding to the burden of my conscience. My running away with her was a bad inspiration, a cowardly audacity, a revenge or at least a blind reaction of my wounded pride. Better than I was, Alida had taken my devotion seriously, and if her faith in me was an attack of fever, the fever lasted and consumed the rest of her life. In myself, the flame was often turbulent and as if battered by the winds; but, from that day, it never died out. And it was no longer vanity only that sustained me; it was gratitude as well as affection.

Henceforth, a sort of calm came into our life, a deceiving calm that hid many spells of anguish always ready to return; but the idea of changing our minds and of separating was never again reconsidered.

That day we took some good resolutions, considering our hopeless position. We turned our temerity into caution, our madness into wisdom. I gave up my hostility against Valvèdre as Alida did her complaints against him. She only mentioned him very intermittently, sadly and sweetly, as she spoke about her children. We gave up our dreams of free triumph, which we had entertained, and we took great care to hide our residence in Paris and our close relations. Alida took the care of explaining herself to her husband in a letter she wrote Juste, as Valvèdre had explained himself to her in his letter to Obernay. She persisted in her plan for a divorce; but she promised to lead a life so discreet that no one could be her accuser in front of Valvèdre. "I know," she said, "that my prolonged absence, my unknown whereabouts, my unexplained disappearance may seem suspicious, and that it would be better if Caesar's wife was above suspicion; but since Caesar does not want to abruptly repudiate his wife, and since we are talking about separating without bitter reproaches, she will keep up appearances and will not make public her future name change. On the contrary, she will hide it; she will see no one who could guess and betray it; she will be dead to the world for several years, if necessary, and it will be up to you to say that she really is in a convent, for she will live under a veil and behind thick curtains. If this is not all that Caesar wishes and advises, it is at least everything he can demand, for he never wore the crown of a despot and did no more kill freedom in marriage than he means to kill it in the world. May he allow me," she added, "to refuse the interview he is requesting. I am not strong enough to withstand the sorrow of resisting his influence, but I am too strong for any human consideration to weaken my resolve."

She finished the letter after, in her turn, having asked her sister-in-law's forgiveness for her unfairness and her prejudices, notifying her that she did not want to accept any financial help, however small it might be.

When she wrote to her children, and to Paule and to Adélaïde, she cried so much that she covered with tears a note to Adélaïde in which she was settling, with playful seriousness, the great matter of the shirt collars. She had to write it again, making generous and naive efforts to hide from me how heart-wrenching this was. I threw myself at her knees. I begged her to leave for Geneva with me. "I shall go with you to the border," I said to her, "or I'll hide in Moserwald's country house. You'll spend three, eight days, if you want, with your children, and we'll escape again; then, when you feel the need to kiss them again, we'll go back to Geneva. It is definitely the life that you would have led if you had gone back to your Valvèdre estate. You would have visited them two or three times a year. So don't cry or don't hide your tears from me. I admit that I am glad to see you cry, because every day I discover that you don't deserve the reproaches made against you and that you are as much of an affectionate mother as you are a loyal lover; but I don't want you to cry too long when I can dry your tears with one word. Come, come, let's go! Don't start your letters over. You will see your friends, your sons, your sisters, and *Ilion*, which you sacrificed for me but which you haven't lost!"

She refused without giving any explanations about the causes of her refusal. Finally, pressed by my questions, she told me:

"My poor child, I did not ask you what we were living on and where you found money. You must have committed your future, borrowed on the income of your future successes... Don't tell me; I know that you have made for me some great sacrifice or something quite foolish and I find this quite natural coming from you; but I must not, for my own satisfaction, take advantage of your devotion. No, I don't want to; don't insist, don't take away from me the only credit that I have to repay you. I must suffer, do you see? It is good for me; it is what purifies me. Love would be really too easy if we could give in to it without breaking off one's other duties. It is not the case, and Valvèdre, if he were listening to me, would say that I am saying a blasphemy or a fallacy, he who did not understand that what he called a guilty idleness could be the ideal devotion that I demanded of him. But for me, the fallacy consists in believing that passion is not the holocaust of the dearest and most sacred things, and that is why I want you to let me come to you, divested of any other happiness that is not you..."

Yes, today I too think that the unfortunate Alida was expressing a frightening fallacy, that Valvèdre was right and that she was wrong, that duty done makes love more ardent and that duty alone makes it long-lasting, whereas remorse drains or kills; but in the triumph of passion, in the elation of gratitude, I was listening to Alida as the oracle of divine mysteries, as the priestess of the true God, and I shared her immense dream, her yearning for the impossible. I also said to myself that there was more than one way to reach up to the truth; that if perfection seems to be in the religion of legitimacy and in the sanctifying virtues of the family, there is still a haven, an oasis, a new temple for those whose fate has toppled the altars and homes; that this right of sanctuary on the heights was not cold abstinence, voluntary death, but invigorating love. As refugees from society, we could still build a tabernacle in the desert and serve the sublime cause of the ideal. Weren't we angels in comparison with those vulgar pleasure seekers who become depraved in the abuse of positive life? Was not Alida, who was shattering all her life to follow me, worthy of a loving and respectful pity? As for myself, in accepting her questionable past and the dishonor she was braving, wasn't I a man more scrupulous and more noble than the one who loses himself in debauchery or cupidity in order to forget his dream and to get rid of his pride?

But public opinion, anxious to maintain the established order, does not want people to stray away from it, and is more tolerant of those who indulge in easy vices, in common faults, than of those who retire from the world and who seek merits which it has not sanctified. It is ruthless for those who ask nothing of it, for the lovers who do not want its forgiveness, for the thinkers who, in their relation to God, do not want to consult it.

Thus Alida and I were entering solitude not only in actuality but also in the realm of feelings and ideas. It remained to be seen whether we were strong enough for this frightful struggle.

We held this illusion, and as long as it lasted, it strengthened us; but one needs either a great intellectual ability or a great experience of life to remain thus, without tedium or terror, on a desert island. Fear was my torment, tedium the canker worm gnawing at my unfortunate companion. She had taken the necessary steps for the dissolution of her marriage. Valvèdre had not opposed it, but he had left for a long journey, people said, without presenting his own petition to the competent court. Obviously he wanted to force his wife to think things over for a long time before she tied her life to mine, and as his absence could last indefinitely, the waiting period required by foreign law threatened my passion with a delay beyond my strength. Was it what this strange man, this mysterious philosopher wanted? Did he trust his wife's chastity to the point of letting her face the danger of my impatience, or did he prefer to know that she was completely unfaithful, and thus protected from my lasting passion? Obviously he held me in great contempt, and I was obliged to forgive him and recognize that he had no other preoccupation than that of softening Alida's bad destiny.

This poor woman, seeing infinite delays to her union, overcame all her scruples and acted with magnanimity. She offered me her love without restrictions, and, overcome by my flame, I almost accepted; but I saw what sacrifice she was forcing upon herself and with what terror she was facing what she thought was the utmost sign of love. I knew what ghosts would be engendered by her dark imagination and the thought of her downfall, for she was proud to have never betrayed *the letter of her vows*; this is how she expressed herself when my anxious and jealous curiosity asked her questions about the past. She also thought that for men desire is the only food for love, and thus she feared marriage as much as adultery. "If Valvèdre had not been my husband," she would often say, "he would not have thought of neglecting me for the sake of science; he would still be at my feet!"

This fallacious notion, as wrong with regard to Valvèdre as it was to me, was difficult to eradicate in an intractable thirty-year-old woman and I did not want a happiness drenched in her tears. I now knew her well enough to be aware that she was unmovable and unbending and that, to find her always enthusiastic, one had to leave her to her own initiative. It was in her power to sacrifice herself, but not to avoid regretting the sacrifice perhaps, alas, at every moment of her life.

I was right in this, and when I rejected happiness, proud to be able to say that I had a superhuman strength, I saw, at her increased affection, that I had understood her. I do not know if I would have been able to exert this self-control for a long time; alarming circumstances forced me to turn to other preoccupations.

Last Part

For three months we lived hidden in one of those wide and quiet streets which, at that time, were adjacent to the Luxembourg Garden. We would stroll in the park during the day; Alida always wrapped and veiled with the utmost care, I leaving her only to take care of her comfort and safety. I had resumed none of the acquaintances, which were but few in any case, that I had made in Paris. I had called on no one; when I had happened to see an acquaintance in the street, I had avoided him by changing sidewalks and looking the other way. In this regard, I had even acquired the percipience and the presence of mind of an Indian in the woods, or of an escaped convict being watched by the police.

In the evening, I sometimes took her to the various theaters, in one of the lower-level boxes where you cannot be seen. During the bright days of autumn, I would often take her to the countryside, seeking with her the solitary spots that, even around Paris, lovers can always find.

Her health had thus not been affected by the change in her habits, or by the lack of diversions, but when winter came, the dark and mortal winter of large Northern cities, I saw an abrupt change in her face. A dry and recurrent cough, to which she did not want to pay attention, saying that she suffered from it at the same time every year, worried me enough, however, that I convinced her to see a doctor. After examining her, the doctor told me with a smile that there was nothing wrong with her, but he added for my ears only as he was leaving, "Madame your sister (for I had introduced myself as her brother) has nothing of concern now, but she has a delicate organization, I must warn you. The nervous system is too dominant. Paris is not good for her. She needs an even climate, not Nice or the Island of Hyères, but Sicily or Algiers."

Henceforth I had only one thought, to tear her away from the pernicious influence of an execrable climate. I had already spent, in order to provide for her a life in agreement with her tastes and her needs, half of the sum I had borrowed from Moserwald. He was writing me in vain that he had in hand the funds deposited by M. de Valvèdre for his wife: neither she nor I wished to receive them.

I inquired about the cost of a trip in the southern regions. The printed guides promised wonders in terms of savings; but Moserwald was writing to me: "For a refined woman who is accustomed to comfort, do not expect to live in those countries, where anything beyond the strict necessities is rare and costly, for less than 3,000 francs per month. It will be very little, too little if you are not careful; but don't worry about anything and go quickly if *she* is sick. This must remove all your scruples, and if your madness is carried to the point of refusing the husband's allowance, poor Nephtali is always here with all he has, at your service, and only too happy if you would accept!"

I was resolved to take this last option as soon as it would become necessary. I still had a future of 20,000 francs on which I could borrow, and I hoped to work during the trip when I saw that Alida was cured.

I won't tell you anything about Africa in this intimate narrative of my private life. I took care of establishing my companion in admirable quarters, not far from which I took for myself a most humble lodging, as I had done in Paris, in order to remove any pretext to the malice of the neighbors. I was soon reassured. The cough disappeared, but soon thereafter, I was alarmed again. Alida was not consumptive, but she was exhausted by the constant overexcitation of her mind. The French doctor whom I consulted had no specific opinion about her. All the organs of life were threatened in turn, then cured, and then affected again by a sudden debilitation. Nerves played such a great role in this that science could very well risk taking the effect for the cause. Some days she thought she was and she felt cured. The next day, she relapsed stricken by a vague and deep affliction which drove me to despair.

The cause! It was in the depths of the soul. This soul could not rest an hour, an instant. Everything was an object of somber apprehension or senseless hope. The least breath of wind startled her, and if I was not near her at that moment, she thought she had heard me scream, the last call of my agony. She abhorred the countryside; she had always disliked it. Under the imposing African sky, in the presence of a nature not yet quite under the influence of European civilization, everything seemed to her wild and terrifying. The distant roaring of the lions which, at that time, could still be heard around inhabited places, made her shiver like an unfortunate leaf, and no safety measures could assure her sleep. At other times, under the influence of other states of mind, she thought she heard the voice of her children coming to see her, and she would dash forward, delighted, mad, soon filled with despair when she saw the Moorish children who played by her door.

These examples of hallucination which I mention were among thousands of others. Seeing that she disliked living in ———, I brought her back to Algiers at the risk of not being able to keep our incognito. In Algiers, she was crushed by the climate. Spring, already summer in these southern regions, pushed us toward Sicily, where near the sea and with mountains on one side, I was hoping to find for her warm air and a few breezes. For a few moments, she enjoyed the novelty of things, and soon I saw her deteriorate even more rapidly.

"See," she told me during a spell of invincible despondency, "I can see that I am dying!" And, putting her pale and emaciated hands on my mouth, she added, "Don't mock me; don't laugh! I know the price of your gaiety, and that at night, alone with the inevitable certainty, you mourn your laugh! Poor dear child, I am a plague in your life and a burden for myself. You would do well, for our sake, to let me die quickly."

"It is not a disease," I answered, deeply grieved by her penetration, "it is sorrow or ennui that are wearing you down. That is why I laugh at your so-called incurable physical ailments but I cry about your moral suffering. Poor dear soul, what can I do for you?"

"One single last thing," she said. "I would like to kiss my children before I die."

"You shall kiss your children and you shall not die," I exclaimed. And I pretended to prepare everything for our departure, but in the midst of these preparations I felt prey to a deep despair. Was she strong enough to go back to Geneva? Wasn't she going to die on the way? Another terror overtook me: I did not have any more money. I had written to Moserwald asking him to loan me more, and I could not doubt his trust in me. He had not replied: Was he ill or away? Was he dead or bankrupt? And what was to become of us if this supreme resource failed us?

I had made heroic efforts to work, but I had been unable to continue anything, to finish anything. Alida, sick of spirit as well as of body, did not leave me a moment of peace. She could not stand to be alone. She urged me to work, but when I was out of her room, her mind wandered and Bianca would come to fetch me soon thereafter.

I had attempted to work at her side; it was quite impossible as well. My eyes were always on hers, trembling when I saw them glowing with fever or staring, their spark gone, as if death had already taken her. Besides, I had already recognized a terrible truth, which was that my pen, in terms of profit, was, for the time being, forever perhaps, unproductive. It might have been able to sustain me very modestly if I had been alone; but I needed 3,000 francs per month... Moserwald had not exaggerated.

After exhausting every imaginable lie to encourage my unfortunate friend to be patient, I had to admit to her that I was awaiting a letter of credit from Moserwald in order to be able to take her to France. I hid from her the fact that I had been waiting for the letter for so long that I no longer dared hope it would come. I had brought myself to the horrible humiliation of writing about my distress to Obernay. Was he also absent? But probably he would answer. The time of hope had not run out on that side. In doubt, I overcame the distress of asking my parents for a sacrifice: a few days of patience and some answer would come. I begged Alida not to worry.

That day she had her last courage. She smiled with that heartbreaking smile that I only understood too well. She told me that her mind was at rest and that, besides, she was resigned to accept her husband's gifts as a loan that I would certainly be able to have her pay back later. She thus spared my pride; she kissed me and fell asleep or pretended to do so.

I withdrew to the adjoining room. Since I had seen her nearing the end, I had not left the house in which she lived. After an hour, I heard her speak with Bianca. This girl, who had few scruples when it came to love but who was admirably devoted to her mistress, who mistrusted and spoiled her alternately, was making every effort to comfort her and to convince her that she would soon see her children again.

"No, I shall not see them again," replied the poor sick woman. "This is the cruelest punishment that God could have inflicted upon me, and I feel that I deserve it."

"Be careful, Madame," Bianca said, "your despondency hurts the poor young gentleman so much!"

"Is he here?"

"I think so," said Bianca as she came to the threshold of the other room.

I had happened to throw myself in an armchair with a very high back. As she did not see me, Bianca assumed that I had gone out, and went back to her mistress, telling her that I would certainly be back soon and that she should not get overwrought.

"Well, when you hear him come back," Alida said, "you will signal to me and I'll pretend to be asleep. He is comforted and somewhat reassured when he imagines that I have slept. Let me talk to you, Bianca; it relieves me; we are so seldom alone! Ah, my poor child, you yourself do not know what I am suffering and what remorse is killing me! Since I have left everything to be with good Francis, my eyes have opened and I have become another woman; I have began believing in God and have become frightened. I have felt that He was going to punish me and that He would not allow me to live in sin."

Bianca interrupted her. "Don't hurt yourself," she said. "I haven't seen any woman as virtuous as you are! Though, you would have every right to do as you please, with such a selfish and indifferent husband!"

"Hush, hush!" Alida rejoined with a feverish force. "You don't know him! You have been in my service for only three years; you have seen him only long after my first infidelity of feelings and when he had stopped loving me. It was my fault! But until recently I thought that he knew nothing; that he had not deigned to know anything and that, unable to judge me unworthy of him, his heart had withdrawn out of lassitude. As a result, I resented him, and without thinking about my own faults, I was irritated by his. My faults! I did not believe I had any; I said like you, 'I am so virtuous really; my husband is so indifferent!' His kindness, his politeness, his liberality, his thoughtfulness, I attributed to another motive than generosity. Ah, why would he not speak! One day finally... See, it is today the same day of the year! A year ago... I heard him speak about me and I did not understand. I was mad! Instead of throwing myself at his feet, I threw myself in the arms of another man; and I thought I was doing something great. Ah, illusion, illusion! You plunged me into such misfortunes!"

"My God!" Bianca went on. "Now you are missing your husband? Don't you love this poor Monsieur Francis?"

"I cannot miss my husband, whose love I no longer have, and I love Francis with all my soul; that is with whatever was left of my poor soul!... but you see, Bianca, you a woman, you must understand this:

one only really loves once! Everything one dreams afterward is the equivalent of a past that will never come back. One says, one believes one loves more; one would like so much to convince oneself of it! One does not lie, but one feels that the heart contradicts the will. Ah, if you had known Valvèdre when he loved me! What truth, what greatness, what genius in love! But you would not have understood, dear girl, since I myself did not understand! All this became clear for me at a distance, when I was able to compare, when I met those sweet talkers who do not say anything, those burning hearts who do not feel anything..."

"What! Francis himself..."

"Francis is something else; he is a poet, a true poet perhaps, an artist certainly. He lacks reason, but not heart or intelligence. He even has something of Valvèdre; he has a sense of duty. He fell short of it when he took me away from mine; he does not have Valvèdre's principles, but he has his great instincts, the sublime devotion. However, Bianca, try as he may, he does not love; he cannot love me! At least, he does not love me as he will be able to love someday. He had dreamed of another woman, younger, kinder, more educated, more capable of making him happy, a woman like Adélaïde Obernay. Do you know that he could have married her and that I was the obstacle that prevented it? Ah, I did him much harm and I am right to die!... But he does not blame me for it; he would like to make me live... You can see that he is great, that I am right to love him... You look like you think that I am contradicting myself... No, no, I am not delirious; I have never seen more clearly. We got excited the two of us; our strength broke against fate, and presently we forgive each other; we respect each other. We did our best to love each other as much as we said, as much as we had promised each other... and I, mourning Valvèdre still, he pining for Adélaïde for all that, we are going to give each other the kiss of the last good-bye... Well, it is better than the future certainly awaiting us, and I am happy to die..."

As she was uttering these words, she burst into tears. Bianca was also crying, unable to find anything to comfort her and I was paralyzed by terror and grief. What! Such was the last word of this fatal passion! Alida was dying mourning her husband and saying *"The other* does not love me!" Of course, by desiring the love of a woman whose husband was beyond reproach, I had given into a bad and sinful temptation, but great was my punishment!

I made a supreme effort, the most praiseworthy in my whole life perhaps: I came near her bed and without complaining in any way on my own account, I succeeded in calming her down.

"Everything you have just dreamed," I said, "is the effect of fever, and you are not really having these thoughts. Besides, even if you were thinking so, I would not believe it. So do not restrain yourself in front of me; say anything you want; it is your illness that is speaking. I know that at other moments you will see my heart and yours in a different light. Your belief in God, your fairness to Valvèdre, your blaming yourself for not having understood a husband who was anything but virtuous and who may have known better than anyone else how to love, all this is good; I grant it and I knew it. Haven't you told me a hundred times that this belief and this remorse were good for you and that you were offering me this suffering as a credit and a reconciliation with yourself? Yes, it was good, you were in the right, but why would you lose the advantage of these good inspirations? Why excite your imagination precisely to deprive yourself of the merit of repentance and to wrench from me the hope of your cure? Everything is consummated. Valvèdre has suffered but he has long resigned himself: he is traveling; he is forgetting. Your children are happy and you are going to see them again; your friends forgive you, if indeed they have anything personal to forgive you. Your reputation, if indeed it is compromised by our absence, can be salvaged, either by your return or by our marriage. Do justice to your destiny and to those who love you. Submissive in everything, I shall be for you whatever you want, your husband, your lover, or your brother. As long as I can save you, I shall be rewarded enough. You can even think what you said, not believe in *the second love*, and grant me but the remnant of a soul exhausted by the first love, I shall be satisfied with it. I shall overcome my stupid pride; I'll tell myself that it is more than I deserve, and if you feel like talking about the past, we shall talk about it together. I only ask one thing: don't keep any secrets from me, your child, your friend, your slave; don't fight against yourself and exhaust yourself in hidden sorrows. Do you really think that I have no courage? Yes, I do, and for you I can have enough to the point of heroism. Don't spare me, if it relieves you a little, tell me that you don't love me, as long as you tell me what I must do and be for you to love me!"

Alida was moved by my resignation but she no longer had the strength to recover through enthusiasm. She put her lips to my forehead crying like a child with whimpers and tears; then, exhausted, she fell asleep at last.

These emotions revived her for a while; the next day she felt better and I saw her looking forward again to our departure. That is what I feared the most.

We were living near Palermo. Everyday I would run there to see if there was something for me at the post. That day was a day of hope, a last ray of sun. As I was coming near the town, I saw a hackney carriage which was leaving and came toward me at a gallop. A mysterious warning cried to my soul that it was help coming to me. I hurled myself, haphazardly, at the head of the horses. A man leaned over the door; it was he; it was Moserwald!

He asked me to climb up next to him and gave orders to continue, as he was going to our house. The way was so short that we hastily exchanged the most urgent explanations. He had received my letter, with the one I was sending him for Henri, two months later after I had sent them, because of an accident suffered by his secretary, who injured and seriously ill, had forgotten to give it to him. As soon as the excellent Moserwald had been apprised of my situation, he had burned my request for money to Obernay; he had taken the post; he was rushing to us: money, help, affection; he was bringing me everything that could save Alida or prolong her life.

I did not want him to see her without my taking the time to announce to her a meeting brought by chance, as I would say. One always fears to enlighten patients about the worry that they are causing. I also feared that Alida's fierce prejudices against Jews would cause her to give a cold welcome to such a trustworthy and devoted friend.

She smiled her strange smile and was not deceived about the reason which brought Moserwald to Palermo, but she received him gracefully, and I soon saw that the distraction of seeing a new face and the pleasure to hear about her family was doing her some good. When I was able to be alone with Nephtali, I asked him what impression he had of the state in which he was finding her.

"She is dying!" he answered me. "Don't have any illusions. It is now only a question of making the end more comfortable."

I threw myself in his arms and I cried bitterly; I had held back for so long!

"Listen," he said after drying his own tears, "I think, first of all, that she should not see her husband."

"Her husband? Where is he?"

"In Naples; he is looking for her. Someone who had seen you as you were leaving Algiers told him that his wife seemed to be dying and that she had to be carried ashore. He was in Rome at that time, inquiring about her and asking in all the convents because his older sister had led him to believe that she was not with you and that she had really gone for a retreat."

"But so you saw Valvèdre in Naples? Did you speak to him?"

"I did. It was impossible for me to avoid it. I kept your secret in spite of his gentle entreaties and his cool admonitions. I may have succeeded or not in escaping him: he has not been able to follow me, but he is quite obstinate and quite clever, and unfortunately a lot of people know me. He will ask questions; he will easily discover what direction I took. He has certainly guessed that I was going to join you. I should not be surprised to see him arrive here a few days after me. Make no mistake about it; he still loves the poor woman; he is still jealous. In spite of his quiet looks, I saw through him. You must hide; I mean to hide Alida farther from town, or in the harbor on some boat. I have more than one at my disposal. I have many friends, that is many people who owe me favors everywhere."

"No, my dear Nephtali," I replied, "this is not what we should do; it is quite the opposite. You must be on the lookout for Valvèdre's arrival and let me know as soon as he reaches Palermo, so that I can go meet him."

"Ah, you still want to fight? Don't you think the poor woman has suffered enough?"

"I don't want to fight; I want to take Valvèdre to his wife; he alone can save her."

"What? What does this mean? She misses him. She has reasons to complain about you?"

"No, she has no grounds for complaint. Thank God! But she misses her family, that is certain. Valvèdre will be generous, I know him. Jealous or not, he will comfort, he will strengthen the poor broken-hearted soul!"

Moserwald returned to Palermo and placed the most trustworthy of his fellows on the lookout in the harbor; then he came back to stay in my small lodging in order to be at hand for help at any time. He showed admirable generosity, kindness, and thoughtfulness. I must say it and never forget it.

Alida wished to see him again and to thank him for his friendship toward me. She did not want for a single moment to look like she suspected him of having been in love or of still being in love with her; but in a strange way quite typical of this childlike and charming woman, she had with him a surge of coquetry at death's door. She had Bianca paint her eyebrows and her cheeks and, lying on her couch, wrapped in fine Algerian cloth, she reigned one more time in the languor of her expiring beauty.

This was perhaps cruel; for while she could no longer revive the desires of love, she could still seize the imagination, and I saw Moserwald being stricken by a painful rapture. But Alida was unaware of it: she was instinctively following the custom of her life. She was flirtatious in mind as well as in physical appearance. She encouraged our guest to tell her the gossip from Geneva, and, crying when she went back to talk of her children, she had fits of nervous laughter when, with his mocking good nature, Moserwald recounted to her the absurdities of some characters in her former circle.

Seeing her thus, Moserwald regained hope. "Diversions are good for her," he was telling me at the end of two days. "She was dying of boredom. You supposed that a society lady, accustomed to a little court, could blossom in a tête-à-tête, and you can see that she withered like a flower without air and sun. You are too romantic, my child, I cannot repeat it enough. Ah, if she had wanted to follow me! I would have taken her from party to party; I would have created for her a new circle. With money, you can do what you want. She has aristocratic tastes: the Jew's mansion would have become so luxurious and so agreeable that the biggest wigs would have come to greet beauty, queen of hearts and wealth, queen of the world! And you, you did not wish to understand; your pride, your conscience made of your home a cell in which you have been unable to work and she has been unable to live! And what did you need for her to feel excitement, for her not to have time for regrets and for missing her family? Money, only money. And her husband was giving her money, and you had some too since I do."

"Ah, Moserwald," I rejoined, "you are hurting me to no purpose! I could not do as you think, and even if I had been able to, can't you see that it is too late?"

"No, maybe not! Who knows? I may be bringing her life; me, the fat Jew who is so prosaic! The day before yesterday I thought she was on the verge of dying in front of me; today she looks resurrected. Let her hold her own like this for a few days and we'll take her away; we'll surround her with comfort and distractions. I'll spend millions, if need be, but we shall save her!"

At that moment, Bianca came calling for me, crying out that her mistress was dead. We rushed to her room. She was still breathing but she was livid, motionless, and unconscious.

I had for her the best doctor in the area. He had given up on her in the sense that he now only prescribed innocuous medication; but he came to see her daily and he arrived just as I was sending for him.

"Is it the end?" Moserwald whispered to him.

"Who knows?" he answered with a shrug of grief.

"What!" I cried out, "you cannot bring her back to consciousness? She shall die like this, without seeing us, without recognizing us, without receiving our good-byes?"

"Speak softly," he rejoined, "she may be hearing you. We have here, I think, a cataleptic state."

"My god!" Bianca cried out turning pale and showing us the end of the gallery, the doors of which were wide opened to allow the air to circulate in the apartment. "Look at *that one man* who is coming here! . . ."

The one who was coming like the angel of death was Valvèdre!

He came in without seeming to see any of us, went straight to his wife, took her hand and looked at her attentively for a few seconds; then he called her by her name, and she moved her lips to answer him, but her voice could not be heard.

There was still for a few moments a horrible silence, and Valvèdre said again as he leaned toward her and with a tone of infinite kindness, "Alida!"

She grew agitated and arose like a specter, fell back, opened her eyes, let out a heart-rending cry and threw her two arms around Valvèdre's neck.

For a few more instants, she regained her voice and her eyes; but what she was saying, I did not hear. I was standing rooted to the spot, struck by a conflict of emotions beyond words. Valvèdre seemed, I was told later, to pay no attention to me. Moserwald took me vigorously by the arm and led me outside the room.

I fell prey to a veritable fit of deliriousness. I no longer knew where I was or what had just happened. The doctor came to rescue me in my turn and I helped him with the full effort of my will, as I felt I was becoming mad, and I wanted to be strong enough to accomplish to the end my terrible destiny. When I came back to my senses, I learned that Alida was calm, and could still live a few days or a few hours. Her husband was alone with her.

The physician withdrew, saying that the newcomer seemed to know as much as he did about the care to give in such circumstances. Bianca was listening at the door. I had an outburst of ill-temper against her and I abruptly pushed her outside. I did not want to allow myself to hear what Valvèdre was saying to his wife at this supreme moment; the girl's curiosity, however well intentioned, seemed to me a profanation.

Left alone with Moserwald in the drawing room next to Alida's room, I remained dazed and as if struck by a religious terror. We had to stand there, ready to assist if need be. Moserwald wanted to listen as Bianca had done, and I knew you could hear by coming close to the door. I made him stay near me at the other end of the drawing room. Valvèdre's voice came to us soft and reassuring but no distinct words could confirm to us its inflections. Perspiration was running down my forehead, so difficult was it for me to bear this inaction, this uncertainty, this passive submission in the face of the supreme crisis.

All of a sudden the door opened quietly and Valvèdre came to us. He greeted Moserwald and apologized for leaving him alone while asking him not to leave; then he turned to me to say that Madame de Valvèdre wished to see me. He had the politeness and the seriousness of a man who does the honors of his own house in the midst of a domestic crisis.

He went back to Alida's room with me and, as if he were introducing me to her, he said, "Here is your friend, the devoted friend to whom you want to express your gratitude. Everything you have told me about his care and his infallible affection justifies your desire to shake his hand; and I have not come here to keep him away from you at a time when everyone who feels affection for you wants and must prove it to you. It is a consolation for your suffering and you know that I am bringing you everything that my heart owes you in terms of tenderness and solicitude. Have no fear, and if you have some orders to give which you think will be better carried out by others than me, I shall withdraw."

"Don't, don't," Alida answered holding him back with one hand while she clung to me with the other; "don't leave me yet! . . . I would like to die between the two of you, he who did everything to save my life, and you who came to save my soul!"

Then, raising herself on our arms and looking at us in turn with an expression of hopeless terror, she added, "You are here in front of me so that I may die in peace; but I shall hardly be under the shroud and you will fight!"

"No," I replied with force. "It will not be so, I swear it!"

"I can hear you, Sir," Valvèdre said, "and I know your intentions. You will offer me your life and you won't defend it. As you can see," he added addressing his wife, "we cannot fight. Set your mind at rest, *my dear girl*, I shall never do anything cowardly. I gave you my word, a moment ago, that I would not seek revenge against the man who devoted himself, body and soul, during those bitterly trying times, and I don't go back on my word."

"I am reassured," Alida answered as she brought her husband's hand to her lips. "Oh! My God! You did forgive me! . . . there is only my children . . . my children whom I have neglected . . . abandoned . . . poorly loved while I was with them . . . and who will not receive my last kiss . . . Dear children! Poor Paul! Ah, Valvèdre, is it not a great atonement and because of all this everything will be forgiven to me? If you knew how much I have adored them, missed them! How my poor inconsequential heart was torn by their absence! How I have understood that the sacrifice was beyond my strength and how Paul, who made me sad, who frightened me, whom I did not dare kiss, has appeared to me handsome and good, and forever to be missed in my hours of agony! Francis knows, he does, that I no longer made a difference between the two and that I would have been a good mother if . . . but I won't see them again! . . . I must remain here, under this foreign soil, under this cruel sun that was supposed to cure me, and that smiles while one dies!"

"My dear girl," Valvèdre continued, "you promised me to think of death only as a thing whose presence is as much of a possibility for you as it is for us. The hour of this passage is always unknown, and the person who thinks it is coming may be further away from it than the one who is not thinking about it. Death is everywhere and always, as is life. They go hand and hand and work together for God's purposes. You seemed to believe me a while ago when I was telling you that all is well, for the reason that everything gets reborn and begins anew. Don't you believe me anymore? Life is an aspiration to rise up to higher spheres, and this eternal effort toward the best, the purest, the most divine state, always leads to a day of sleep which we call death and which is a regeneration in God."

"Yes, I understand . . . ," Alida replied . . ." Yes, I saw God and eternity, through your mysterious words! . . . Ah, Francis, I wish you had heard him a moment ago, and I had listened to him earlier! . . . What peace he had brought, what trust he can inspire! *Trust*, yes, that's what he said, *have faith in one's own trust*! . . . God is the great haven, nothing can be a danger, after life, for the soul who trusts and surrenders; nothing can be punishment and degradation for the woman who understands goodness and has no illusions about evil! . . . Yes, I am at peace! . . . Valvèdre, you have cured me!"

She stopped speaking and fell asleep. Moist beads of sweat, becoming colder and colder, dampened her hands and her face. She lived thus without voice and almost without breadth until the next day. A pale and sad smile appeared on her lips when we spoke to her. Tender and broken, she was attempting to show us that she was happy to see us. She called Moserwald with her eyes and with her eyes pointed to her hand for him to press it in his own.

The sun was rising magnificently over the sea. Valvèdre opened the curtains and showed it to his wife. She smiled once more as if to tell him that it was beautiful. "You are feeling well, aren't you?" he asked her.

She indicated that she did.

"You are peaceful, cured?"

Still yes, with a nod.

"Happy, relieved? You are breathing well?"

She lifted her chest effortlessly as if she was delightfully relieved of the weight of agony.

It was the last breath. Valvèdre, who had felt it coming and who, with his look of conviction and joy, had averted its terrible expectation, gave her a long kiss on the forehead, then on the right hand of the dead woman. He took back on his finger the wedding ring that she had stopped wearing for a long time but which she had put back the day before; then he came out, bolted behind him the door of the drawing room, and hid from us the spectacle of his grief.

I did not see him again. He spoke with Moserwald, who took care of fulfilling his intentions. He asked him to have his wife's body embalmed and carried to the Valvèdre estate. He apologized for not saying good-bye to me. He left immediately and no one could find out what road or sea passage he had taken. He probably went to the great spectacles of nature to seek the strength to bear the blow that had just struck his heart.

I had the atrocious courage to help Moserwald to fulfill the funeral task imposed on us: cruel bitterness inflicted by a strong soul to my broken soul! Valvèdre was leaving me his wife's corpse after taking back from me her heart and faith at the final moment.

I accompanied the sacred consignment to Valvèdre. I wished to see again the house forever empty for me, the garden still smiling and superb in the silence of death, the solemn shady trees and the silvery lake which reminded me of thoughts so fervent and dreams so fatal. I saw all this at night, not wanting anyone to notice me, feeling that I had no right to kneel by the tomb of the one I could not save.

There I took leave of Moserwald who wanted to keep me with him, to make me travel, to entertain me, to make me rich, to have me marry, and who knows what else?

No longer did I have the heart to do anything, but I had a debt of honor to pay. I owed more than 20,000 francs which I did not have, and it was precisely to Moserwald that I owed them. I was careful not to mention it to him; he would have been quite offended by my concern or he would have found the means to discharge me of my debt by cheating himself. I had to think of earning, through my work, this sum, which was small for him but enormous for me who did not have a profession and which was weighing on my conscience, on my pride like a mountain.

I was so crushed morally that I could not foresee any work of imagination of which I could be capable. Besides I could feel that to be rehabilitated I needed a rough, hidden, austere life; the rivalries as well as the hazards of literary life were no longer emotions in keeping with the weight of my grief. I had committed a great sin in throwing into despair and death a poor, weak, and romantic creature, whom I was too romantic and too weak myself to know how to cure. I had made her break her family ties, which she did not respect enough, it is true, but which she might have never openly evaded without me. I had loved her very much, it is true, during her torment, and I had not willingly found myself unequal to the terrible trial; but I could not forget that the day when I had run away with her, I had yielded to pride and revenge more than to love. This self-reflection struck my soul with dismay. I was no longer proud, alas! But what a price I had paid for my cure!

Before leaving the vicinity of Valvèdre, I wrote to Obernay. I opened to him the most hidden recesses of my grief and of my remorse. I told him all the details of this cruel story. I accused myself unsparingly. I informed him of my plans for atonement. I wanted to regain someday the friendship that I had lost.

It took me thirty hours to write this letter; I was choking with sobs at every instant. Moserwald, who thought I had left, had started back to Geneva.

After managing to complete my narrative and my thoughts, I went out for some fresh air and, imperceptibly, instinctively, my steps took me toward the rock where, the preceding year, I had picnicked with Alida who, active, determined, up at sunrise, had arrived on a proud and capering horse. I wanted to relish the horror of my suffering. I turned to look again at the villa. I had walked two hours on a fast and tiring path, but in reality I was still so close to Valvèdre that I could make out the smallest details. How proud and happy I had felt on this spot! What future of love and glory I had dreamed!

Ah, wretched poet, I thought, *you will no longer sing joy nor happiness nor grief! You will have no more rhymes for this catastrophe of your life! No, thank God, you are not as hardened as that. Shame will kill your poor muse: she has lost the right to live!*

A distant knell of bells startled me: it was the toll of the funeral. I went up to the highest ridge of the rock and I could make out a sorry sight, a black line which was moving toward the castle. These were the last honors given to the poor Alida by the villagers from the surrounding areas; they were lowering her down in the grave, under the shady trees of her park. A few carriages revealed the presence of friends who felt sorry for her fate without knowing it, for our secret had been faithfully kept. She was thought to have died in an Italian convent.

I attempted for a few moments to cast a doubt on what I was seeing and hearing. The priest's hymn, the servants' tears and even, it seemed to me, children's screams reached up to me. Was it an illusion? It was horrible and I could not escape from it. It lasted two hours! Every ring of the bell fell on my chest and crushed it. At the end, I could not feel it; I was unconscious. I had just felt Alida die a second time.

I only came back to my senses near nightfall. I crawled along to La Rocca, where my former hosts were but one. The woman had died. The husband opened my room without paying further attention to me. He was just back from the *Lady*'s funeral, and as a widower for the last few weeks, he had felt the wound in his own heart reopen. He was prostrate with grief.

I was delirious all night long. In the morning, not knowing where I was, I attempted to get up. I thought I was having a new vision after all the ones that had just haunted me. Obernay was seated near the table on which I had written to him the day before; he was reading my letter. His gloomy face displayed a great pity.

He turned around, came to me, made me go back to bed, ordered me to keep silent, called a doctor, and took care of me for several days with the utmost kindness. I was quite ill, without being conscious of anything. I was exhausted by a year of all consuming agitation and by the atrocious sorrow of the last few months, a sorrow without outlet, without respite, without hope.

When I was out of danger and able to talk and to understand, Obernay told me that informed by a letter from Valvèdre, he had come with his wife, his sister-in-law, and Alida's two children to attend the funeral. The whole family had gone back to Geneva; he alone had stayed, guessing that I would be there, looking for me everywhere and finally discovering me fighting against the most serious illness.

"I read your letter," he added. "I am as pleased with you as I can be after what happened. You must persevere and reconquer, not my friendship, which you never lost, but your self-esteem. Look, here is something you'll find encouraging."

He showed me a fragment from a letter written by Valvèdre: "Keep an eye on this young man," he was saying, "find out what is becoming of him, and beware of the first despair. He too was struck by lightning! He had attracted it on his own head; but destroyed as he is, he deserves your benevolence. He is the most unhappy of us all, don't forget, for he no longer has any illusions about the accursed work he has done!

"Great offenses require great succor before anything, my dear child! Your young friend is neither cowardly nor depraved, far from it, and I don't have to be ashamed for her of the last choice she had made. I am sure he would have married her if I had agreed to a divorce, and I would have agreed to it if she had long insisted. We must therefore set him back on the right track. We owe it to the memory of the woman who wanted to take, who could have taken his name.

"If someday he asks to see the children, do not oppose it. Seeing the orphans, he will deeply feel his duty as a man and the salutary pricks of remorse.

"In a word, save him; let me never see him again, but let him be saved! I myself have been saved for a long time and it is not to me, to my more or less sad state that you must attend. To forget oneself, here is the great issue when one is not stronger than one's ills."

Seven years had already passed after this terrible period of my life when I saw Obernay again. I worked in industry. Employed by a company, I supervised important metallurgic works. I had learned my profession by beginning with the hardest work, manual labor. Henri found me near Lyons, among workers, my face blackened, like theirs, by the fumes issuing from the cave of labor. He had some difficulty recognizing me, but I could feel in his embrace that his heart of past years was given back to me. He had not changed. He still had his strong shoulders, his thin waist, his fresh complexion, and his limpid eyes.

"My friend," he said to me when we were alone, "you'll learn that it is a chance excursion which brings me to you. I have been traveling with my family for a month, and now I am on my way back to Geneva;

but without the circumstance of traveling, I would have joined you, anywhere, a little later, in the fall. I knew that you were at the end of your expiation and I was eager to kiss you. I received your last letter, which did me much good, but I did not need this to know everything about you. I haven't lost track of you for the last seven years. You did not wish to receive from me any favor; you only asked me to sometimes write you as a friend without mentioning the past. I first thought that it was pride again on your part, that you did not even want moral assistance, especially for fear of living under the indirect influence, the hidden protection of Valvèdre. Presently I am doing you full justice. You have and you will always have much pride, but your character has risen up to the level of your pride, and I shall no longer ever allow myself to smile at it. Neither I nor anyone will any longer call you childish. Rest assured, you have managed to have your misfortunes treated with respect."

"My dear Henri, you are exaggerating!" I replied. "I have simply done my duty. I have obeyed nature, which may be somewhat ungrateful, in shirking pity. I have wished to punish myself, and with my own hands, by subjecting myself to a course of study for which I had an aversion, to labors in which I thought imagination was doomed to wither. I have been happier than I deserved, for the acquisition of knowledge, whatever it may be, carries with it its own reward; and instead of becoming dazed in studying something for which one has the least affinity, one becomes less rigid, one becomes transformed, and passion, which never dies in us, turns to the object of our research. I now understand why some people . . . and why wouldn't I name M. de Valvèdre, have been able not to become materialists when studying the secrets of matter. And then I often remembered what you often told me in the past. You found me too ardent to be a literary writer; you used to tell me that I would write wild poetry, fantastical history, or hot-headed, partial, and, therefore harmful, criticism. Oh, I haven't forgotten anything, as you can see. You used to say that very robust organizations often contain a destiny which leads them to exuberance and which thus hasten their premature destruction; that a good piece of advice would be that which would take me away from my own excitation to throw me into a sphere of serious and calming occupations; that artists often die or their minds atrophy from the effect of emotions that are sought and developed exclusively; that performances, dramas, operas, poems, and novels were, for overly keen sensibilities, like oil over fire; finally, that to be a long-lasting and sane artist or a poet, one often had to temper one's logic, reason, and will in rigorous studies, one even had to force one's self to deal with the dry beginnings of things. I followed your advice without realizing that I was following it, and when I began to reap its fruit, I thought that you had not told me enough how beautiful and attractive these kinds of studies are. They are so much so, my friend, that for a while, I felt pity for imaginative arts... with the fervor of a novice for which you would have forgiven me; but today, while appreciating as an artist the rays that science projects over me, I feel that I shall no longer leave a branch of knowledge which gave me back the ability to reason and to think: an invaluable blessing, which preserved me equally from overindulgence and from the disgust of life! Presently, my friend, you know that I am nearing the term of my captivity..."

"Yes," he continued, "I know that with the salary, which has been quite modest for a long time, you have managed to gradually repay Moserwald, who rightfully claims that it is a tour de force, and that you must have imposed on yourself, especially during the beginning years, a life of great deprivation. I know that you lost your mother, that you left everything for her, that you nursed her with an unrivaled devotion, and that, seeing your father quite old, quite tired, and quite poor, you felt very happy to be able to double for him, with a life annuity, and without his knowledge, the small sum that he was keeping for you and that he had entrusted to you so that you could make it grow. I also know that you have led a life of austerity and that you have made people appreciate you for your knowledge, your intelligence, and industriousness to the point of being able to claim now a very honorable and very happy existence. Finally, my friend, in coming here, I have learned and I have seen that you were loved by the workers whom you manage... that you were somewhat feared—there is no harm in this, but that you were a friend and a brother for those who suffer. The region is now full of praise about a recent action..."

"This is excessive praise: I was just lucky enough to save from death a poor family."

"At the peril of your life, the most imminent peril! People thought you were lost!"

"Would you have hesitated in my place?"

"I don't think so! So I am not paying you any compliments; I find that you are following without fail the line of your duties. Come, this is good; kiss me. I am expected."

"What! I shall not see your wife and your children, whom I don't know yet?"

"My wife and my children are not here. The little ones do not leave for such a long time the grandfather's school and their mother won't leave them for an hour."

"But you said you were with your family."

"As a way of speaking. Relatives, friends... But I am not saying good-bye for long. I am taking my people back to Geneva; and in six weeks I shall come back to get you."

"To get me?"

"Yes. Will you be free then?"

"Free! No, I shall never be free."

"You'll never be free to be idle, but you will be free to work wherever you wish. Your contract with your company expires at that time; I shall then come to propose to you a plan which you may find to your liking, and which, by creating for you great occupations which fit your current tastes, will bring you closer to me and my family."

"To be closer to all of you!... Ah, my friend, you are too happy for me! I have never considered the possibility of moving closer, something which would constantly remind me of a past that was terrible for me; that town, that house!"

"You will not live in town, and that house, you won't see it again. We sold it; it has been pulled down. My old parents missed their routine, but today they are not missing anything. They live with me, in the countryside, on a superb spot, on the side of Lake Geneva. We are no longer squeezed in premises that have become too small for a larger family. My father only takes care of our children and a few selected pupils who come respectfully to his lessons. I have succeeded him in his professorial post. You see in me a serious professor of science no longer exclusively possessed by botany. Come, you have lived alone long enough! You must leave your retreat; your presence is necessary for my complete happiness, I must tell you."

"All this is quite tempting, my friend, but you forget that I have an old invalid father who leads an even more lonely and sad life than I do. The whole effort of my newly recovered freedom must aim at bringing me closer to him."

"I am not forgetting anything, but I say that everything can be worked out. Don't remove hope from me, and let me arrange things."

He left me with such effusive kisses that the spring of sweet tears, which had long been dried up, opened up again. I went back to work, and a few hours later I saw in one of my workshops a young boy, a child of fourteen or fifteen, with a determined and intelligent face who seemed to look for someone and whom I approached to find out what he wanted.

"Nothing," he replied with self-confidence. "I am looking."

"But do you know, my sweet little bourgeois," an old worker told him mockingly, "that you are not allowed to look like this at what you don't understand?"

"And if I understand," the child rejoined, "what do you have to say to that?"

"And what do you understand?" I asked him, smiling at his self-assurance. "Tell us."

He answered me with a chemic-physic-metallurgic demonstration that was so well expressed and so well thought out that the old worker was stunned and stood like a statue.

"In what textbook did you learn this?" I asked the small boy, for he was small, strong, and ugly, but it was the kind of uncommon and charming ugliness that is suddenly attractive. I examined him with an emotion that made me tremble. His eyes were quite beautiful, somewhat divergent, and they made him two profiles with different expressions, one kindly, the other mocking. His nose, delicately carved, was too long and too narrow but full of audacity and sensibility; his complexion was dark, his mouth healthy, filled with strong, strangely cut teeth, with something indefinably caressing and provocative in his smile, a mixture that was at once graceless and charming. I could feel that I liked him very much although my entire being was in a terrible state of shock. I was hardly surprised when he answered me: "I don't study textbooks; I am reciting my master's lesson, Professor Obernay. Do you happen to know Obernay senior? He is far from being stupid, isn't he?"

"I do, I do know him. He is a good teacher! And you, are you a good student, M. Paul de Valvèdre?"

"Well!" he continued without any surprise showing in his expression. "So you know my name? And you what is your name?"

"Oh, me, you don't know me; but how come you are here all by yourself?"

"Because I am here for six weeks to study, to see how things are done and how metals react in experiments on a large scale. You cannot judge that in a lab. My professor said, 'Since he is hooked on this, I'd like for him to be able to see how a large specialized factory works,' and his son Henri answered him: 'It's quite simple. I am going near a place where there are some and I'll take him. I have friends there who'll show him everything and will give him good explanations'; and here I am."

"And is Henri gone? He is leaving you with me?"

"With you? Ah, you said that I did not know you! You are Francis! I was looking for you and I was almost certain I recognized you right away!"

"Recognized me? Since..."

"Oh! I don't remember you much; but your portrait is in Henri's room, and you are not so different!"

"Ah, my portrait is still in your house?"

"Still! Why wouldn't it be? But, by the way, I have a letter for you; I am going to give it to you."

The letter was from Henri:

I did not want to tell you what was bringing me there. I wanted to leave you the surprise. Besides, you might have scolded me. You would have needed perhaps one hour to recover from that emotion and I don't have an hour to waste. I left my wife on the verge of giving me a fourth child, and I am afraid her zeal may anticipate my return. I don't need to tell you to take care of our Paolino as you would the apple of your eye. You will love him; he is an adorable little devil. In six weeks, to the day, you'll bring him back to Blanville, by Lake Geneva.

I kissed Paul with quivers and tears. He was surprised by my agitation and looked at me with his inquisitive and penetrating eyes. I quickly regained my composure and took him to my house where his little luggage had been left by Henri.

I was quite nervous but really besides myself with happiness to be in a position to serve and take care of this child who reminded me of his mother, like a blurred image seen through a broken ray. At times, it was her during her all too rare hours of trusting cheerfulness. Other times, it was her again in her deep reverie but, as soon as the child opened his month, it was something else: he had, not dreamed, but sought, and meditated upon a fact. He was as positive as she had been romantic, passionate like her but for his studies, and eager for discoveries.

I took him with me everywhere. I introduced him to the workers as a son of the workroom and he immediately gained the affection of these good people. I had him take his meals with me. I had him sleep in my bed. He was my child, my master, my property, my consolation, my forgiveness!

But two days went by before I had the courage to mention his parents. He had hardly forgotten anything about his mother. He especially remembered having seen a coffin come back after one year of absence. He had gone back every year to Valvèdre since that time with his brother and his aunt Juste; but he had never again seen his father there. "My dad no longer likes that place," he would say. "He never goes there now."

"And your father," I asked him with a shyness full of trepidation, "he knows you are with me?"

"My father? He is still very far! He went to see the Himalayas. Do you know where it is? But he is on his way back. We'll see him again in two months. Ah, how wonderful! We love him so! And you, do you know him, my father?"

"Yes, I do. You all are right to love him. Has he been absent for? ..."

"For eighteen months; this time, it's very long! The other years, he always came back in the spring. Anyway autumn will soon be here! But say, Francis, what if we went for *a lick* of work instead of chatting endlessly?"

"What have you done?" I later wrote Henri. "You entrusted this child to my care; I love him already, and his father does not know about it! And he might blame us, you for introducing him to me, and me for accepting such a great happiness. He might order Paul to forget even my name. And in six weeks I shall part from my treasure and never see him again! ... Did I need this new wound? ... But no, Valvèdre will forgive our foolishness; however, he will be hurt to see that his son feels affection for me. And why make him suffer, he who has done nothing wrong!"

A few days later I was to receive Henri's answer: "My wife has just given me a gorgeous little girl. I am the happiest of fathers. Don't worry about Valvèdre. Don't you remember that during the saddest days of the past, he wrote to me 'Let him see the children if he wants to. Above all, let him be saved, let him do honor to the memory of the one who almost took his name!' You can see that, without daring to say so, you needed this since you are so happy to have Paolino! You will see the other one too. You will see us all. Time is the cure of all things. God wished it so, He whose eternal work is to erase in order to rebuild."

The six weeks went by quickly. I had become so fond of my pupil that I was ready to do anything in order not to part from him irrevocably. I refused to renew my contract; I accepted Obernay's offers without knowing what they were, the only condition being that I could convince my elderly father to come live near me. As I no longer owed anything to anyone, it was not difficult for me to set him up properly and to devote my attention to him.

Blanville was a glorious place, with a simple but spacious and pleasant house. Lake Geneva's beautiful waters gently lapped away at the feet of the park's great oak trees. When we drew near, Obernay was coming to meet us in a rowing boat with Edmond Valvèdre who, tall, handsome, and strong, was rowing with consummate skill. The two brothers loved each other and embraced with a touching ardor. Obernay kissed me hastily and urged us to go back. I could see that he had arranged some surprise and that he was impatient to see me happy; but the dramatic surprise held in store for me failed because of the hero of the celebration. More impatient than all the others, my old gouty father, running and dragging himself partly on his crutch, partly on Rosa's young and strong arm, came toward me on the shore.

"Ah, my God, it's too much happiness!" I cried out, "To find you here, you!"

"You mean, to find me here for good," he answered, "for I am not leaving this place! Things have been worked out as I wanted; I am modestly paying for room and board, and I don't miss my Belgian fogs as much as one would think. I would not mind dying in full light on the shore of the blue waters. Do you understand all this? It is to tell you right away that you are staying and we shall not part again!"

Paula also ran toward us with Moserwald, whom she reproached with being less nimble than a nanny carrying her small charge. I saw at the first glance that they had become close to him and that he was proud of it. The excellent fellow was quite moved when he saw me. He still loved me and better than ever, for he was forced to respect me. He was married; he had married Israelite millions, a good, vulgar woman whom he loved because she was his wife and because she had given him an heir. He had finished the novel of his life, he said, on a page soaked with tears, and the page had never dried.

Obernay's father and mother had hardly aged; the safety of domestic bliss made the autumn of their life majestic and pure. They welcomed me as they had in old times. Did they know my story? They never let on.

Two persons, for sure, did not know, Adélaïde and Rosa. Adélaïde was still magnificently beautiful and even more beautiful at twenty-five than at eighteen; but she was no longer beyond dispute the most beautiful among women in Geneva: Rosa could, if not surpass her, at least hold the scale even. Neither of them was married; they were still always together as before, always cheerful, studious, teasing, and loving each other.

In the middle of everyone's affectionate welcome, I worried about the one Mademoiselle Juste held in store for me. I knew that she lived at Blanville and was not surprised that she did not come to meet me. I asked about her. Henri answered that she was not feeling well and that he would take me to pay my respects.

She greeted me with gravity but without hostility, and after Henri left us alone together, she spoke about the past without bitterness. "We suffered much," she told me, and when she was saying *we*, she always meant her brother, "but we know that, since that time, you haven't spared yourself or forgotten yourself in a life of pleasure. We know that we must, I don't say forget, this is not possible, but forgive. A great strength is necessary to accept forgiveness, a greater one yet than to offer it. I know this too, I who am proud! I thus respect you very much for having the courage to be here. Stay. Wait for my brother. Face the first encounter, whatever it may be, and if he utters the terrible and sublime words, "I forgive," lower your head and accept it! Then, only then, you will be absolved in my eyes . . . and in yours, my dear Monsieur Francis!"

Valvèdre arrived eight days later. He saw his children first, then his older sister, and Henri—who probably pleaded my cause; but it did not suit me to wait for his judgment. I provoked it. I presented myself to Valvèdre before perhaps he had made a decision in my regard. I spoke to him effusively and loyally, boldly and humbly, as it suited me.

I laid bare under his eyes all my heart, all my life, my faults, and my qualities, my moments of weakness, and my renewed strength. "You wanted me to be saved," I said to him. "You were so great and so vastly superior to me in your conduct that I have finally understood the little that I was. To understand this is already to be worth more. I have understood it increasingly every day for the seven years that I have chastised myself unsparingly. Thus, if I am saved, it is not owing to my grief and to the kindness of others, however great; this kindness did not come from high enough to be able to conquer a pride like mine. When coming from you, this kindness broke me and I owe everything to you. Put me to the test; know me as I am today, and allow me to be Paul's devoted friend. Through him, I have been brought here in spite of myself; my father has been settled here without my knowing it. I am offered an important and interesting position in the area that I studied and which I think I know. I have been told that Paul had a definite vocation for the sciences to which this kind of work is essentially linked, and that you approved of this vocation. I have also been told that you might agree to his doing with me and under my direction his first training... But this, I have had difficulty believing! What I know, what I have come to tell you is that if my presence was to send you away from Blanville, or only to make you enter it with less pleasure, if the good that they want to do me seemed to you to be too close to my fault, and that, judging me unworthy of devoting myself to your child, you disapproved of the trust given to me by Obernay, I would withdraw immediately, knowing fully well that my whole life is subordinate to you, and that you have right over me on which I cannot put any limit."

Valvèdre took my hand, kept it in his own for a long time, and finally answered me: "You have mended everything, and your atonement has been such that you are owed a great relief. Know that Madame de Valvèdre was deathly ill before she knew you. Obernay has just revealed to me what I did not know, what he himself did not know and what a physician, a serious man, told him recently. So you did not kill her!... I may be the one who did! I might have made her live longer if she had not broken away from me. No one can probe the mystery of our actions on destiny. Let us submit to what has happened and let us not speak about the rest. Here you are. Someone loves you and you can still be happy; it behooves you to attempt to find happiness. The wretched who are so willingly are not useful for long. God abandons them; He wants life to be a blossoming and a fructification. Marry. I know that Obernay, in his secret thoughts, intends one of his sisters for you; which one I don't know; I did not ask him. I know that these children have no notion of his plan. Their family is too religious for any imprudent or even frivolous act to be committed. Henri, for fear of putting you ill at ease in case of repulsion on the young girl's part or on yours, will never mention it; but he hopes that affection will come of itself and he knows that this time you will trust him. Try then to come to life again; it is time to do so. These are the best years in which to found your future. You are consulting me with the deference of a son; here is my advice. As for Paul, I entrust him to your care and I have little merit in doing so since I intend to stay in Geneva for at least a year and I'll be able to see if you are still getting along. I shall often come to Blanville. The factory that you are going to improve is quite near. We shall see each other and if you have other advice to ask of me, I shall give you the advice, not of a wise man, but that of a friend."

For three months, all I did was to set up my industrial plant. Everything had to be created, everything had to be directed; it was an enormous task. Paul, always at my side, always good-humored and attentive, was getting to know the details of the practice, thereby charming by his presence and his good humor my terrible task. When I had learned the business, the main director of the factory, who was none other than Moserwald, assigned me a pretty house and a salary that was quite respectable.

I was coming back to life, to friendship, to the blossoming of the soul. Everything brightened the dark cloud that had weighed on me for so long, every friendly word shone a ray of sun over it. I came to think with a feeling of hope and terror about Henri's plan which Valvèdre had revealed to me. Valvèdre himself often alluded to it, and one day, when lost in my thoughts, I was looking from afar at the two sisters who were walking, radiant and pure like two swans, on the grass by the lake, he startled me, knocking softly on my shoulder, and said with a smile: "So, which one is it?"

"Not Adélaïde," I answered with a spontaneity which had become my heart's habit with him, so much had he conquered my confidence, my trust, and my filial respect.

"And why not Adélaïde? I want to know why! Come, Francis, tell me why!"

"Ah, that, I can't."

"Well, I am going to tell you, for she told me, *she who is no longer suffering*! She was jealous of her, and you are afraid that her ghost will come crying and threatening during the night! Set your mind at ease; these are blasphemous beliefs. The dead are pure! They fulfill elsewhere a new mission, and, if they remember us, it is to bless us, and to ask God to repair their errors and their mistakes by making us happy."

"Are you so sure?" I asked him. "Is it really what you believe?"

"Yes, absolutely!"

"Hmm, ... Well! Adélaïde, a splendor of intelligence and beauty, divine serenity, charming modesty ... all this will never lower itself down to me! What I am next to her? She knows everything better than I do: poetry, music, languages, natural sciences ... perhaps metallurgy, who knows! She would see in me too much of her inferior."

"Pride again!" said Valvèdre. "Does one suffer from the superiority of what one loves?"

"But ... I don't love her! I revere her, I admire her, but I can't love her! ..."

"Why not?"

"Because she loves someone else."

"Someone else? Do you think so?"

Valvèdre remained pensive and as if he was deep in thought figuring the solution to a problem. I looked at him carefully. He was forty-seven years old but he could have hidden ten or twelve of these years. His manly and gentle beauty, with such a lofty and serene expression, was still the only one that could arrest the attention of a woman of genius; but had his soul remained as young as his face had? Hadn't he loved too much, suffered too much? *Poor Adélaïde!* I thought, *you may grow old alone as Juste, who was beautiful once too, who was a superior woman too, and who, perhaps like you, had placed her dream of happiness too high!*

Valvèdre was walking silently beside me. He resumed the conversation where we had left it.

"So," he said, "do you like Rosa?"

"She is the only one whom I would dare think of if there was a hope she would like me."

"Well! You are right; Rosa is more like you. There has always been some fire in her, and it won't be a fault in your eyes. With this, she is gentle in the practice of life, not resigned, not ruled by convictions as set and as reasoned as that of her sister, but convinced and led by the affection that she feels and inspires. Less educated, she is sufficiently so for a woman who has a taste for housekeeping and family instincts. Yes, Rosa is a rare treasure, I already told you a long time ago. I don't know if she will like you. There is so much peace in the chastity of these two girls! But there is a great way to be loved, do you know? It is if you yourself love, love with your heart, faith, conscience, with one's entire being, and you haven't yet loved like this, I know it!"

He left me and I felt invigorated, as if blessed by his words. This man held my soul in his hands and now I only survived, so to speak, because of his beneficent energy. At the same time that every glimpse of his luminous spirit opened to me the horizons of the natural and celestial world, every movement of his generous and pure heart closed a wound or revivified a faculty of my own heart.

I soon opened this renewed heart to my dear Henri. I told him that I loved Rosa, but that I would never give her the slightest hint of it without the approval of her family. "Come," Obernay told me with a hug, "here is what I was waiting for! Well! The family agrees to it and wishes it so. The child will love you when she knows that you love her. That's how we do it in our family! We don't throw ourselves into romantic dreams, even if we are inclined to be convinced; we wait for certainty, and we don't lose our color or our appetite in the meantime. And still we love for a long time, forever! See my father and my mother, see Paule and me. Ah, Valvèdre would have been so happy if . . . !"

"If he had married Adélaïde? I have had that thought a hundred times!"

"Hush!" Obernay told me as he was clasping my arm. "Never a word about this . . ."

I expressed my surprise; he again imposed silence with authority.

Still I came back to the subject; the day after my wedding with my beloved Rosa, I insisted. I was so happy. At last I loved, and I almost fought passion, as its older brother, love, seemed to me to be more beautiful, and truer. Thus, far from being inclined to be selfishly happy, I could feel the urgent need to see happiness in all of my loved ones, especially Valvèdre, the one to whom I owed everything, the one who had saved me from destruction, the one who, after having been wounded to the heart by me, had held out to me his liberating hand.

Overcome by my affection, Obernay finally answered me: "You think you guessed that for a long time, already quite a long time, ten years perhaps, Valvèdre and Adélaïde have loved each other deeply; you may not have been wrong. And I too, I have had this thought, a hundred, a thousand times, which at some moments, became almost a certainty. Valvèdre directed my sisters' education almost as much as that of his own children. He saw my sisters when they were born; he seemed to love them with the same affection. Adélaïde received from my father the most brilliant education and from my mother the example of all virtues, but it is to Valvèdre that she owes the sacred fire, the inner flame that burns without sparkle, hidden at the far end of the sanctuary, protected by a shy modesty, the grain of genius which makes her idealize and bring pure poetry to the most arid studies. She is thus not only his grateful student, but his fervent disciple; he is her religion, her enlightener, the intermediary between her and God. This faith dates from her childhood and will only perish with her. Valvèdre cannot not know it; but Valvèdre does not think he is loved except as a father figure, and although he has been more than once, especially recently, very moved, more than paternally moved when looking at her, he believes he is too old to be attractive to her. He has fought his inclination ceaselessly and has repressed it so valiantly that one might think it has been overcome . . ."

"My friend," I interrupted Obernay, "since we have broached such a delicate topic, tell me all . . . Already I have been relieved of a terrible remorse when learning, thanks to your investigations, that Madame de

Valvèdre was deathly ill before knowing me. Tell me now, what I have never known, what I have never dared know, what Moserwald thought he had guessed: tell me if Valvèdre still loved his wife when I eloped with her."

"He did not," Obernay answered, "I know it is not the case. I am certain of it."

"He told you so, I know. He spoke of her with the deepest indifference; he thought he was quite cured; but love has mysterious inconsistencies..."

"Passion, yes! But love, no! Passion is illogical and incomprehensible; such is its character, and I shall tell you here a *mot* by Valvèdre: 'Passion is a love that is sick and that has gone mad!'"

"One could as well say that love is a passion that is healthy."

"You can play with every word; but Valvèdre does not play with anything! He is too much of a great logician to lie to himself. The soul of a true scientist is honesty itself because it follows the method of a mind given to scrupulous perspicacity. Valvèdre is very ardent and even impetuous by nature. His rash marriage is proof of the spontaneity of his youth, and in his mature age, I saw him fighting against the furor of the elements, as he was carried away beyond caution by the fury of discovery. If he had felt any love for his wife, he would have conquered his rivals and yourself. He would have pursued her, brought her back, and provoked her passion again. It was not so difficult with a soul as changing as that of that poor woman; but such a struggle was not worthy of a man who was undeceived, and he knew that Alida, returned for a while to her duties, could not be saved. Besides, he feared destroying her in mastering her, and above all, by instinct and by principle, he abhors causing suffering. So, do not exaggerate, calm the excess of your remorse, and do not make extravagant heroes of human beings. Indeed, Valvèdre, in love with his wife and bringing you back to her deathbed in order to forgive you in her presence, would be more poetic; but he would not be true, and I prefer him true because I cannot love what is contrary to the laws of nature. Valvèdre is not a God; he is a man of honor. I would quite distrust a man who could not say: *Homo sum!*"

"Thank you for telling me all this, especially since this does not take anything away from Valvèdre's greatness. If he has been in love and jealous, he could have, in his generosity, only given in to the weaknesses which belong, as much as violence, to the realm of passion. The great compassionate friendship, which, in him, had survived love; the need to soothe the wounds of others while respecting their moral freedom; the religious care with which he gently led to her grave the mother of his children, to save her soul at least, all this is beyond ordinary human nature, whatever you may say!"

"Nothing that is beautiful is above it in the realm of true feelings and coming from an exceptional soul. Thus you can imagine that I no longer fight your enthusiasm when Valvèdre is its object. You are now reassured on some points, but you must not go from one extreme to the other. You may not have inflicted the torture of jealousy, but you have deeply saddened and worried the heart of the husband, still a friend, and of the father, concerned about the dignity of his family. Great characters suffer in all their affections because all are great, whatever kind they may be. At his wife's death, Valvèdre thus suffered cruelly at the thought that she had lived without happiness and that he had been unable through no devotion and sacrifice, to give her anything but a moment of peace and hope on her deathbed. Here is the whole of Valvèdre; but Valvèdre in love with a purer ideal becomes mysterious again for me. The respect of this ideal goes as far as fear. I, seeing the gradual cooling of his familiarity with Adélaïde, whom he still addresses in the familiar *tu* form but whom he no longer kisses on the forehead as he kisses Rosa, I saw she was no longer for him like the other children of the household. I also thought that I saw at every trip he started, at the last one especially, a supreme effort, like a duty done, but becoming more difficult by the day. In short, he loves her, I think he does; but I do not know it, and my position prevents me from asking him. He is very rich, with a name famous in science circles, very much above, according to society, this petite bourgeois woman who hides with determined care her talents and her beauty. I do not fear that he will ever accuse me of ambition; however, there are conventions of education above which I am not yet enough of a philosopher to place myself, and if Valvèdre has been hiding his secret from me for so long, he must have reasons that I don't know and that would make my approaches painful for him and humiliating for me."

"These reasons, I shall learn what they are," I exclaimed. "I want to know what they are!"

"Ah, be careful, be careful, my friend! What if we were mistaken about Adélaïde? What if at the moment when, encouraged and regaining hope, Valvèdre realized that he is not loved as he does? Adélaïde is quite a different myth than he is. This girl who looks so happy, whose eye is so pure, whose character is so even, the mind so studious, the cheek so fresh, whom neither desire, hope, nor fear seem to be able to reach; this

Andromeda smiling in the midst of monsters and chimeras, on her alabaster rock inaccessible to stains as well as to storms..., why is she not married at the age of twenty-six? She has been asked in marriage by men of talent placed in most honorable circumstances, and in spite of her mother's wishes, in spite of my entreaties, in spite of Juste's and my wife's advice, she said with a smile 'I don't want to marry!' 'Never?' Valvèdre asked her one day. 'Never!' "

"Tell me, Henri, was Alida alive then?"

"Yes, she was."

"And since she is no longer with us, has Adélaïde repeated 'Never'?"

"Many times."

"In Valvèdre's presence?"

"I don't remember. Now that you remind me, he might have been far away. She might have lost hope."

"Really! You haven't been very observant yet. It is up to me to apply myself to decipher the great enigma. Stoic philosophy, acquired through the study of wisdom, is a godly and beautiful thing, since it can nourish such pure, constant, and peaceful flames; but any virtue has its excess and perils. Isn't it a great one to condemn to celibacy and to an eternal inner struggle two human beings whose union seems to be written in the most beautiful page of divine laws?"

"Juste Valvèdre has lived very peaceful very dignified, very fertile in kindnesses and affections... and yet she loved without happiness and without hope."

"Who?"

"You have never known who it was?"

"And I don't know it now."

"She loved your mother's brother, the uncle who cherished you, Valvèdre's friend and master, Antonin Valigny. Unfortunately he was married and Adélaïde has given much thought to this story."

"Ah, that is why Juste forgave me for having offended and grieved Valvèdre so much! But my uncle is dead, and death does not leave any agitation. You can be certain, Henri, that Adélaïde suffers more than Juste does. She is stronger than her suffering; that is all. But her happiness, if she has any, is the work of her will; and I too thought during seven years that one could live on one's fund of wisdom and resignation! Now that I live with someone, I know that yesterday I did not live at all!..."

Henri kissed me and let me take action. It was a work of patience, of innocent cunning, and devoted obstinacy. I had to catch by surprise words in snatches, and stolen glances; but my dear Rosa, more daring and more trusting than I was, helped me and saw the truth before I did.

They loved each other and thought the other did not return their love. The day when, through my care and my encouragement, they understood each other was the greatest day of their life and of mine.

words in snatches, and stolen glances; but my dear Rosa, more daring and more trusting than I was, helped me and saw the truth before I did.

They loved each other and thought the other did not return their love. The day when, through my care and my encouragement, they understood each other was the greatest day of their life and of mine.